Mike Carter trained as an actor at the RADA and has worked extensively in films, television and on stage in the West End, the National Theatre and on Broadway, the Moscow Arts, the Rustavelli Theatre in Tbilisi, and the ancient theatre of Epidaurus in Greece.

He played Bib Fortuna in *The Return of the Jedi* (Episode 6 of the *Star Wars* series) and has consequently been immortalised as a series of dolls ranging from one inch to two feet high.

Other jobs have included white van driver, Spike Milligan's gardener, barman, stage crew member, stage set builder, university lecturer and training video writer.

Carter deviated from acting unemployment later in life to gain a masters degree in psychology and trained as a counsellor.

He co-wrote a film, which starred Anthony Hopkins just before he became a mega star, and has returned to screenwriting (and counselling).

He is married, has two adult children, a grandson, and lives in London with his Californian wife and a black Labrador.

The UnAmericans is his first novel.

THE UNAMERICANS

Michael Carter

Published by nthposition press, 38 Allcroft Road, London NW5 4NE

British Library Cataloguing-in-Publication Data
A catalogue record for this book is available from the British Library

Library of Congress Subject Headings
Cold War – Fiction; Spy stories; Noir fiction

BIC Subject Categories
FHD (espionage and spy thriller); FA (modern and contemporary
fiction, post c.1945)

ISBN 9780992618506 (paperback); **ISBN 9780992618513** (ebook)

Once, when I worked at the New York bureau I tried to get through a day without lying. I got up, had breakfast, caught the train to Grand Central, walked to the bureau, dumped my coat and case – so far so good. Apart from a 'good morning' or two, I hadn't spoken to anybody. I was standing at the coffee machine watching my cup fill when someone asked me a question and I lied.

Plano, Texas – 8 December 1962

What Tomas has lost with the Batista days burns in him. The Havana bars and beaches, the honey girls in the crimped bathing suits that decked out his younger virility, ghost in his slipstream across the cheap room in Plano.

"Papa and Mafia put him the White House. He is a bought man with no fucking balls!"

"His balls are a Federal concern," says Peter and we Americans laugh to defuse things.

Since breakfast Tomas and the other Cubans have presented their case with an Hispanic dignity that highlights our gracelessness. We have nothing for them but the news that there will be no second season for their show and the circularity of the debates degenerates into hostility. Tomas is left pacing and turning, an old caged leopard with power to do nothing but buffet anger into the winter evening.

"Eisenhower! A soldier! Now you pick an Irish horse thief! A nigger lover! What's wrong with you people? The going gets tough and the tough get fucking going! Over there outa fuckin' sight!" His finger jabs at the purple clouds and the scar of light in the west.

"Tomas, we are skinning this cat differently." Jerry plays the reassuring card, Pete presides, and Henry can get heavy when necessary. My job is to suggest I'm sitting on a pile of information, but of course what I'm really sitting on is information I can give no one in this room.

"Castro's lost his missiles, Tomas. All he's got is sugar cane and propaganda."

No one delivers a hard message as sweetly as Pete. Cuban exiles have booed and hissed our unwillingness to remount an invasion after the missile crisis panned out okay. We know a deal has been struck – they don't, but there is mucho Hispanic indignation at the reduction in funds for the struggle against Castro. That money made them big men in their Miami ghettos. Now they're just Joe Schmos with sideburns.

Tomas scans the infinite space of the Texan twilight and continues his invective against the horse thief filling the White House with Guinness and dung. Frustration has broken into bitterness and for counter revolutionaries like Tommy and his coxcomb cohorts, the liberator's garland has been withdrawn forever. Calls are not returned and they feel the same chill as all the other objects of Kennedy's affections – feted, fondled, fucked and finally forgotten. So the office dispatches us with flowers and Kleenex down to this backwater to assess if the Mambo Band are likely to fade into their own kind in the Florida ghettos, or continue defining themselves by their old island's rape and become a pain in the White House ass.

I remain on the touchline observing the night gather on two contradictory cultures: one sensuous, full of false pride and easy indignation, intolerant of those who do not play the game by their arcane rules; the other conformist, repressed, and intolerant of anyone who does not play by their mercantile rules. Both are bound by the urge to cleanse all heresies so's a man can walk free down the street, buy a Frigidaire and ignore Darwin.

I once observed my father's spleen at a female neighbour who regretted John Garfield got in trouble with McCarthy, because she liked him so much. Witnessing the intensity of Dad's patriotic rant across the fence as he set her right on a couple of things shocked me. I reassured our neighbour later that I liked John Garfield, but she blanched and moved away. The Un-American message was getting across. Ten years down the line we have a Catholic President and coloureds calling themselves American, but Dad stuck to his prediction that no Catholic would enter the White House while he was alive by dying two days before inauguration. "That man – the catholic – killed him," my mother declared to the grim family. Maybe he did.

The cluster of bottles on the table catch my eye. Bright labels conjure

palm beaches and ochre missions: rums and daiquiris, Hawaiian shirt
drinks winking in the darkness which I – as junior member of Corporation
USA – had been sent out to buy for our guests. I could do with one now.

I watch brother-in-law Henry. Do you know what your beloved little
sister and I get up to Henry? Do you know she loves having the bacon
brought home to her on all fours across the kitchen table?

"Tomas," I start from the back of class, "Washington coordinated more
than fifty million dollars in food and medicine as ransom for the twelve
hundred captured at Bahia de Cochinos." I reason with quiet cadences
that contrast Tomas's barrio melodramatics and remind him he is not
dealing with the local bookmaker. I tell him about the billion dollars in
assets expropriated by the revolutionary government, how we have good
cause to take issue with Castro, but that President Kennedy has reasons
for examining options other than the military, options which will have a
powerful impact on Cuba.

"You banned cigars. That'll bring the fucker down."

I move on before his rage finds a toehold and reveal one of the things
the administration is examining is a way to secure permission to leave for
Cuban nationals who wish to come to the United States.

Tomas has heard the same stuff twelve different ways but I know the
permission to leave is new to him. His daughter is in Havana. He wants her
in Miami but knows – and of course, we know – that she hates him and will
cleave to Castro rather than join the animal who left her mother rigid with
fear every time the front door opened and rigid with rejection all through
the nights it didn't.

He slides the window and spits. The sudden noise of fat tires on the
highway startles us and we watch his string of spit cartwheel across the
Denny neon. Tomas watches an old pick-up struggle along the highway
with a hump of Christmas trees lashed down in the back, then pulls at the
window to shut it, but it won't shift. The runners are clogged. Henry moves
to help when under the force of Tomas's anger it slides like a toboggan, and
sends him into a small stumble. Tommy was probably the kind of guy who
slipped on a lot of banana skins in his Chief Tom Cat existence.

"Maybe we need to change options. There are other guys."

It's nothing more than a codicil to his window rage. Peter casually looks across to me and crosses his eyes. Henry hears the choked-off giggle and it's round the room in milliseconds, affecting only the sober-suited Americans. The whole class is about to fall out of order. I dredge up a solemn expression that just makes everything worse.

The *coup de grâce* comes from my loving brother-in-law, Henry, who pulls his Jack Benny look. I keep my mouth tight shut, but Jack Benny does as Jack Benny does, just stares till I'm like a twig holding a logjam. Something whinnies through my nose. I bluff it into coughs. Tommy glares, Jerry's looking down covering his mouth with his hands, Henry is turned to face the wall and I see the muscles on the back of the bastard's neck twitching. The dam is about to burst big time.

"Go get a drink of water," says Peter. I propel into the bathroom and spend the next five minutes running taps, flushing the toilet and keeping my fist in my mouth to prevent another Cuban uprising.

Then I sit on the toilet and catch my reflection in the mirror and a sensation of complete solitariness grips me again, a feeling that's plagued me as long as I remember. As a kid I felt a stranger in my own house and was convinced my parents weren't my real parents and that one day a limo would draw up in the street, the door would open, I would graciously forgive the dumbos who had masqueraded as dad and mom, wave the neighbourhood goodbye, and step into the limo to be taken off to my real inheritance. I gave up waiting around eight.

I don't want to go back into that room. I can't take any more of Tomas and the Cubans grief about Castro and his nickel and dime pin-up Che, and the vitriol about the Hollywood President with more mouth than guts and how everybody is betraying them.

There is another betrayal none of them know about. It is buried in me, embracing not just Tomas and the other friends of Batiste, but also my boss Peter, my brother in law and colleague Henry, little Jerry who's queer as a coot and thinks no one knows, the Hollywood President, and finally, the whole American road show. Everything that goes on in this nicotined room in bum fuck Plano, chosen that its cheapness might convey to our Cuban guests that the trust fund is no longer paying out, will pass across a Kremlin desk in the next few days. Alone in the bathroom I hold this secret in me, deep and guarded, a gem of power and magic, that sometimes terrorises and sometimes nourishes me, that lets me walk down the street past faces that know nothing of what I have, and gives me a sublime sense of difference.

The irony is that my adolescent discontent crystallised into clandestine communism at Harvard where it might have remained a harmless intellectual anomaly had not the CIA come looking for bright law graduates and dropped temptation in my lap. I was led to the treasure trove of classified files with promises of improved pension deals and generous expense accounts. My communist attitudes were hardened by many of the hardened attitudes I found in the Agency I pretended to serve. My hesitation was dissolved by many of the things I knew we were doing in those foreign states that would not kneel at the corporate altar. As I handed over confidential information to my Russian contacts I felt no hatred for my own people, just a sense that I was balancing the excess. The poignancy is that I like most of my American colleagues. I am genuinely fond of the team I work in, particularly Henry; he is as good a brother in law as a man could want.

Usually I swim in the morning to rinse out my hangovers, but in the remote fastness of Texas there are no wives to limit the after-work martinis, so I swim when work's finished; the later I get to the bar, the longer I remain un-drunk. When the others shuffle up the little wooden hill, a couple of strong ones usually get the click and float me to bed at peace with the world. I can go without the stuff for months, but if I lift just one drink it takes off like an un-braked truck. Peter, educated in England and never missing an opportunity to bring his European literacy to bear on any vacant moment, compares my drinking to that of Dr Johnson: "often abstinent but never temperate." At least I'm in good company. The other he levels at me is the one about the chains of habit being "too weak to be felt until they are too strong to be broken", and that quote leaves me wondering if Peter has an insight into me that might one day lead to the denim suit and the body harness. These fears around Peter come like storms and leave me exhausted. Something about the man, something beneath the affection, the words, looks and gestures of friendship leave me wary and vigilant. Then it passes and I indulge a nephew like love for him. I pinball between fear and love, suspicion and trust; my life is a racket of motion, strikes, ricochets and flippers. I sit and think sometimes is there a moment when I am truly relaxed, when something in me is not firing around the walls? And there isn't. I am constantly whirring. Time doesn't pass; it stretches me. I hate time. Stalking me. Always there. I don't know why I have this odd fear of it. I only wear a watch because they would ask if I didn't. I would have no clocks in my house if I could – I have a feeling they're going to play a dirty trick on me. But the clocks stop for JD. That's it, the bottle of peace, the Jack Daniels that soothes where the restless nature cannot and dampens down the background whine that tears a hole in space-time and lets you breathe. It may be an imperfect meditative state, but it's one I can switch on at will, as long as the bar is open.

The hotel is new and the pool at the back open to the flat Texan landscape. The underwater lamps and blue bottom create a sapphire in the velvet night. I cut up and down, fifteen-yard lengths in a couple of strokes. I aim for a hundred lengths in these little pools but usually lose count around sixty. Nevertheless, the rhythm sucks me into a kind of Zen nothingness, till some natural message says enough, get out.

Peter sits by a lamp working and whisking away drizzles of winter insects drawn to the blue pool and the solitary cliff of lights in the Texan night. Jerry and Henry will be in the bar mocking the absent Cubans.

I arch out onto my butt. The effort has swollen the muscle into slabs. I'm still a strong boy and I like it. My chest is heaving as I towel myself, I can feel the stuffiness of that room with Cuba's fate in it slowly clear from my body. The moon tears through flying clouds. Suddenly they're gone like smoke and the sky is sprayed with stars. There is a billion acres of silence.

"They say there's no sound in space."

"What a pleasant place that must be."

Moonlight spreads like pale paint to the horizon. I comment on how flat this country is, more to myself than Pete, but he responds with a quote about the flat lands of Cisthene from some Greek tragedy about Prometheus he thinks I know nothing about. Put a penny in him and he's off. I enjoy pandering to Peter's orotund classicism by playing the blue collar monosyllabic. I know more about this stuff than I let on, but I keep all my candles under the bushel on principle. For example, I have a minor musical talent and after a few drinks I might get on the piano, but always play bar taste: Liberace, never Liszt. So, I sit there, lug-like by the pool, while he pronounces on the ancient world.

A figure in a gown at a high window closes the drapes and checks me out. I vector the floors and windows to her bedroom to Peter's riff about the ancient Greeks' fascination with the movement from chaos to rational compromise.

"Somewhat akin to our salaried obsessions, though I sometimes feel we move in the reverse direction."

"It's a living."

The moon has laid a silver thread on the horizon. I am lounging in my chair and I hear the snick of Peter capping his fountain pen. He declares softly that fountain pens don't work in planes, and time begins to bend.

'Fountain pens don't work in planes' is one of my code phrases. These phrases can crop up innocently, so it's important to assess the moment. In a Texan night the Sphinx's riddle smacks me by a blue pool. Get it right I live, get it wrong, I die. Reason advocates that Peter has led me to my Gethsemane and the Judas kiss is being applied with regret. He waits, the admired old hand, the patrician with the extraordinary war record who has laboured at the heart of his country's security since the trials at Nuremberg. I feel ashamed to have let him down.

Surface patterns whisper across the pool. A curtain draws behind soundproof windows. I can hear a moth breathe or grass grow; all the Texan night sounds crowd in to my private ear.

"They've found your snow prints."

What are you talking about I ask. When we're afraid we speak in clichés.

"Don't be naïve. They're following. It's only a matter of time."

I try to remember if they electrocute spies or hang them, and determine to go to the bathroom before execution in case my corpse shits my prison issue pants.

"Your reply is 'I use a pencil'."

That was the best they could come up with, pencils and pens.

"Why didn't you use the reply?"

"I don't know what you're talking about. Fountain pens and pencils."

"I'm not getting through. Ring Yura for confirmation. I'm all you've got."

Yura is my contact from the Russian Embassy in Washington. So, Peter knows. I have been hooked. Peter is playing me into his part of the shallows and the waiting gaff. I know he has always seen me as the overgrown adolescent who can't lose face, replete with the pride that leads to lives of small and larger disasters. I look at him. His face is haggard with worry and I know in that second, for some indefinable reason, that I am safe. Of all people, Peter is my angel. I am no longer alone.

Peter had fought Nazism, had seen the bony bodies and the charred ovens, the monuments to hate, and then sensed a kindred spirit flickering around the Great Democracy. His was a considered conversion, reached after a long debate with himself. I am an 'idealist', a 'walk-in', a person of passion, cause for suspicion; young leftists often become old fascists. Later I will learn Peter has his doubts, even there by the poolside as he was guiding me, fundamental questions nagged him, and over the years in Moscow I will follow the fading of his commitment. By the Prague Spring he will have long dropped out of the landscape. These things happen, Alexei will say with a shrug. A few years before Glasnost he will die in Palm Springs, the great historical concerns of the twentieth century lost to the last great obsession of his golf handicap.

"You have to go over." The fountain pen is put back in a pocket. My fear seeps out and twists a question mark into the enemy night. I ask in a mouse's voice if I can take Peg with me. He reminds me I'm not asking her to change her shopping from Macy's to Gimbels, sheathes his papers into his briefcase and turns towards the hotel, "Don't be long."

Postcard, September 1998

Dear Mom,

This is Tverskaya Street, Moscow's Park Avenue. If you half close your eyes you could be in Cleveland except everybody's thinner. To think millions died in the Gulag for Paradise on Earth and got Pizza Hut. Heading south for Tbilisi in Georgia – not Willie Nelson's Georgia, the other one – but I'll probably be back before you get this. If you get it.

Regards to Arnold.

Lucy xxx

Under crimson balconies, fretwork shutters, peeling paint and pillars warped by centuries of scalding summers, she was conscious of nothing but her own ridiculousness. Dark eyed women and children hanging over balustrades scrutinised her with the incomprehension of primitives eyeing a disc jockey. Her blonde head had a radiance that was an asset on a Californian beach but in a shabby Tbilisi courtyard stamped her as a foreigner.

In a basic Russian, twanging with Valley Girl inflections she asked for the apartment of Mr Max Agnew. The question galvanised nothing but more stillness among the women, then a language she did not understand, full of aspirates and glottal stops, flickered between the balustrades.

"He's not here" was returned with uninflected finality.

Everyone protected her from her father. No questions were ever answered by her mother, her uncle, or the American nation; he was left an unmentionable enigma, but his neighbours probably had good reason to vet strangers.

"I'm his daughter. Lucy. From America."

"His daughter?"

"From America?"

Their shock hissed through the courtyard in Georgian. They knew nothing of an American daughter.

"Your name is Lucy?"

"Yes."

Her name was all her father had left her.

"Lucy?"

"Lucy Agnew."

Faces blanked, heads shook imperceptibly, a child's face peeped at her between scarlet banisters, then a tall mother unfolded from the group and etched her concern up at an apartment leaning into space and beckoned. Someone called "Lucy", and they were off, floating her up wooden steps through sudden mixes of perfumes and clouds of mustiness from flower baskets and rugs airing on the balustrades, whipping her through a portal in time. Distant hills shimmered in the heat haze, traffic noise skimmed across the River Mtkvari way below; she seemed to be walking in the sky. The old apartment building canted over a park sloping down to the brown river by which the first settlers had paused six thousand years before.

Then the women halted, sunlight burned a door, bounced off small windows, and everyone had fallen back. Answered prayers sometime materialise as nightmare. This was the door, the one to which she had beaten a long and winding path and now she had reached it, it mesmerised her. Arteries beat in strange parts of her body. The women saw the last drops of her resource drain away and began to sense she was real. Her father's name burst huskily around her. It was the first time she had heard it outside the walls of her home. She panicked about how to introduce herself when he appeared at the door.

But it was true. He was not there. There was a house on the Black Sea, they said; he comes he goes. The ordinariness pricked the apocalyptic shock. I told you so, they would say back home and shake their heads, you should have rung him.

This journey to her father had begun in her child's head and become a Holy Grail that sustained itself into adulthood, but when she sorted out certain problems in her life and the great day to make the arrangements arrived, her courage deserted her. Even the banal parts of the trip – the flights, the hotel booking for the stopover and change in Moscow – had her moving as if adrift in a monstrous dream. The vital call to her father announcing who she was and asking his permission to come and visit, was simply beyond her. When her boy fiend Timmy enquired if she had called him he had his face chewed for his concern. She preferred the path of spiritual fatalism: "If my Higher Power wants me to meet my father, I will. If not, then so be it. What ever happens is meant to happen." and this elevated approach calmed her. She would go with faith that he would be there and agree to see her, but as her plane banked above LAX and started its long haul east, the notion that she was a fraud taking her cowardice on a round the world trip nagged her. More vigorous prayers to the Higher Power were made, asking, handing over, promising to accept his will for her, but standing before her father's unanswered door all she could wonder was why, just for once, her Higher Power couldn't sign the shit shovel over to someone else.

The women ushered her to the window, every movement and gesture formal, polite, graceful and gracious. Face pressed to the pane, her eyes adjusting to the light, the first artefacts of the mystery that was her father began forming in the dimness. Small kilims, books and soft furniture materialised in shadow, lines of light slowly edged a baby grand piano. She had never known he was musical, but the women confirmed he was very musical, that he had taught a couple of kids in the apartment block, that he was practically a concert pianist. She was astonished.

The building was buckled by age and shabby, the courtyard cracked, the roof short of tiles, paint flaked everywhere, and within this architectural entropy her father's undistinguished apartment provoked her first sense of disappointment.

An old neighbour swung up, saw Max in her and was shocked. Back home the family dynamic was amnesia and suggestions of resemblance were cut dead. Dad was not to be mentioned; Dad did not exist. The same dynamic obviously prevailed behind her father's door, but with Lucy as the non-person – she had obviously not merited a mention.

Questions came like humming birds. She had no memory of him; she was three weeks old when he left. There were more slow nods, more understanding, the picture was forming and in the mix of conversation it became clear her father was a popular neighbour, but could be tricky and reclusive about the world beyond his gates. The women glossed over the fact that she had arrived without any previous arrangement with her father. They took her American address and promised to tell him when he returned. "He may not be interested", said Lucy. The old woman replied that he was always interested in a pretty girl and cued a gallery of knowing smiles. A Brit from the embassy in Moscow had claimed he "drank like a Georgian". So he was a drunk who liked women. She'd been avoiding those assholes since she got sober.

The city was all hills. When she got back to the hotel, her buttocks smarted and her cleavage was glossy with sweat. The agoraphobia of Moscow, that had her clinging to the Amex and Citicorp neon among the Cyrillic, or hanging out in the hotel lobby for American voices, was now replaced by a bubbling excitement. Lucy had to take difficult things in small bites; she had got to his door, declared herself in his courtyard and to her that was no small triumph.

She showered, fought the hotel hair drier for a while, and put on a fresh summer dress that hugged her curves. In Moscow her Californian looks attracted men like flies and she was warned by the hotel receptionist that the Georgians were worse. But as an American blonde who had served time in the sewage runs of LA she had good sleazeball radar and an armoury of feints and put-downs.

On her knees by the bed her Higher Power was thanked for bringing her to her father's door, for keeping her sober so far that day, and asked to keep her sober for the rest of the day. A humble request for knowledge of His will for her and the power to carry that out was added. Her AA sponsor had been promised regular phone calls, but the time difference between Georgia and California defeated her.

Downstairs the manageress with the beehive hairdo who looked at all guests as if they were something brought in on the sole of a shoe gave her the time difference and the codes for a direct call to California as if Lucy had never used a phone before. A brief desire to spit on her retro winged glasses was suppressed for a "Spasebo" with Valley Girl inflections. Then a bright 'Hi!' cut through the cigarette smoke shrouding the old Cossack doorman as she breezed out onto steep, ex-Bolshevik streets to tighten her butt and discover the city her father had made his home.

The long swim out to the raft was almost beyond him now. Flat on his back, sucking air, he waited for the freshening of the pain in his lungs, and the narcotic of muscles detumescing. Under the pulse squeezing through his good ear, trees that feathered the shore and headland rocks like green clouds a kilometre away whispered to him. Distant sand, blood red cannonades of bougainvillea, pale houses, and tiny Georgians and Germans baring their breasts to a tourist sun, rotated into view on the bellying sea.

He would miss the raft when the swim finally defeated him. Life was intrusive, inconvenient and noisy. Max had never moved easily among others; his great conversations were always with himself. The rest of humanity triggered a reflex to contradict, to bounce opposing views at any opinion, like a man searching for a belief in nothing and the safety of loneliness.

He had flown to the raft from Masha. His intention to thaw the chill between them had disintegrated under a Tourette's hail of jibes about her religious faith. Once released, the words could never stop until the target was driven off, even when that was the last thing he wanted. When he suggested that when she died she would finally get to the pearly gates only to find no one was in, he saw the hurt and felt the stab of triumph and then the immediate regret. But this game played him without asking and she turned and left him cradling his loneliness.

His life, by the standards of most others, had been one of adventure and high office, but left him with the sense of being stuck somewhere, snapping, like a yappy dog at any passing ankle. Some buried connection spontaneously sparked cruelty in him to any one close, then sluiced up tsunamis of regret and sympathy to salve the hurt. But Masha was finished with being batted from one side of his nature to the other. She had read, marked, learned, inwardly digested, and finally dropped him and his flinty atheism, marooning him in the suspicion that a Kafkaesque Heaven's gate awaited him where his call *would* be answered but the hatch slammed against him. He would turn away. He always turned away. Things happened. Nothing happened. He never happened. It never happened. So he swam, drank occasionally, disappeared into boltholes in the head. Distance was his harmony, the raft, a kilometre from land and mankind his hermit's cell, the sky, with its great silence and indifference, his strip of peace.

The Party gave him the little house in the 70s, and barring hangovers and official business, he would swim to the raft most summer days to get away and reflect. But from a mountain of reflection there seemed barely a molehill of conclusion. He had been brought up to believe in the common things, and rejected them, but replaced them with nothing, just more rejection. And as the world surrounded him with corruption, bigotry and greed, his position had no need to change. His was a spirit constantly in flight, feeding upon the latest abominations on the wing. Occasionally he was shot down and doubt came in little painful moments like wounds.

He lay watching a silver dot stretch a silk thread of vapour across the cobalt sky. The thread hung, sagged, broke, and then slowly dissolved to nothing.

The swim back was murderous. When he hit the beach it had emptied. Only two Muscovite girls remained, Mercedes Eurotrash wearing little but the vacant expression of the habitual drug-user. Topless women on the beach were still a rarity in Georgia and flirted dangerously with the old permissive attitudes towards rape that still hung on in the last breaths of the century. They were both face down, their backs glowing with the day's sun.

The smaller, vulgar one had lavished some of the euro-roubles flooding Moscow on a set of new breasts to match the new Russian robustness. As she rolled onto her back the bosoms followed the rotation of her body like jet nose cones. They were so grotesquely inflated that he imagined them exploding in moments of high excitement. It was also a reasonable assumption that she had been a flat chested kid who watched her developed friends gather the boys, while she remained ignored. There was about her the exhibitionism of the nouveau attractive as well as the nouveau riche, that celebration of trashy, expensive jewellery and the over-priced car with the gold trim. And the breasts, that bounced out of a dead communist past like new chicks.

Her tall, dark friend was thin as a stick, and as he walked past, pretending his eyes weren't slanted sideways to take in the huge tits, he caught the contempt in her eyes. For that contempt he had respect. For the prole flaunting the monuments to social mobility vulcanised on her chest, he had only his own withered derision, alongside an urge to discharge himself all over them.

He picked up his towel and sank down among the wild flower on the edge of the beach to let his pulse calm, his chest settle and the stillness recharge him. Something deeper in the ordinary was occasionally touched in these moments, and a sensation of blending into peace lifted him. But when these moments passed he felt drained and depressed and all the problems rushed in to claim their place again.

Thoughts coalesced round Masha and Gia, the two others in his tiny world: she once a lover, he once a surrogate son, now betraying him together. Women who seek the older man in youth often seek younger men in their maturity, and Max was simply past his use-by date. She was a 'mature' woman, much younger than he but still vigorous and beautiful, still in the race. He was out to grass. He let the sand run between his fingers, felt its coolness race down his old skin, and glanced across for the breasts again. It was known both girls spent their nights with Gia. Masha must know, he thought, everyone knew about Gia and his overactive member. She would have her own pain round that, as he had his around her. Hers was a history of sexual generosity anyway, but as Max discovered several times, those who dish it out are often least able to take it when it is dished back to them.

The sun blushed the sea and hammered copper into the headland treetops. Half way to the horizon the raft melted into twilight. Another summer was ebbing, leaving the morbid thought that it might be the last beached in its quiet, dissolving evenings.

The lights went on in the village. The Moscow girls sloped into the dusk. He could hear the 'phone tinkling in his little house and was relieved he was too far away to answer, but it rang persistently. He counselled himself to be calm. He often spoke to himself as if he were a son in need of reassurance; father and child in one, a whole family in him all trying to make their point at the same time. The 'phone stopped, and the evening settled into peace again.

Then it rang again, but not for long this time.

"Sober, you're welcome. Drinking, no. No way, Max."

Insects orbited lamps slung from concrete arches. Cicada tapped syncopations with the sea. Light glowed through bottles of brightly coloured alcohol on the bar: rubies, deep blues, green limonvodka.

"You know I'll just go to Shota's and drink there."

"Max, don't drink anywhere."

The lamps caught the two Moscow girls from the beach. Bionic Woman's cantilevered magnificence strained her Tommy Hilfiger top to bursting. Their faces, waxed by the light, stoned him with derision then dipped back to their shisliks. A mosquito bit him as he left.

Max knew the disapproval bristling Shota's moustache would give way to the mercantile instinct. A small bottle of vodka was purchased on condition that Max drank away from the tourists in the bar, so he sloped under the huge magnolia to the farthest corner of the patio hanging over the sea. The headland soared above him; light bulbs strung through the magnolia branches formed a sickly cone glowing in the Black Sea night.

Perched on the edge of the land above the waves, he released the genie in
the bottle.

One bottle wasn't enough: an hour – maybe it lasted slightly longer.
He didn't want to rush it, look like he needed it. He always wanted to
smoke when he drank, but had given up when someone said it withered
the erectile nerves. Half the second bottle had gone before he tried a song.
Shota silenced him with a shout from the bar. Max swaggered towards him
via several small diversions and inflated his chest. "It's fucking Schumann!"

"Behave, Max."

He drank to his own sullenness. Among the tourists scattered under the
branches, two locals recognised he was back on it and chose a table on the
far side of the tree. He watched them avoid his stare.

"Normally I would drink wine, but it dehydrates me."

Still they ignored him.

"And Georgian wine is piss."

They went inside, and the tourists followed.

Now the brooding started. There was a library of disappointments that
required redress but the infidelity of Masha and Gia smouldered at the
heart of everything. She was an artist whose paintings were sold by the old
Georgian émigré community in Paris. Max had been partly responsible
in setting her on the road to artistic success; she had been his woman for
decades, protected by his position, plucked from mental hospital, tolerated
and loved, with a few excursions to other bedrooms – nothing serious, and
as for Masha, she outstripped any sexual run of his, sprint, middle or long
distance. The ones he married annoyed her because he never married her.
But the wives meant nothing to him, they were married for ... well, there
must have been reasons. Except his first wife of course, certainly there were
reasons for her, but he had to bale out of that one, he had to. No doubt, if
the circumstances had been different, it would have ended the same way as
the others. Whenever he thought of young Peg, his American wife, he felt
uneasy and in drink this expanded into something so painful, it required
more anaesthetic. Young Peg, of course, would now be old Peg, just a few
years short of his own decrepit state.

The other partner in this conspiracy of ingratitude was Gia, a dyslexic,
warped by a family feeding on rage and despair. Max and Masha provided

sanctuary from Gia's brutal family and Max watched him become a prototype for the child Masha wanted and he didn't. When Gia revealed a talent for carpentry, it was he and Masha who had him apprenticed and when he started producing astonishing furniture they set him up and Masha sorted the export of his work to fashionable Parisian stores. He had, Max supposed, brought a sensation of parenting to him, albeit of an avuncular kind, but as the boy grew he developed a second talent that made him popular with the lady tourists and finally with Masha herself. Everyone knew about this triangular arrangement, everyone talked about it except its three members. Ignoring the little complication, they hung together; adult orphans keeping a breath on a fading cinder of thin, herd love. But the ember was dying; the old male was now in the way. Max, the former star, was being sidelined.

He stood aggressively, "Judas!"

"Shut up!" shouted Shota from the bar.

Masha drained Gia. The Moscow Beach girls were currently draining him too; anyone sunshine side of vomit ugly drained him. But Gia refilled and emptied with the ease of a flush toilet. Masha had emptied many others in her time too. Max's head roared with the sound of flushing toilets.

Past fantasy now: third bottle, only the odd bewildering thought penetrating the thickness. He was refused a fourth bottle. The customary splutter of indignation ended with the drunkard's pout and the angry stagger, the swaying bow over one of the jaywalking tables, the bump off a vine post, and the list into darkness.

He encountered the two Moscow girls as he dipped and rose vaguely towards home. Their faces were half seen masks of disgust, giving as wide a berth as the road allowed, but the uncontrollable, drunken lurch threatened face-first intimacy with the mighty bosoms. "Say something," the dating agency in his head counselled. Involuntary dance steps teetered him within the tall one's domain, and a beautiful face burned contempt down from the night sky at his slurring apologies. For the first time he noticed the astonishing beauty that transcended her gutter origins; the flower from the dung heap hidden from sight behind her friend's vulcanised pheromone triggers. Then all was caught in a swift totter as he fell over and everything disappeared.

Early 1964

I do nothing. It's a kind of epic indolence in me often misinterpreted as a death wish. Fear springs some men into action, but sends me to sleep and my inactivity becomes a crisis. I go from invaluable to liability in double time.

Kennedy is assassinated and Oswald's shots ricochet around the world. In my cups, I present inappropriate theses about the bed mating Cubans and Mafiosi as the shadows on the knoll and dismiss the misfit in the Book Depository. Peter gives me the flea in the ear about that and my lack of action on defection. Tomas died of heart failure before Kennedy threw himself in front of the cornering bullet, and was nothing anyway; all those threats were Hispanic piss and wind, so zip it with the wild allegations and look to your responsibilities and danger.

Things are complicated. I have been an expectant father for some time, a cause for celebration that I have never mentioned. Peg was bewildered at my request to keep it from her brother as long as possible, but held out for a few months. As soon as Henry knew champagne corks popped all over the office, and everyone, including Peter – consummate actor that he was – grinned and gave me the expectant father jokes and advice.

It was not deliberate. The pregnancy sent me into a tailspin of panic and rage at Peg, all smiles and momsy, collecting magazines with crib and baby clothes ranges, happy as she was entitled to be. I did wonder if it might throw my investigators off track; surely anyone under suspicion wouldn't start a family unless he were innocent?

Away from the office celebrations, Peter accuses me of irresponsibility to the point of cruelty. Why hadn't I told him? What was I hoping for by concealing it? What was I hoping for by making her pregnant? Now there would be two to be abandoned. I have no answers; I tell him it wasn't intended, even Peg didn't want to get pregnant I say, but it makes no difference, this is a terrible situation.

I know he's worried. My vulnerability is his vulnerability and I suspect he is making arrangements for his own defection, just in case. He has a huge family he won't want to leave and I know he blames me for putting him in that position.

My Russian contact Yura says I'm not consciously cruel, simply careless enough to let cruelty in through my legs each time I open the door.

Ironically, they arrange a going over point in an alley behind the baby store where Peg and I bought the pram and a bundle of things. That was the rendezvous, the beginning of the trip that would end in some dacha behind the Iron Curtain writing love poems to my abandoned wife that could never be sent. I was in the habit of calling in on the way home from work, so it wouldn't arouse suspicion. It had a neon stork carrying a baby in a sling that switched from pink for girls to blue for boys and traded under the name 'The Happy Stork'. Yura suggested it, so I knew they were watching me too: both sides watching, maybe watching each other watch.

But I was trapped by my own inertia. The concept of free choice is a delusion; it only exists as a therapist's bait to keep you booking more sessions and signing the cheques. We are powerless over ourselves. I called off two pick-up days with feeble excuses that children could have seen through, and I knew the panic bells were now ringing all the way to the Kremlin. The star boy was losing his nerve and there is no one more dangerous than an operative who has lost the plot.

It's night in the Washington bar where we drink. I shoot back too many martinis and ignoring the discomfort of buddies in the company of someone they know to be under investigation, launch into my lecture about the Cuban/mafia connection to Dallas. Peter comes in, sees I am drunk and doubting the Official Version. He makes a gun with his hand, aims, 'fires' and immediately turns his back. It is the presentation of his back that collapses every last redoubt of resistance. The choice is clear: it's the bright red star above the Kremlin or Peg in widow's weeds.

September 1998

Max sensed death sniffing him out. As they left the village, the clutter of houses and the bay receding in the wing mirror reflected back as the last glimpse of a place where so much of his life played out its farces and tragedies. Everything seemed to be ending: Masha was receding with the

houses; the century was drawing to its close; the ideas to which he had
dedicated his life were buried and millions danced on their graves.

The village was preferable to Tbilisi, which had become derelict and
dangerous in recent years, but the difficulty with Masha was best dealt with
by distance. As the van whined up the hill road she and the village would
soon be out of sight – out of sight, out of mind, as with much of Max's life.

Gia's van slowly filled with the smell of perfume. The lingering presence
of the Moscow girls who had decorated the beach and Gia's bed deepened
Max's nausea. He knew Gia would have crept out before they woke.
Goodbyes scared him and threatened to open up secrets that he could not
define. When little Gia was sent in to make his final farewell to his dying
mother, she made him wait for an hour by her bed before turning her
martyr's face to him and saying "Just go away". She made sure it was the
last thing he heard from her, and Max supposed that moment from a bitch
who took her sadism right to the grave was the reason why Gia could only
deal with women one way. In the bedroom he was a master. Beyond the
bedroom he was a mouse. His sexual hunger always ended in flight. But
there was no flight from Masha. She had him netted, and Max watched the
pained sufferance of the slave quietly set in his face.

"Past their sell by date?"

"What?"

"The Moscow bints."

"Don't get on the moral.. You know.."

"High ground?"

"Yeah."

"There's something worrying about Russian women with money. "

"Lots of people in Moscow have money now.."

"They have drugs?"

"No."

Gia's denials betrayed exactly what he was at pains to hide. Max could
visualise it: the inelegant image of the huge bosoms rising and sinking
under sleeping arms like trapped buoys would be the one Gia woke to when
the drugs wore off. Their epic proportions that no doubt had him vibrating
like a tuning fork the previous night, would repel him in the morning. As for
the tall dark beauty who seemed to have energy for nothing but contempt,

what would she provide? Sex was probably multi-tasked and practised while smoking and reading a magazine.

"Gia, are you driving into these potholes deliberately? You trying to punish me?"

"No."

"I can get drunk once in a while. It does no harm."

"Sometimes Max you are two metres of bullshit."

"Gia I can't stand this self righteousness."

"Give it a rest, Max. You're still pissed."

Max turned his mouth to the air slipping past. They were on the crest of the hill now. The village was behind them and slipping out of sight. Below them the sea sat to the horizon like grey glass, broken by tiny flickers of foam.

Twice a year Gia delivers his furniture and Masha's paintings to Tbilisi for their journey to the galleries and shops of Paris. Max does the export and EU paperwork and they oversee the precious cargo being loaded into the trans-continental lorries for their long haul across Turkey, the Bosphorus, Bulgaria, and the long roads to France. Gia has no idea where the countries his furniture will cross are; Max points them out on the map but it means nothing. Gia can't imagine it, a complication of his dyslexia Max supposes, an inability to conceptualise space and direction.

But Gia waits for these days like a child anticipating a birthday, and in the van rattling over the long and broken road Max knows he's raining on Gia's parade. "You shouldn't have got drunk last night. You could have waited," he mumbles to himself.

An unavoidable hole in the road flew Max's brain against his skull and produced a loud bang somewhere in the back of the van.

"Shit!"

Gia stopped and got out to check and Max took the opportunity to hover his dry old member over the roadside weeds while the precious cargo in the van was inspected and re-roped. The sun was tapping on layers of cloud over the Russian side of the sea.

"'The quality of pissing is not strained, it droppeth as the gentle rain from Heaven.'" And the gentle rain caressed a few weeds, then paused, then started again, then paused, then didn't start again, then did.

Patches of the sea and coast were still mixing light and mist into low sprays of incandescence. Gia was drawn towards the cliff's edge to contemplate the day smoothing away the remnants of night. He was a dyslexic who could barely read a thing, a condition that condemned him as a child to the fist fights and rage of the pack outsider, but Max knew that behind this was a strange, battered poetry, a sensitivity that plugged him into mystery, almost like an animal, a Dao quality of knowing something the rest didn't get. The balancing cost was word blindness and hopelessness with women. He was a tortured soul but not on an operatic scale. His was a life of everyday difficulties exaggerated because of his handicap, the type who would always find life difficult, and when he wasn't arguing or being driven close to insanity by him, Max loved him for that.

"What's that word for you know, poems or music about dawn?"

"Aubade."

"Yeah. All that peace. You could be an alien, just landed, and you wouldn't know there were people."

"Nice thought."

"The bit just between night and day. The world's changed. People have died, people have been born."

"I hate it."

"How can you hate that peace? Before the shit starts."

"It's death's light. I wake, and I know."

"You know what?"

The vomit rose up like lava and was over the wild flower before the brain transmitted the previous evening's vodka was on its way back.

"Jesus!" said Gia and watched till the vomit production ran dry. Max seemed as shocked as Gia at this sudden flight from his stomach and took his jitters off to a little rock to calm down. Light as a rag, a canvas wrap of bones and skin, glowing with illness high above the ocean, he seemed as skeletal and warped as the surrounding trees that a century of winds had deformed.

"Jesus, Max. Why do you do this to yourself? What kind of a manly thing is this? Getting helpless drunk?"

"Oh, for Christ's sake!"

"You remind me of my old man. Drinking and spewing. Have you any idea how bad it makes me feel?"

"Not as bad as me."

"I nearly didn't bring you this morning. I was so disgusted with you."

"Who would deal with your EU paperwork?"

"That's the only reason I brought you."

"Well, we must be grateful for small mercies."

"Your door was open all night. The room was full of mist. Wet everywhere. Inside the piano. How can you do that? Musical instruments... They're the masterpieces of carpentry."

"I threw up in it once. It survived."

"Your room stank like a lavatory. You pissed the bed again."

Max let out a death rattle sigh and the arteries on his temples channelled pain into his brains.

"We can't hang about."

"A minute."

Gia pouted and waited, then the shifting light and the first seabirds moving across the pewter sea caught him again. Max spoke with the energy of a man running out of time.

"You know those books I gave you? With the photos. Gaudi, Art Deco, Japanese minimalism, you know, for your ideas."

"I have my own ideas."

"I know, but there's nothing wrong with plagiarism. It's the privilege of the gifted and the only recourse of the mediocre. These books have beautiful photographs, but why not go there and see the real thing? Stand under Guadi's spires tickling the old Barcelona dusk. You've got the money. Most people here haven't got an arse in their pants. Go to Japan and feel what its like to sit at a tea ceremony in a Shinto temple or wherever they have tea ceremonies in Japan." Max felt a foreign body in his mouth and spat it at the wild flower. Gia turned back to the sea birds in disgust. "You get wound up about being dyslexic, poor me, everyone else can read. So what? Idiots can read. Idiots write. How many of them have a real gift? Like you? Though you wouldn't think it, the amount of whining you get through in a day.

"You can pick up some scrap of wood and hand back civilisation. Jesus Gia, how many people can do that? A chunk of that old tree over there,

that twisted, old, knackered thing, transformed into a... I don't know.. A
beautiful chair that will sit in a Parisian home for generations. That people
will get fond of – 'Oh I love that old chair, don't you? So get off it will you?.'"

"Get off what? The chair?"

"Not the chair! You! Poor me. The 'poor mes'. 'Think of how upset I get
when you have a drink!'" Max spat again into the long grasses soaking his
legs. "Trees are pregnant with your furniture. You're a fucking midwife. A
forest is just a big family to you." He aimed another gob of murky phlegm at
a clump of wild flower.

Gia grimaced, "D'you save that stuff up?"

"Money really does grow on trees for you. Well, spend some. See the
world. Everything stays little in a place like this. Yes, the littleness of life."
He looked at the palm of his hand as if he were reading it, "I've always had a
dread of the littleness of life."

"Look where it got you. Honking up on a hillside."

"Thank you. As I was saying before your astute observation, get out of
here. Before you shrink away."

"You've shrunk into a bottle."

"We're talking about you. What have you got here? Your loving family?
Who only stopped beating you when you got rich?"

"They're family. You don't know about that."

"You really are pissed off with me." Max hauled himself unsteadily to his
feet.

"You're not going to throw up in the van?"

"Oh, get off the pity pot."

Lucy found an old cafe, solid in a proletariat past. Steel coffee machines
and samovars hissed and dribbled; cakes turned stale in glass cabinets, and
women in white bonnets brandished fleshy forearms pink with dishwashing
at porcelain sinks at the back. It hadn't changed since Stalin's Five Year
Plan had them dancing in the streets. But a cream éclair, like a queen bee
on a white saucer spun a membrane of narcotic sugar and white noise
between her and the outside world. She fought it till the door-bell clanged
in half a dozen German office workers.

"Does this have alcohol in it?"

"No."

"And another coffee please."

The day tunnelled down to Big Bertha hovering the cream drug across to a fresh plate then hulking beyond focus into the background and the coffee machine. Saliva formed in pressure balls and squeezed Lucy's tongue root. Her heel started moving up and down in a rapid flutter. All noise was baffled and distant; she could see the coffee machine and the slender black rope filling the cup. Time and space were warping. Einstein was right; he too was a cake-eater.

The coffee was made. She lifted the cup and éclair, turned and shouldered through the Germans, across the cafe floor to the safety of her table and the relief as her teeth tore through the éclair.

Four coffees and another chocolate hit after the éclair pulled her back to a familiar basin of despair. The power of this cycle suggested her weakness had more stamina than her strength and the optimism of the new sober and disciplined life was simply delusion. Normally she could call on a tribe of Alcoholics or Overeaters Anonymous members to talk her through whatever storm of self-destruction she induced. Once through these crises she seemed to forget things very quickly, her world became benign again and she felt safe, never questioning if the sense of grace she aspired to were as delusional as the despair that hounded her. Then a flare of temper, another sweet binge or just a feeling of uselessness fired her back to the dungeon it seemed her life's work to escape. She was a psychological recidivist; out, back in again, out – this time it'll be different – back again. Give yourself time they would say. How long she would ask, and they would just shrug, as long as it takes.

Inevitably she found herself at her father's window, cupping her eyes against the light. Imaginings of him playing the piano lazed past like fish. The room photographed on her mind. Over the river, hills began to bake. Should she haul out to the Black Sea? Her calls had been unanswered. The only transport was taxis; the road was long and dangerous and in this country financial empires had been founded on seed money from kidnapping. The arguments against banked up, then the silent tirade against her own fecklessness replied, citing another grand scheme that

would achieve nothing more than a crater in her bank account: the babe
who was all start and no finish.

A firm decision not to make a decision till noon next day was made,
but on a bench above the river, home began to reclaim her. She put on
her Black Flies; white framed surfer lenses from Southern Cal, with
its beaches, and abundance of AA meetings. East of the Brandenburg
Gate the Fellowship was still a pioneering movement, hacking its way
into the hinterlands of historical alcoholism. She had made one English
language meeting in Moscow, stuffed with Brits, Americans and Russian
businessmen looking for trade openers, where she remained discreet about
her identity with the Americans, but made a British connection that led to
a room at the Embassy. Under the disdainful stare of Her Royal Britannic
Majesty, she was given her father's addresses and asked not to let on where
she got them.

Maybe AA had reached Tbilisi; it usually followed Citicorp and
MacDonald's into the vacuum left by communism. The American Consulate
would know; all she need do is lift the phone. But it seemed such an effort.

Daily life for the Georgians was buoyed up on collisions of anger and
resignation. The disappointments and abuses of the new freedoms were
an insult and Lucy was aware of a dangerous rumbling discontent. She
could almost smell the threat. The gulf between the new Mercedes class
and the rest shuffling the downside of economic freedom was huge. For
most, things were going the wrong way since the Soviet collapse. Answered
prayers brought poverty, electricity and water shortages, and a corruption
unmatched in the dead days of socialism.

As the darkness gathered, swathes of the city had disappeared. Patterns
of light broke out only in patches and across acres of darkness the hideous
high rises on the edge of town where the residents had rigged illegal taps
into the electricity systems, glowed dimly. Moscow was rough but eager
to seize the capitalist dream, her classical streets garish with neon, but
Georgia, once regarded as the California of the Soviet, was reeling from the
shock of freedom. It had first brought a brief, bloody civil war that left parts
of the city a mosaic of bullet holes; architectural war wounded reminding
the visitor that the juncture of a corrupt past and a corrupt present was a

graveyard.

As an addict Lucy understood the hit of cruelty, how hatred makes junkies of mankind and how killing was the greatest high of all. When placed beside that greater addiction, her problem was insignificant. She had survived the excess of her own nature; thousands of innocents had been swept away by others' insatiable habits of violence. The town touched her sentimentally; both were slowly dealing with their own historic rubble.

As a child, she had taught herself Russian and infuriated her mother who wanted all links to her former husband erased. Tolstoy, Dostoyevsky, Chekov, Gogol, Gorky, Pasternak, Turgenev, Lermontov were pored over without necessarily being understood. She couldn't talk about this in the Valley; anything beyond Mork and Mindy was cause for persecution. She had written to Solzhenitsyn and never received a reply; watched Eisenstein, listened to Tchaikovsky, Rachmaninov, and wondered if her father listened to the same composers. She had never known he was musical. Her mother had soaked him in mystery, the various houses of her peripatetic childhood painful with unasked questions, and above everything squatted the unpatriotic fear of a war with Russia that might kill her father.

The brown Mtkvari river beneath her slowly mesmerised her on its long way to the Black Sea. She should take something back from this place; not dismiss it because of its unfortunate association with her father. It had a sense of surviving everything that history threw at it. She would ask the hotel where the monasteries were – perhaps pick up a repro icon for Timmy her cartoonist fiancée. She should ring him, she should find a meeting, she should do this, do that; 'shoulds' buzzed like wasps. She switched them off and stretched. The morning was bright and lovely. The trees made zigzag silhouettes against the river and the sun boiled up the hills.

Just as her buttocks and calves began to smart from the gradient, she heard a dog snarling and felt a burst of adrenalin, but pushed on praying to her Higher Power for protection. Foreign dogs always had rabies. Then she thought she heard a sharp, helpless sound like a desperate puppy or even a child.

Her senses sharpened; she could hear wind spreading leaves in the park a hundred yards downhill. The gradient pulled her butt, "Keep going – this is doing you good," she exhorted and bent into the hill but a scream yanked her straight. Fifty yards up the slope to her right was her hotel basement, to her left the terrace of houses stepped up the hill. A car was parked in front of one house. The first house had a walled garden stretching down the hill from the gable end. Trees draped over the cracked facing of the wall, rusted hinge pins fanged an empty doorframe and the throaty vibrato of the dog roared somewhere in the garden. She whipped herself on, no one would blame her for walking past, but another yell drew her into the garden, scanning bushes, vegetables, fruit trees, freshly turned earth, seeing nothing, then a big, ugly shadow at the bottom wall violently shaking something. From her place in the light, she couldn't distinguish what it had in its jaws then she heard the child's screams again.

She shouted for help in English and Russian. A woman sprinted in from the street and started pelting the dog with shopping from a string bag, then anything she could get her hands on. Its nose crinkled out of shadow and the sun highlighted blood on one fang. The mother rained oranges and onions, clods and flowerpots on the fiend's head; a plover defending its chick against an eagle, drawing it as far from her child as she could. The little girl soughing in a red and white dress at the foot of a tree began repeating a word from some half alive retreat of pain and shock. Lucy dashed back to the gate as if to fetch someone, whom, she didn't know, but on cue a police car drew up. "In here! Mad dog!" she bellowed in Russian. The cops rolled up their window and stared. "You cunts!" she screamed in English.

Like rubbish rolled by the wind, the child bowled along the wall for a couple of turns into sunlight, then stopped, her self preservation instinct dying. Against the other wall the mother fended the beast off with an old canvas and tube chair. It flipped like a fish and was at her again. From the safety of their car, the police sucked radio.

Some impulse rushed Lucy over the seedbeds, releasing earth smells around her and she swore at the soft soil for ruining her Birkenstocks. While the mother blocked the dog to her right she went for the kid, now cursing that she had not been born athletic and panicking like a slow catcher going for the line, knowing an avalanche of defence is about to bury her. Her breath exploded in hisses and half screams and she berated the child for lying there so she had to stoop to grab her, "Make it fucking easy!"

but the child was an inert, useless weight not helping in her own rescue and Lucy yanked the arm hard so it would hurt the little fucker who had got her in this trouble, and turned for the escape hatch to the street a thousand miles across the garden.

Dragging the kid like a rag doll towards the street and the cops she saw in the corner of her eye the lacerations in the child's neck and arms widening with each pull and the little thing's eyes Exorcist up in their orbits, then the dog baling off the mother. Now she was caught. The dog raced at her and the stolen prey. It was happening, and she felt mesmerised, like she did in a vertigo attack. A garden fork by a vegetable bed presented itself, she lifted it and lunged at the savage blur ripping towards her and the load of the prongs bursting into the dog's chest knocked her onto her knees. The animal convulsed into an epilepsy of shock and whined its pain into the Tbilisi morning and the fork spun and perforated her palms with splinters, but she held tight and watched the prongs yaw and widen the wounds as the dog fought to free itself. Suddenly the prehistoric racket faded. The dog put a paw up to dislodge the thing in its chest. Some primitive instruction told her to push; she sank its hindquarters into the soft earth and on the edge of her vision, saw the mother skedaddle off with the bloodied parcel, saw the police open their car doors and get them inside, then heard an engine rev.

"Don't fucking leave me!!"

The dog convulsed back in zigzags, she slalomed with it into a haze of stinking breath pleading with it to die but it was still unbelievably strong and whisking her closer to malignant teeth. She was beginning to lose. Then a stocky, crop haired man bounced over the wall at the bottom of the garden, and spat a command along a huge automatic rifle.

"I don't speak Georgian, you cunt!"

"Take him that way!" he said calmly in Russian. She dragged the dog flank on. Foam blurred its jaws.

"Shoot the fucking thing!"

The detonations were very fast and loud. She felt the ground convulse, the dog dropped like a stone and the fork was wrenched from her hand. She knew it was dead before its big ugly body hit the earth, but he kept firing and she watched the sudden perforations in its hide and the bullets exit

through the other side in little bursts of fur. The firing stopped and she was
in the suffocation of cordite and burnt dog hair, seeing the man's mouth
move, hearing nothing through the fire alarms in her head. The bullet holes
were tiny and there was no blood.

A strong hand gripped her upper arm and pulled her away from the dead
dog. It was one of the policemen. The man with the rifle shoved the dog
with a toe. Words babbled under the ringing in her ears. There was blood
on the lower part of her dress. A cloud shaped like a human foot drifted
slowly over the gable.

The drive to the hospital was all horns and swerves. The dog's eyes accused
her of murder. In a room of antique cabinets and medical equipment, she
watched her blood fill a hypo and felt the edge of mortality. God won't give
you anything you can't handle, they say. How about rabies?

Then she was out with Joseph the rifleman into the afternoon sunshine,
ricocheting between feeling lucky and worrying about infection and death.
They progressed through Dopplers of horns along a wide avenue by the
river. On the other side the town lifted from dark wooded banks to hot roofs
wedging out of blue shadow. Hazy figures drifted across a stone bridge.

Among chrome dryers and oscillating fans at his wife's hairdresser's
shop Joseph told the story while Lucy waited in the car. The door was open
because of the heat and Lucy watched two women in aprons flicking their
cigarette ash onto the linoleum and a third, tall, sturdy woman with dyed
black hair stepping into view and putting her hand over her mouth. The
solitary customer rotated in her nylon bib in shock, then like an under
funded Greek Chorus they turned and peered at Lucy. The big one looked
the way only a wife looks at a blonde. A tie-dye coloured comb rose from
one fist like a small cleaver.

Narrow streets spewed them into a square. A drink winked, a drug,
something to wash away the morning's contamination. She asked to be let
out; the hotel offered nothing but solitude to brood, here she could feel the
crowd and let them tease her back to life.

Joseph's ease with the gun and his unfussy calm alarmed her. She
sensed old survivals haunting her companion, milliseconds where death
whips past and the sensation of life sharpens. Someone standing on

another experience of life, looking down at her innocence and naivety. But she sensed his interest in her. It was innocent, devoid of the usual sexual charade she expected from men. His nut-brown head gleamed through the sunroof teasing her to shoot the breeze and unload her father on him over a Georgian coffee, but the words stayed locked up and it didn't matter.

The passing citizens and groups at café tables became background to a sensation of owning a moment, as if time had slowed just for them. Who or what her bullet headed companion Joseph was, was of no importance. Perhaps he was named after the fourteen-year-old Stalin, the local boy who came to this square from his seminary to read Darwin and a hand written copy of Das Kapital, before growing the other most hated moustache of the twentieth century. It didn't matter. None of the old nonsense mattered to her at that moment. Everything felt clean and pure, and free.

"I could have shot the thing. Its been hanging around for days. It went for a guy last night in the street. He stood on my car roof to get away from it. "

She saw faint claw marks on the bonnet. Joseph was shaken with guilt.

"Don't be hard on yourself." She could imagine him teasing the little girl and doing his bit to help her enjoy being a child.

"Who is this Monica Lewinsky?" He lit a cigarette with a match from a box, swirling with tiny Cyrillic. "And Judge Starr", he smiled, "Ringo Starr" and laughed his way into a mild smoker's cough. His head was almost spherical; his hair cropped to stubble to disguise his baldness, his huge, prominent eyes the colour of amber resin. She felt close to this stranger.

"Pretty matchbox."

He offered it to her but she declined politely.

"Most people wouldn't have done what you did."

Courage was beyond her understanding. She felt a pair of invisible eyes on her wherever she went, judging every action, and a horror of publicly exposing her cowardice had pushed her through the gate. But in the garden she had experienced the urgency of survival and it was exhilarating. Killing a dog had made her feel authentic.

He suggested they meet; insisted he and his big hairdresser wife would take her to a real Georgian restaurant where they served good Georgian wine. It wasn't the time to say she didn't drink, but it reminded her that she was an alcoholic who hadn't been to a meeting for too long.

Joseph gave her his card and she accepted his emphatic invitations. He made her promise she would call next day. He was offering friendship. She promised. She could see how much her acceptance meant to him.

"Don't forget your Kalashnikov in the trunk."

The dried blood blended with the burgundy leaf patterns of her dress. Now the city's bullet holes made a visceral sense; she felt connected. But as his car left the square she knew she wouldn't call him.

Down in that part of the city where the electricity was rationed, a principle stirred in Max when touched by the 'people' and their struggle. The broken streets where they dream of a second Stalin had grip on some withered corner of his imagination, and whenever possible he shopped among the 'people' in stores where candles guttered over a few hanks of rope or tins of olives under no credit signs and portraits of Uncle Joe. Then he would haul back to his respectable neighbourhood and listen to Bach.

He progressed out of the candle nebulae towards the boulevard brightness up the hill where native Georgian played host to the tiny vanguard of European and American businessmen. The evening crowd streamed past, music tinkled from battery-powered radios, scooters revved, herbs and cooking engulfed the wheezing Peoples Hero in smells and teases of alcohol. A coffee would help – the hangover was still strong – a coffee would gee up everything.

At the point in the descent to the chair where the bony buttocks hit the seat with a happy bump, he heard American voices. His quadriceps reflexively strained him vertical and hauled him two cafes distant from his former countrymen. A boulevard of pavement tables and lamps scattered up the hill to dark trees melding into an indigo star swung sky. There was no power cut where the tourists and foreign businessmen hung out.

Eventually, when the arteries in his throat calmed he ordered coffee and water and sat back to watch the rooftops silhouette against the first lightning flash. Now the day's static would be discharged, the air would sweeten and soften his hangover. A glass of wine would help, hair of the dog, but no, he wouldn't. He was hitching to the wagon again. For a while.

Gia's and Masha's stuff would be well over the Turkish border. The paperwork was in order and all was well again with Gia.

English voices drifted from a far table, businessmen laughing with the gracelessness he had come to associate with that greedy little island. In Moscow at the Old Spies Network – a club with no premises where the members socialised with the gay abandon of actors who know they've done their last job – the Brits were particularly loathsome. He recalled Maclean and his English rose wife, trailing scents of tea and Cambridge lawns in their wake, and how after a bucket of whisky the old-school-gentleman performed the Mr. Hyde twist into violent ass bandit. At the other end of the scale festered the bickering of Moris and Leona Cohen, a union made in Limbo of a man feeding his insatiable dissidence by railing against Soviet plumbing, and a woman refusing to be critical of anything east of the Brandenburg Gate. How hopeless could principle become, Max wondered? Didn't it all boil down to incontinence and fear in the end? The philosopher Locke said we are what we remember. Fine by me, thought Max, because I can't remember a fucking thing.

Sweat pattered on the ground between unpolished shoes. Two small vodkas would stop this confounded shaking. He looked up and an anonymous Georgian kid strolling past with his father looked at him as if he were deformed. The kid's stare knocked him from his drunk's disdain into a puddle of shame. He jammed his tongue out aggressively. The lad turned back into his father; dad's hand rested on his shoulder and they continued down the hill, leaving the old heap in a bluster of righteous indignation at the contempt of the young. He banged back his coffee and snapped at the waiter to bring him another.

A flurry of 'fucks' burst from the Brits. "Weaned on sophistry and hypocrisy", Modin said of the English. Particularly Philby, a man for whom treachery was oxygen, and a twenty-five carat drunk till his Russian wife put the mockers on that. "Two whiskies only or he gets his arse spanked" Alexei used to crow.

He had shared propaganda tours with Philby – speeches, awards, and hatred in the street, dinners with grim Hungarians and Czechs, and functional sex with waitresses in freezing eighteenth century bedrooms overlooking the Vistula in spate. Philby was surface and meretricious glitter, a calibration of balances and gyroscopes absorbing every blow, twist, breeze and vibration, hiding and storing, multiplying meanings; born to treachery. Two beers would do, get rid of the shaking. Ames apparently drinks too, he'd read. Burgess died of drink. What's this thing with spies and drink? Fuck that kid. Staring at me like that. I could go to the bar near the apartment. Shit. I'm barred there.

As he lifted his shopping the tendon on his hip pulled and the limp home was divided into short relays with pauses for rest and back rubbing. Many a bar mocked him on the way, but he passed by and got to the last junction before his apartment. It was now eighty metres of pavement and thirty-six stairs to the triumph of arriving home vodka free and thwarting Gia's doleful disapproval. His breath came in miserable rations, his arteries beat in toothache thumps, his tendon nagged like a persistent wailing child till he wanted to give it a damned good thrashing; body and age conspired against him.

He bent with his bags to the pavement, laid them down and placing his hands on his lower back near the source of the pain, hauled himself vertical in steps, moving his palms up his sacrum with each upwards creak till he was able to stand tall and empty another bag of quiet curses into the Tbilisi night. To his left the road rose steeply to Rustavelli Street and on a high balcony of the hotel a woman in half silhouette stared out over the city, her blonde hair haloed by the light from her room, a goddess of capitalism, in tourist luxury high above the penury and darkness below. He looked the other way across the river at nothing, at black blocks of an invisible city. No streetlights burned; no tourist hotels bathed blonde visitors in light; pinheads of candles were the only evidence that people existed out there.

What difference does it make, he thought, the universe will die one day like a rotting cat and leave God waiting for Welfare. That is a scientific fact and there will be nothing the priest, the Mullah or the philosopher will be able to do. "We shall have strutted our stuff across existence and left no print" he said quietly to the blonde on the balcony, exhorting her not to be so fucking pleased with herself. But up above him she sipped her coffee unconcerned, then turned her head, and light shimmied across her hair and a chill went through him, perhaps simply because she had seemed like a statue, then moved as if she had heard him. But she was too high and far away to have heard him and the fear shocked him and left his rattling

arteries scurrying and leaping like a chorus of frightened ring tailed lemurs
against the bars of their cage.

He stooped to his bags on the pavement and his tendon sent a twinge
across his hips and all philosophy was eclipsed by lower back pain.

Early 1964

I let all lines go dead, hoping the investigation would run aground; many
have in the past and many innocent officers have been investigated for a
host of mysterious and misguided reasons – it is part of the landscape. If
worst came to worst I could take my chance with the interrogators, but this
was a desperately foolish place to be and I knew I was probably holding a
loser's hand. I also knew Yura and the Russians knew why I was holding my
ground and resisting an immediate defection. Peg was the fatal weakness;
for her Marxism was no alternative to moving up to three bedrooms.
She was not designed for the political debate and too woven into the old
Eisenhower fabric of nation, family and marriage for the subject to be
broached.

"We know you are in such a painful place, but the consequences of not
going over will be much more painful" said Peter, "at least this way Peg
knows you're alive and perhaps one day something can be worked out. Who
knows? But we can't negotiate with the electric chair."

I met Peg when she was a schoolgirl, Henry's kid sister; the bobby
dazzler who had the High School boys almost reading Rimbaud. I
thought nothing more of her; she was funny and very beautiful and we
communicated on a level of mischievous insult whenever Henry took me to
his Mom's for Sunday lunch.

I was a swimmer, county freestyle champion at sixteen and although
the martinis rapidly began to inhibit my training programme, in those days
I swam almost every day. One night I saw a white blonde head pushing
a swell of water up a lane and lo and behold when she touched the side it
was Henry's kid sister. She was a swimmer too – school captain and on
the verge of State representation. So I took her for a hamburger and we

exchanged swimming notes and it first occurred to me that the twinkle in her eye might not just be for my coaching hints. This flummoxed me and I took it to Henry.

"Of course. It's puppy love."

"Maybe I should stop coming round to your mother's for a while." And I did. For two years, and next time I returned the young girl had become a woman, self-assured, calm, operating with a different set of coordinates in the human map. Her mature beauty had a force to it that overwhelmed me. In this I was no different to the rest of the male population outside her door, yet she was modest and decent and often complained about how she hated being stared at.

Who could blame the passer by for staring? Some beauty places the bearer beyond the norms of sexual reaction and they become a human aesthetic, an ideal by which the mass can place itself, and Peg was like that. Hers was a lonely place because it isn't easy being natural around someone blessed with such extraordinary looks. Small talk is impossible. However the wit still bubbled under the elegance. Her swimming career had stuttered; a series of back strains had edged her out of the State side; the ladder to national level and maybe even Olympics had been pulled up.

I took her to the theatre a couple of times and a feeling between us could no longer be ignored. So it went on, sweetly, clandestinely, chastely, till we had to tell the family. They seemed thrilled and confident I would conduct myself like a gentleman, and I did – her mother scared me too much for anything else. Away from Peg I drank like a lumberjack, but she was the decency in me. Seven years younger, she nonetheless anchored me to a sense of being normal.

Our courtship was chaste, formal and conducted within the classic rituals of that time of Schwinn cantilever bicycles, tin coke ads and drive-in movies, when being an American really seemed the greatest blessing in God's world. Kent State, Oswald, drugs and Vietnam lay in ambush in the next decade.

Peg had had boy friends, but she was a virgin, a not altogether exceptional state in those days, and remained so until her marriage night. I, on the other hand had negotiations of a less pure nature with Boston girls when I was at Harvard, and my barroom hobbies occasionally led to waking to strange ceilings with an unknown face on the pillow beside me. I had also begun to pass information across.

When I told Henry that I had proposed to his sister and she had accepted, we waltzed arm in arm through the Washington snow from bar to bar to celebrate our new affiliation till poor Henry couldn't drink any more.

September 1998

Coffee went over the white tablecloth and her suede Birkenstocks. Her second Tbilisi morning started badly and as waiters fussed around, the fuck-this default position clicked in. She could fly back from Tbilisi with connections in Vienna, but when the receptionist asked if she would like to book, her resolve stumbled. The morning continued with a bad fall on her father's stairs and she hung from his courtyard gates, rotating her foot like a dancer till the nausea subsided. Now she hated the city, her father, and everything east of Highway 5. The dog garden and Joseph's house were passed without notice and the ankle became so painful she had to turn and walk up the hill backwards.

Limping into the refreshment bar on the stout arm of the Cossack doorman, she hid her bruised dignity behind indignation. She was finished with her father. The Cossack nodded, and lowered her onto a banquette by the big windows then brought her a glass of tea in a silver Georgian holder.

Her head tilted back onto the top of the leather banquette and the sun haloed her exhausted face. Shoots of ruby bounced from the maroon Formica into the smoking tea in her shadow. Morning sunshine shrouded her into a ghost. She was fading like an unfixed photo of herself, dissolving in light.

Max left early and spent the morning in a music shop, browsing the manuscripts and discussing politics, music and soccer – about which he knew nothing – with the proprietor over an endless succession of coffees. He bought a Schubert manuscript he didn't really need because he had to leave the shop with a gesture to the morning's goodwill.

Approaching home he saw a woman hanging onto his gates and the old alarm in his head blasted off. Automatically he hid in the park trees on the other side of the road. Hugging the Schubert sonatas to his chest, he saw Peg waiting for him at the gates, rotating her foot like a ballet dancer. Turning profile to limp along the embankment, Peg faded and something of him washed glassily underneath. Then the woman was round the corner and gone.

He was shaking. I'm in shock, he thought, this is a hangover hallucination. But all the rationalisations were swept away by some unquestionable force of evidence and instinct.

Strolling casually across the junction he saw her struggling up the hill. She was obviously in physical distress, and for an eerie moment he felt concerned. Something about the shape of her head, the angle of it to her shoulder as she leaned against the wall and the way her hair tumbled down the side of her face left no doubt that this stranger extended his line on Earth.

He always wondered if the child might turn up. He had told no one about her; only Party colleagues in the old days knew about little Lucy from official sources. Now all the resurrected ghosts pulled his thinking back to his baseline state of escape and the logarithms and binary systems of his nature rolled out the automatic fight instructions.

Gia had gone skirt-hunting the previous night, but might have been back when she called and the beans may have been spilled. He imagined Gia's shock. Masha's reaction did not bear thinking about. Friends would hide him without questions; he should run back, pack a few things and vanish – explanations could come later. But some other buried thing pulled him a new way and sucked him after, squinting along Rustavelli's walls for a hand helping the injured ankle or the blonde head shining in the crowds. In a hotel entrance he glimpsed the Cossack doorman supporting her.

He had occasionally allowed himself to think about her. He remembered the baby vividly. Asleep on her mother's chest, she had been preserved tiny and helpless, locked in time, although he had sometimes worked out the years and tried to imagine what she might look like as she grew. Now an adult from a future he left behind replaced the tiny thing he had last seen in his kitchen. There was no doubt. He was shaking, he should go; this was far too dangerous. But he found himself in the lobby, positioning himself

so the archway wall bisected him and edge-framed her. A slight lean to his
left and he would disappear. Twenty metres away he and his ex-wife's youth
shimmered in the sunlight, ghost dancers preserved in living aspic. Peg's
throat shifted under his jaw, a bigger bosom than Peg's drew his eye, but his
wife was much younger than this woman, slight and vulnerable compared
to the buxom blonde who seemed mother to the breast he watched feed
her. A spoon tapped a glass and clattered Formica. She had his mouth. He
hoped she didn't have his teeth.

"Hello Max."

The Manager shook his hand; the Cossack had the other in a vice. He
had fallen for the classic pick-up. The Cossack retrieved the music from the
floor.

"Schubert! Wonderful." They were gliding forward. "Come on Max" said
the Cossack.

"Nothing to worry about" added the manager.

"Please stop this...."

Eyes floating above smoking teas followed his humiliation.

"Miss?"

The sunlight switched up the blue and he saw Peg. When her face tilted
into shadow the eyes became grey and Peg dissolved.

"Miss, this is your father. Max, meet Miss Lucy. Your daughter."

Like workers not certain something will stand, they waited for a
moment. Schubert was laid on the table; sunlight bleached his portrait on
the yellow cover. The manager and the Cossack smiled discreetly and left
for guard positions by the arch.

He was thinning but not bald. She had thick eyelashes, like Peg's, corn
coloured beneath the mascara. Her hands were disproportionately small.
His shadow flitted in a spray of light dancing on the ceiling. Voices scattered
sibilants through slanting sunbeams. A man standing at the corner table
turned a page and flattened it.

"Hello" she said.

"Hello" he replied. "How's your ankle?'

"I fell on your stairs."

"Oh, they're vicious.' His hands were intertwined in front of his belt;
his thumbs moving vertically round each other slowly and smoothly. "I've

fallen down them myself."

No shit Sherlock, she thought. He drinks like a Georgian the Embassy Brit had said. Max saw the spray of light above and glanced out the window for the source. One of the women in the corner burst into hysterical laughter.

"I'm sorry I'm such a mess." She fingered the abrasion on her knee.

"No, don't apologise. Please." A silence seethed at them. "Can I get you another tea?"

"Actually I'd like a strong coffee."

"Excellent idea. I'll have one too."

The manager watched Max from the lobby. Lucy's chest was tight as a drum; she took a couple of deep breaths and the man at the corner table peered over his glasses at her swelling breasts.

For Max the immediate problem was coping with the engulfing sense of public shame. His conviction was that all eyes were on him and he embellished his walk to the counter with a ham actor's insouciance. As yet he couldn't bridge beyond embarrassment to the reality of what had happened.

As he brought the coffees and sat she observed him leave a discreet space between them. He loaded sugar into his and started slightly at a noise or movement she could not detect. She dropped three sweeteners into her coffee and felt naked revealing her sweet tooth and weight concerns. But all alcoholics have a sweet tooth she counselled in her head, he has a sweet tooth, look at him taking coffee with his syrup.

"I haven't spoken English for some time. Although I occasionally teach it. On an informal basis."

"You translate, don't you?"

"Ah. You've been checking up on me."

"Have you ever checked up on me?"

He felt a hot rose unfold under his ear and spread through his skin like warm water. Another smile greeted the empty space in front of them. Sipping coffee and looking up at the dancing light, he unconsciously turned the music manuscript over so Schubert couldn't see him.

"When did you arrive?"

"Yesterday. No. Day before. I was in Moscow for two days. Three days.

Two days. I leave tomorrow." She didn't know when she was leaving. She was letting him off the hook and cursed herself for it. Already she was giving in.

"What's the coffee these days in America?"

She shrugged. "Starbucks. Chains. Lots."

"I can't remember what it was in my day." His face lifted to the ceiling. "Maxwell House!"

The pigment under his ear was pale again and blended into a leather neck, cracked with fine lines like old stucco or baked earth or cookies. These observations were a pushing against the suffocation closing on her, a trick developed in the unbearable moments of childhood; look at the thing in front of you, give it your concentration, don't look up. Then the hotness would go and another little drawer was safely locked. She had known he was old but now experienced it. She had shocked him; she must give him a chance.

"You lived in Wisconsin." He had checked up. "All those Norwegian Lutherans who don't dance in case people think they're having sex standing up." The woman in the corner gagged on some different gem of wit and Max wondered what she found so fucking funny. "I mean... they don't have sex standing up in case people think they're dancing. I think in Georgian and I never could tell jokes, but you probably follow my..."

"Drift."

"Drift."

"How did you know we lived in ....?"

He knew. Idaho, Indiana, Iowa, Michigan, Minnesota, Mississippi; they had dragged themselves through an alphabet of unhappy locations under a series of pseudonyms. He had been fed the information by a poisonous shit at the Lubyanka precisely because he knew Max didn't want to know, and had occasionally caught himself browsing maps of the States.

Cutlery was being shifted somewhere; the pair of them strained to end silences. Max asked what she had seen. The dog was mentioned and he seemed to listen with intense concentration while keeping his head partially turned away. He wouldn't look at her. He coughed then rapidly barked into a brief, hanging dry heave that gathered looks from the women and tempted Lucy to announce he was nothing to do with her.

The man in the corner pressed the spine of his book again and the
women turned back to their gossip. The laughing woman had fallen into a
depression. Sunlight blanched the white haired Cossack as he watched the
passing trade in the street. Outside and in, people passed with the troughs,
peaks and long flat-line of lives wrapped in ordinariness. She wanted a
drink. He wanted a drink. They could handle each other if they had a drink.

"From certain angles you look like your mother." It took courage for him
to say that and he hoped he hadn't revealed that Peg still had some strange
hold on him.

Lucy let him in a little on her mother's Long March from Day Zero and
described her third husband without trace of her own antipathy to him.
"He's a paint millionaire from Phoenix Arizona. Made millions out of house
paint. They live in the Biltmores. It's kind of like a gated Nirvana for her.
She likes to shut herself away anyway, so she can finally do it in style." She
could remember nothing about Peg's second husband who was gone as
quickly as he arrived.

"Well, I'm one divorce ahead of her."

"Yeah?"

"Two Russian wives. One was the daughter of an eminent scientist, the
other was well, it doesn't really matter, it's a long time a..."

"Any children?"

"No."

"So, no Russian stepbrothers or sisters?"

"I'm afraid not."

He had opened up dangerous avenues of conversation and braced
himself for an assault, but it didn't come; she seemed as wary of this
minefield as he.

"You two made a lot of divorce lawyers happy."

"Yes, I suppose we did."

"I'm to be married soon."

"I hope you break the pattern."

"In Maui. Next to Hawaii."

"Hawaii? That sounds very exotic." He coughed at the ceiling, said
"Good luck" and brought the beat of that small exchange to an end.

He was pining for control; everything was picked over and evaluated as a potential threat; he realised he and his daughter were communing on the outer edges of paranoia. He felt her need to find something at the heart of this fragile exchange and she owed nothing in this story. All the debt was on his side.

"I don't expect anything." Her affected honesty was merely an old negotiating technique that usually meant precisely the opposite of what she said, but it swiped the legs from under him. "Kinda like unfair of me to arrive unannounced, you know, invading your private citadel like some Trojan horse."

"No, no.. You have every right to ..."

"I should have phoned and asked but I was scared you would have said no. It's kinda childish uh? Just arriving here."

"Well I don't know, sometimes it's good to catch a passing wave, you know. Throw caution to the wind and all that. Anyway you're here. And I'm here and... Are you familiar with Homer?"

"Homer?"

"Wooden Horse of Troy?"

"I read it."

"I read it in Greek."

"Wow. Greek! You speak Latin?"

"I did. A long time ago." He moved Schubert an inch forward. "I can't remember a thing now." He continued to cover a noise snaking up through his lower intestines. "We stuff ourselves with all that education and.." a loud bowel groan reddened him. Something in his lower trunk bayed for release and he excused himself and rose. The intensity of her fear shocked him; he reassured her he was only answering Nature's call, and as he entered the lobby the manager and the Cossack rose like bouncers. He explained himself, they looked at Lucy and she smiled and nodded in a way that suggested it was a desperate emergency and they should let him through. That little gesture revealed wit and he felt strangely pleased as he headed down the stairs to the basement lavatory.

In the lavatory a benign state settled on him. One of the nightmares that ran through his exile had come true. Oddly, he felt lightened now it had happened. At the moment it was academic, it could not be grasped except as cold information and shock. The irony that he had given the

most sophisticated security service in the world every chance to catch
him and had been brought to ground by someone he last knew in a state
of helplessness in his American kitchen was not lost on him. He detected
a fine anger and wit bubbling beneath his daughter's diffidence; she
was attractive and bright, although perhaps frail psychologically. But
that of course could simply be because she was in a vulnerable position.
Nevertheless, from what he could see so far, he would have no need to be
ashamed of her in public. She had grown up to be a bonny woman too,
and it intrigued him that the little pile of sleep he had first seen behind a
hospital glass screen had grown into this fine looking person.

A curious relief motored him along the corridor back towards the stairs
and his daughter. But Max was a slave of fantastic organs that gainsaid his
best intentions. An invisible arm would reach out of his chest for the drink
he wasn't going to have, his mouth would say "no" when it meant, "yes".

A door was open on the basement corridor. Heat, city sound and light
beat through. Outside a driver and a hotel porter were unloading crates of
Pepsi from a truck. The crashing sound of the bottles caught his attention,
the invisible arm ushered him through the door and he said good morning
to the men as he walked past into the street.

She caught the flare of the Cossack's lighter as he lit his fortieth cigarette
of the day and looked at her watch. Still an hour to lunch. Max had been
gone some time. Relax, she said, old men and lavatories are sometimes long
negotiations.

She had never considered what she hoped for by coming, but arrived as
unconsciously as an amoeba attracted by an agreeable stimulus, and now
was blank. He was nothing like the fictional father she had carried from
childhood; in some ways he was rather repellent. All the booze graffiti was
hung out to view: the chafed pink patches on the skin, the liverish eyes,
pitted nose, the deep shake and stale smell of wind dried hide. It might
have been worse had he stayed, dry heaving his way through her childhood.
But he had been a member of the generation who created the peace and
black rights movements and the last turbulent shake down of a nation that
had since gone cosily to sleep in its dollar papered nursery. All her life she
was aware of the American-Way being fed into the national consciousness,

in movies and marine corps rhetoric, in the steady voices of patrician newsreaders, the perfection of advertising, and the reverence for the Flag and the Dow; a tranquilizing narcotic that produced a national absence of curiosity. Perhaps the best thing Clinton had done for somnambulant America was to take his dick out in the Oval Office. She reflected wryly how her disagreements with the national mores had usually been articulated in bars and toilets with dollar bill tubes and Jack Daniels in a campaign to become a legend in her own mind. She had wanted to be a person of principles but never found the technique. Her father has at least acted on his convictions – questionable though they had been, but the great dynamic that ripped him from country and family seemed to have left no visible marks. Instead a suspicion of being lost lingered about him, of something huge having leaked and left.

Tilting back to absorb the warmth, the light and the quiet sounds rustling through the hotel, hunting him down suddenly seemed a bogus act. All the problems of abandonment, absence, the resentments and problems, drugs and alcohol, the sense of being an outsider had orbited around the conviction that it could all be traced back to Max as source. But she was three weeks old when he vanished in the baby shop, nineteen weeks when the first news was allowed to hit the headlines. He was nothingness: an enigma, a romantic tragedy, a stranger in another country. She had to be told about him. Was this dowdy pensioner with colonic problems really the hole in her childhood she could never fill?

"How much is your father, how much is your shit?" had been an AA theme. She could see how Max was the excuse for her mother's sustained misery. At school her friends cast her out with the chant "traitor's girl" but kids love cruelty and instinctively sniff out everyone's weakness.

The Cossack rose and looked at her.

"Shit..!" she hissed. Everyone abandoned Lucy and that information loaded her to her seat. Noises distanced. Tinkling spoons were a mile off on the far side of the tea bar. The tea drinkers conversed in a free world, while she watched from behind the wire. She had seized her life for a moment, but with the seat beside her still warm from her father's ass, it had been torn back.

She knew everyone in the tea bar knew. The radio signals were being received loud and clear; the two women stood in embarrassed silence, eyes cast down while the eyes of the man with the book scanned the words without reading them. She was pinned in a time warp. They all witnessed the manager and the Cossack swing round the arch with the burden of her humiliation and watched her go down like a street execution.

"He went out to buy music and hasn't been back."

She remembered Schubert, lying face down on the tea bar Formica. A man, much younger than she stood at her father's door with a proprietorial confidence that suggested he had certain rights. The Cossack who had accompanied her and now took command of the crisis, spoke to him in Georgian. The young man was neatly dressed and handsome in a haunted way. It crossed her mind that her father may have gone across in more ways than one. But what would this young man find in a figure who would not be out of place on a park bench sucking a quart of Coors? Still, she thought, it takes all kinds and if Max had gone gay in his dotage, it would be the crowning evidence to her mother that her youth had been steered into a marriage with a complete aberration. And it also offered Lucy a rationalisation of why he had abandoned her for a second time. He was too embarrassed to let his daughter know.

The neighbours picked up the threads of Max's latest defection and made universal noises of sympathy. An old bony hand stroked her hair like a child's and Lucy wanted to bat it away. The man introduced himself as Gia and made way. The women pressed them into her father's house where perfumes from jugs of flowers mixed with the aggression of furniture polish. Lucy expected the apartment to smell and look like her father, but it was neat; the hoover was plugged in; they had interrupted Gia's housework. Was this relationship one of a young ingénue keeping the clutter of an old eccentric's life at bay? Yet there was something eerily sexual in the attention Gia gave her. He spoke Russian to her but she was convinced the real meanings were being conveyed in the Georgian arcing between him and the Cossack and keeping her out.

"I didn't know."

"About me?"

"Yes."

"Join the club."

"Sorry, it's just a shock." His face betrayed everything he felt and this awkwardness thawed out an edge of her resentment. Both had been betrayed by the same man. "He just walked out?" asked Gia.

"Yes."

"He does unpredictable things."

The Cossack spoke Georgian to him and Gia shook his head.

"He left some music at the hotel. Schubert."

"Schubert?"

"Yes."

"He likes Schubert."

"Well, it's at the hotel."

She saw how difficult he found it to look at her directly. There was some history in him with her father, but she was beginning to doubt that it was a gay one. "What's your relationship with him?"

"He sort of looked after me when I was a child."

"Lucky old you" she said in English.

A brief Georgian sentence from the balcony cued an outburst of laughter from the neighbours. Gia's crimson signals flagged up again. But she had had enough of secret subtexts around Max, and of the futility of her pursuit. She looked at the Cossack. "I want to go."

"If he turns up, I'll bring him to the hotel."

"He won't turn up."

"If he does, I'll bring him."

The Cossack helped her climb the hill back to Rustavelli. She gave in to the pain in her ankle to keep the anger and everything else at bay till she reached the privacy of her room. There she lay on her back and stared at the ceiling, watching the light change as the day wore on, trying not to think, just feel, letting the disaster drift through her, snag and hurt, release and move on, compress her with pain, shame and anger, shake out of her, let her sleep for a while, wake her to a deeper sky and the morbid facts, unchanged and present.

A drink would numb it all. Where would be the harm? Could she be blamed after what she had gone through? Just till she gets home. Then she'll deal with it. Fuck off Lucy, what would that solve? Nothing is improved with a drink and she would settle into the knowledge that even this awful day would pass and become an anecdote.

The phone rang and her pulse trebled. Her mind convinced her she didn't care, her body told her the truth. But it wasn't her father but Gia, down in the basement bar, if she felt like joining him, which she didn't but she did because she didn't know how to say no and perhaps he had some news. His vulnerability mirrored something in her, and she found herself adjusting her make up as she left the room. The wrong kinds of whispers were taking breaths by her ear.

"I've tried everyone I know. But.. No sign of him. Don't know. The neighbours are keeping an eye out now. If he turns up while I'm here, they'll march him round. Don't you worry about that; they're all on your side."

Gia is courteous and considerate, shielding her from the cut-price gigolos stalking the bar where they meet, but he smells of damage and danger.

"I'm dyslexic and Max tried to teach me to read. When I was a kid. Not much success, but he tried."

Dyslexics scent things no one else can smell, hear notes the rest can't hear, can speak to dogs – she looks at the tell-tale fold in his chinos and knows what he is and how everything is foreplay.

"Masha would like to meet you."

"Who's Masha?"

"She was your father's long term, you know, lover," he said the word as if it might be inappropriate, "I rang her. Its been a bit of a shock, you know, your father never.. Anyway its about a five hour drive, so she should be here soon."

She feels threatened by the attention and the curiosity, and the winking liquids in the glasses and bottles, by the loud camaraderie of a bar and the stink of cigarette smoke. "I have to get out."

They sit in the tea bar waiting for Masha, and her eyes are fixed on the banquette.

"They were lovers?"

"Yes."

She looks up for the dancing reflections but the ceiling is growing dim as the evening moves through twilight. The day is draining itself out of her.

"They looked after me. My family was.. I would stay with them sometimes" said Gia.

"Didn't they want their own children?"

"Masha did."

The way he said it told the story.

"It turned out she couldn't have them anyway.."

Lucy looks up at his face as he struggles to hide some tortuous message. A strange bond binds him to Max and Masha and she cannot see what it might be. But she is on her knees anyway, taking the count. The last thing she needs is some ex-lover full of curiosity and shock arriving to give her the once over. She feels dangerously vulnerable, but she always feels vulnerable. Maybe she should stab another dog. The local AA meeting waits for her somewhere in an unknown street where she could get it out, but she is weighed down with the lethargy of the defeated, and sits sharing silences with Gia till Masha arrives.

Masha comes in trailing a sense of tragedy. Her beauty is earthy, exotic, and makes Lucy feel like a beauty parlour product. But her hands are repellent, deformed, white scars tear across broken knuckles. They are the hands of gargoyles.

Dinner is proposed and Lucy doesn't have the strength to decline. Tinny noises and faces bleat and shift mistily. Fine silver threads in Masha's hair, spider-webbing voices and tinkling plates, cups and piano notes from the in-house pianist weave into the hallucinogenic tapestry of the night. Gia insists on paying. When Lucy argues, Masha tells her to let him. They sit with her till the last diners float towards the door.

Gia is leaving. The moments move like liquid. He patches together a speech telling her she mustn't leave thinking her father a bad man, he was good to him when things were tough, when he was a kid Saint Max was there for him, suffering the little children. Nobody else was. Except Masha obviously. It hovers between them as subtle as a flying mallet. How big is his cock, Masha? How big was Dad's in its communist heyday?

"Just leave, Gia." Masha commands.

"Thank you for the meal. And thank you for your kindness."

He is gone and the two women are marooned with each other, across a no man's land of white tablecloth.

"Masha isn't my real name." It hung under the high ceiling as a statement of the self as enigma and Lucy wondered how some people found themselves so fucking interesting. "I was a cellist once.." aah, thought Lucy – musician, artist, moody, interesting, deep, different, plugged into secrets of the universe, I am not worthy...

"You know Chekov?" asked Masha obviously expecting a negative.

"Some."

"*The Seagull?*"

"Yes. Masha, who dresses in black in mourning for her life?"

Masha was impressed.

"My fellow musicians nicknamed me after her." She laughs and it blows a spit of self-mockery onto the smooth patina of her eastern chic. "I was such a drama queen. Now I'm a painter. Everything I do is hideous." She holds up a fist and puts it down gently. "But people pay good money for hideousness. They think it's profound." She looked down at the fists, lying between them like rubble. "They can hold a paint brush, but not a musical instrument. Except piano a little. But no cello."

"But they could at one time?"

"I wasn't born like this." The hands smoothed a wrinkle of tablecloth. "I was a child prodigy."

You would be thought Lucy.

"A little Soviet star. Hauled across Europe from concert hall to concert hall as an emblem of the cultural genius of all the Russias. We didn't have light bulbs, toilet rolls, but my God we had culture. I was a star turn in Europe. But as soon as the applause died they would shut me away. Just past teenage, young enough to want some fun, to meet an Italian or a Frenchman, paraded for the West then the West shut away. Puritan bastards. So I demanded to be taken off the foreign tour circuit. They would have none of it of course. More lectures on social deviancy, more concerts planned and I thought I'm going to defect. I asked your father to arrange it. He betrayed me."

"You have evidence?"

She laughed. "Are you acting in his defence?"

"If he betrayed you why did you stay with him?"

"Because he stayed with me." She ordered a brandy. When Lucy declined there was a flicker of curiosity.

"Perhaps he just couldn't stand to lose you."

"Sure. It worked. I was dropped from the European tour and sent round factories in the Soviet as a punishment. So one day after a lunchtime concert for workers in Minsk they were showing us the production lines – as if we were remotely interested – and there was this small power hammer punching metal sheets."

Lucy's own hands flew to her chest for protection. She saw fingers bursting over metal and workers stepping back in shock and disgust. Blood on Party officials; a young girl sinking to her knees and the machine hammering on rhythmically above her impervious to the national insult and the pain of an individual pushed by the clash of an unstable nature and political conformity. She thought of a cello, abandoned in a corner somewhere, and then locked up in its case, put away and forgotten.

"I woke in a mental hospital. They fed me drugs that really did make me insane. No one was paying attention anymore." She made a fluttering movement with a hand that was graceful despite the deformity. "Except your father. Everyone has constancy for something in them somewhere."

Not for me, thought Lucy. She wanted a cigarette though she didn't smoke, and looked round for the Cossack who always smoked. All curiosity about her father had suddenly drained away. What little of his background she had picked up slightly repelled her. It seemed so overly dramatic: love triangles, art, broken fingers. She'd got away from the damage in her own past and the passionate and the eccentric in others now bored her.

Silence bumped across their rocky histories and they sat with it for a while under the high classical ceiling. Tall pot plants stood around the room like ancient retainers weary with waiting. Lucy contemplated the brandy glass turning in Masha's fists, following the fish eye reflection of the dining room over its bell curve. Little spectrums glowed and faded as the liquor smear dissipated on the inside of the glass. More shards of her father's past drifted across the tablecloth.

"We went to Cuba. Fidel? Aaah... You meet him, he's all over you, he forgets you. You have to meet him in the middle of the night.

"They had a film festival in Havana years ago – Czechs, Russians and some American radicals who shouldn't have been there. I think they were Jews. Anyway one day we were sitting near these young Americans, outside a cafe. I caught the way your father looked at them. Eventually he spoke to them. I've no idea what he was saying – my English – they shook hands and the Americans ambled off. He was so disappointed."

"Why."

"Because he told them who he was and they had never heard of him."

Peg obviously held a fascination for Masha. Closed down in a non-drip marriage to a man who made his fortune from non-drip paint, Lucy had a whole vaudeville script about her mother, but didn't want to do it. However, for form she gave Masha a teaser. "When I was drinking, her husband – her current husband – bailed out my money problems. I should be grateful but it just pissed me, you know?"

"Did you ever say no, thank you?"

"No. I know, but.."

Masha shrugged.

"Yes I should be grateful but...."

"So many of your sentences have 'yes but' in them."

"Yes... yes..."

"Like your father 'yes but' 'yes but'. Or just 'no'."

"Yeah." Masha's riff of complaints about her father left little space for Lucy. She had things to say too. She pressed on. "I can understand what a shock it must have been for him. I put him in an awkward position. Maybe this trip was a piece of vanity."

"It isn't your fault your father is an arsehole."

"Whenever we settled in a new place I went to the library. The newspaper archives, you know, and read about him? Same stuff everywhere: enemy of liberty, betrayed his country, family..."

"Max betrays. It's his calling."

"Maybe."

"No 'maybe'. Except perhaps me, I suppose. Perhaps that's why I get so angry with him."

"Yeah..." Masha was interrupting her flow; Lucy wanted to dip her oar. "Anyway. In the libraries? Weird, you know, like sitting a few feet away from some library assistant with all this stuff about your father? Then handing him back and leaving. As a kid I always felt something when I passed a library, as if they were where my dad lived."

The pianist finished packing away his music and as he passed, bowed to the two women and said goodnight in Russian. Masha spoke to him in Georgian. He indicated the piano and she rose and crossed and the sensitivity with which she played confirmed her musical past. Lucy had a tin ear but the piece struck a distant bell; a night with a black boyfriend at an art house cinema in the days when she only watched sub-titled films and only hung out with ethnics, lifted up like Proust's stage set, and rekindled a lost feeling of the future as a cornucopia of waiting glories.

The music drew the Cossack in and settled him against the arch by the pianist. Thin pipes of smoke from his cigarette fluttered towards the ceiling in double helixes.

Masha was present only in the music, a component of a higher aspiration, counter-pointing the absence of any such thing in Lucy's life. The music disembowelled Lucy and her journey to truth and healing felt pathetic; the road to the Oracle, only to find it shut for the season.

As the last chords resonated into the recesses of the dining room Lucy's robotic applause was cut short by the pianist's and Cossack's reverential compliments. Masha replied to them and Lucy sat alone with her unmusical self until the chatter and bonhomie ended with another courteous bow from the pianist as he left, and a smile from the Cossack as he took himself back to wrap his chair in another cloud of cigarette smoke.

"The theme from *Solaris*?"

"*Solaris*?"

"The film. Tarkovsky."

"I don't watch films. Bach. Prelude 'Ich ruf zu dir, Herr Jesu Christ'."

"I'm a child of the Spielberg/Lucas nexus... I don't suppose you've heard of them either... I'm not very sophisticated."

"You don't need sophistication. You're American." Masha stroked her knuckles gently. "Your father plays that much better than me."

"How did you meet?

"He came into my dressing room one night. Full of vodka." She laughed. "He was an important person. Though I couldn't understand why he would leave America for Moscow." The fists were raised again. "After this, in the first nuthouse they put me in, a male nurse gave me paper and charcoal for sex, and I started drawing." her eyes blazed with Georgian melodrama. "A triptych of God taking a shit flanked by the Madonna baring her arse and Christ with an erection. No more charcoal. They weren't worried about blasphemy; they just needed an excuse. My drawings were 'degenerate'" She lifted the brandy. "Here's to degeneracy. In the second hospital they gave me the liquid cosh and…"

"Liquid cosh?"

"Drugs. Like a zombie, sleepwalking for months. Then your father turns up. He's tracked me down, and he brought a small tin of watercolours. He told them to lay off the drugs and they did. He was quite a man in those days. I started painting: eerie visions of the hospital and its inmates, the way I saw them off my head on Nembutal and Largactyl. Strange. He liked them. They hated them but they weren't going to argue with Max. Then he brought oils and canvases and it got serious. I painted an old woman Natasha who had spent most of her life in asylums, I painted her bare breasted. Then the hospital as it really was: toilets crawling with filth, patients who had soiled themselves left naked as a punishment. Max would smuggle some of them out. But they caught me. That was going too far. Even Max could do nothing about that. So, more drugs. Materials confiscated. Sleep and nothingness till Max secured my release. That was how it started. The art. Sex and madness."

The deep drone of a plane coming in through the night grew overhead. They listened as its dark vibrations passed.

"I'll drive you to the airport tomorrow."

"Thank you but I can get a cab."

"I'll drive you." Dark hair cascaded down Masha's face and long brown neck. What was a woman like this doing with her old dad? What had been her problem apart from loneliness and insanity?

"Okay."

Blue shadow spreads under the leaves where the dog trapped the child.

From her balcony she studies the streetlight casting the wall's shadow up to the vegetable bed and the shards of light lying on the dark town like broken teeth. Somewhere in the gloomy city her father hides from her.

The phone rings. Someone is at reception for her. Her spirits rise in hope it's her father with some late olive branch, but it's a young gentleman who has come to retrieve a music book. Her father's Schubert sonatas lie on the bed. She knows why Gia has come back, and why he waited till Masha left and it enrages her. But he may have secrets about her father, or even a message. No. The old spy won't fall to a sudden rush of sentimentality, the stroke will be played to its conclusion; he is gone and she should accept it; kill the hope; it is a cancer to her growth, her peace. But she can feel the lure of an old easy road and is tempted for spite's sake. AA ruins everything they say: anything below best standard just pricks the reawakened conscience and those who have gone back to the gin bars and low dives talk about how it ruined their drinking too. There is no comfort, anywhere.

"Send him up."

She instantly regrets it, hides the Schubert in her suitcase, then removes it and puts it back on the bed. Why pretend? Why play victim? Why not give Gia a message for her father? Father I forgive thee. Not. Go fuck yourself. No. Drop it Lucy. No messages either way, the only message Gia has is in his pants. Don't open the door to him. Don't give him the music. She re-dials reception.

"Hi. Could you send up a bottle of vodka, please?"

March 1964

The last few weeks before my defection were like a dream in which I floated from terror into periods of normality where I could laugh and go to bed as content as any man and expectant father. What was happening and what was going to happen seemed to be parts of two different lives. One would possess me for a while then the other would take over. By this stage I never knew how I was going to feel ten minutes later. Life was unpredictable, except that I knew it could only get worse.

Peg was moving slowly now with her pregnancy. We were ticking off days to the birth and had spent Saturdays at the Happy Stork baby store picking cots, buggies, and the inexhaustible complex of mysterious things attached to birth and the early days of a small human being. How a bush woman gives birth with nothing more than a length of biltong to bite on is beyond me.

I was prone to some pretty crazy thinking in those days. I thought about handing myself over to the authorities about forty times an hour, or of kidnapping Peg and burying ourselves in some Peruvian mountain village or taking up fish curing in the Shetland Isles under a new name.

I picked up a message from Yura at a safe drop. They were concerned that everything was taking so long and wondered why I couldn't cooperate? What was the problem was there anything they could do? They appreciated my position was difficult but they could not hold on forever. Perhaps my wife could be persuaded to come with me? She and my child would be well looked after in Russia.

The soul of discretion and understanding, Yura knew I was under no illusions, that assassins stood quietly chatting in the wings. It was a last resort though and a desperate one, so desperate I wondered if they really would have gone that far. The killing of a CIA officer would have upped the ante in the Cold War stakes. It would have been a propaganda bonanza for the Agency and the whole American Patriot machine. Washington would not have disclosed my dubious loyalty, but played the murder for everything it could get: I was worth more to them as a dead hero than an exposed traitor. They may even have awarded Peg a pension, and that's another option I considered – playing it out to the end of the rope, setting up some set of false clues for my colleagues back in the office so that it wouldn't be too big an act of hypocrisy to spit in the Russian eye and have me buried at Arlington under the American flag.

I was not entirely powerless, but all I could feel was a rope around my neck getting tighter. A prosecution was being built. It wasn't a case of if, but when I would be arrested. And it was sooner rather than later.

More reasonably I began to entertain the idea of handing myself in with an offer of information and names in exchange for immunity from prosecution. It would be a long shot. Americans were more reluctant to use this arrangement than our British counterparts, who took the view that since all spies are members of the same class, throwing chaps out of the club and making a fuss should be avoided if at all possible. And lying is second nature to the Brits; it's bred in them with rusks and mother's milk.

However, I had one big trading card. Peter. He would have been a gold medal catch. I also had a bag of others whose expulsion would bring out the bunting in Washington and turn a few Kremlin faces as red as their flag. I was a negotiator, probably in a stronger position than anyone. But these realisations came to me from the edge of madness. To me they seemed desperate grasps at straws. Peter knew this of course. We all knew everything, all the moves in the chess game. It was fascinating in a sinister way. These unspeakable negotiations shimmered between us like ghost dancers, unmentioned, un-implied, off limits, but unmistakeably there on our shoulders.

Something else was happening. Although Kennedy was devoutly anti-communist, it was clear he was willing to do business with Khrushchev after the Cuban crisis cleared up. The world was facing a new set of ideas. He was taking America away from the evils of the Klu Klux Klan and McCarthyism and the WASP smugness of the Eisenhower years. A new breeze was blowing across the Plains. It would never change my beliefs but the idea of being beholden to a Kennedy America for my life and freedom, was less repugnant that it would have been five years earlier. If Oswald had missed, I might be selling real estate in Ohio.

So, given the options available – remote though some might have been – why did I go over?

America was my country and yet it was not. Americans were my people and yet they were not. Some subtle, deep difference separated us. Politics was only one of its manifestations. I had no sense of tribalism. No sense of 'us'. Without that sense, a man can go anywhere.

Early 1999

Max bunkered through the winter in Tbilisi. Masha didn't call; Gia rang occasionally. He turned to repopulating his world, hedging against the last nine yards of loneliness by trying to rekindle dead friendships. Invitations to the house by the sea were offered to people he hadn't thought about in a decade and accepted, though everyone knew no one would turn up. Some asked about his daughter but there was nothing to say. Sometimes the best way to handle things is badly.

He attended mass over the Christmas and New Year period simply for the singing. Got a present from Gia, but nothing from Masha, which he thought was graceless; there was no need for such a lack of subtlety. He played the piano most of New Year's day, wished the neighbours well, paced his room, and reread passages of books from his shelves.

Just after New Year Gia picked him up, and they set off towards the Black Sea. En route Max suffered bouts of travel sickness and Gia had to stop to let the nausea settle. "Jesus, this is getting a bit of a habit, Max."

"It's not drink, I don't know what it can be... Probably something I ate."

Perched on the van's bumper feeling the winter wind lance his lungs, while Gia froze the weeds with pee, Max groped for some comforting thought, but found nothing. The landscape reflected his state. Rolling hills and valleys that in summer were soft with grasses and purple shadows, undulated hard and dun coloured to the horizon. Gia scrolled through white noise on the van radio. Tinny music and local ads bled into the wind. Christmas was a new celebration, and it had been miserable.

The little white house was cold but Max felt good to be back. Books would arrive; work would distract him. From nowhere had come a translation commission. Hunter S. Thompson was about to be set on the reading public of Georgia through Max's linguistic skills. The money was a welcome padding to the pensions and guaranteed as much as anything could be in this country. Shota had replaced the dead bulbs in his magnolia tree for the New Year. But up the shore sat Masha's house, shut away from him, a border fort keeping him in his place.

He toyed with the idea of selling the house by the sea. Masha was wound in its fabric and to return there reeked of self-punishment. But the house and village were part of him, the little measure to which his life had shrunk perhaps, but where he wished to shrink the rest of it. His affair with Masha had straddled the best years of his life and he couldn't just dismiss that. And Gia had most of what passed in him for fondness. Who would he take his problems to if Max were not there?

Gia had stocked the fridge with food. Max made a plate of cold meats. On the radio they were analyzing the peace talks between the Kosovars and Milosovic in Paris and he permitted himself an old hand's snigger at the presumption that there could be any other conclusion than failure: it was after all, what the parties had gone there to get. He switched off and dissolved into the sound of the sea.

It had quietly resonated through the house for two hundred years, God's time signature vibrating in wooden window frames and floorboards, fading on the white walls every few seconds. The house was one of the sea's harmonics. Everything happened to its rhythm and reassuring permanence. Outside, the walnut and thuja trees aged to its soft beat. On its huge surface Max could see the raft a kilometre out in the cold. No one remembered when the raft appeared or why, but he felt it belonged to him, and he to it, and both of them to the great sea, his rocking wilderness where he found a stretch of peace. But now the swim out was beyond him. Another thing was stroked off the list. Life shrank a little more.

He took the padded covers off the old Bosendorfer piano. Sea air should have ruined it but its tone stubbornly survived. He dug out his tools, struck the tuning fork and stood it on the case. It hummed into the room.

He had noticed how the church was slowly taking Masha. However, her painting of the Madonna and Child Jesus was the work of a heretic who in the old days would have been flogged to the execution pyre. Her Holy Pair were like heroin addicts twisting up from some dungeon of horrors, encrusted in thick layers of paint on an iron square hacked from a wreck in Batumi dry dock. Oxide rust and barnacles disfigured them with pustules of marine acne. They were strung from the beams of her studio roof on corroded hawsers and shackles, a shipyard Divinity, brittle with pain and starvation.

"Its very..."

"What?" she demanded.

"Startling. Striking. Very..."

"What?"

"Disturbing."

"So?"

He swerved away from the conflict and invited her to join him and Gia for supper at Shota's. She declined with a bluntness that left him with no option but to excuse himself and leave. He had hoped she had softened in the months they had been apart, but if anything, her disinterest had hardened into hatred, and it bewildered him. Had he disappointed her so badly over the years? Wasn't there so much that he had provided? Emotionally? Materially? Set her on a road to success and wealth? What was it, apart from a child that he had failed to provide? He was hardly alone in that respect; she had offered opportunities for impregnation to any presentable passer by, and all had failed.

On the road home he barely noticed the storm howling in from the sea as he reflected on the devastation this final farewell was wreaking on him and how it differed in no way from the first dear john he received from his first girl friend over fifty years earlier. It offered the same sensation of having been examined minutely then deemed not interesting enough, as if his entire life had been inspected and failed quality control. He was a creature of consistent reaction if nothing else, but such an experience in the teenage years is a rite of passage, whereas in someone his age it was a tragedy for the bearer and a farce for the observer.

A dip in the squall filled with the noise of brakes and he looked up at a black Mercedes bucking inches in front of him, engine running. Its lights were off; the wind had baffled its approach. He was about to give these idiots the benefit of his views about driving in a black Mercedes in a dark night with no lights when something about the four shadows inside checked him. From the rear seat, small, dead eyes above Slavic cheekbones scrutinised and chilled him, then the car revved up and disappeared.

"Jesus, Gia, that needs stitching."

Blood dripped onto Gia's shishlik. He put down his fork and pulled fresh dressings and antiseptic from a tooled leather shoulder bag. "I'm sorry if I'm making you squeamish."

"You're not making me squeamish. I'm just saying that's a bad cut."

"An occupational... What's the word?"

"Hazard."

That afternoon a chisel had slipped and left him with triangular wound on the back of his left hand below the thumb and the first finger. He took himself to the bathroom to apply a fresh dressing.

"He needs to watch that" said Shota across the constellation of table candles. Apart from Max and Gia, the restaurant was empty, but Shota always lit the candles. He liked atmosphere. "Infection, you know?"

"He's got more antiseptic in that bag than Batumi Hospital."

"I've got more antiseptic up my arse than Batumi hospital."

Shota returned to his paper. The contradictions of Gia's fastidiousness and carelessness, his life of neatness and sexual disorder amused or annoyed Max, depending on his mood. But he did not want an evening of fractiousness. He would have to draw heavily on patience.

Outside, the wind bounced the coloured lights around the magnolia. Winters were fierce on the Black Sea. This was the last to be completed in the twentieth century and it was not going quietly.

Gia returned with a pristine dressing and pushed the lamb with his blood to the side of his plate. Something was niggling him; Max sensed a point was about to be made, but when Gia spoke the question was unexpected.

"When you were a spy did you kill anyone?"

Under Gia's doe eyes he tried to assess what prompted this one.

"I don't mean shoot or... I mean, were you responsible for anyone's death?"

"Why are you asking this now?"

"Just..."

"Gia, all that's a long time ago."

"I know, but did you?"

"I gave information. Policy decisions. That's all." Gia dipped his head and ate. His hair had lightened as he had grown older. The bewildered child was visible in the big, strong man.

"Are you all right?"

"Yes. I'm fine."

"You seem a bit preoccupied."

Max waited.

"Masha and I sent your daughter wedding presents."

"That was very kind of you." Out of the corner of his eye he saw Shota flick a glance, then drop back to the paper.

"I sent a chest of drawers."

"That really was generous."

A second stretched by and Max fell prey to a sudden anger. "It's nice of you to feel guilty for me."

"I don't feel guilty for you Max. Please don't start. I just thought you should know."

"And what did Masha send?"

"The rough of that painting she's done. The little version."

"Of the Christ and Madonna?"

'Yes."

"That'll go down well in Christian America."

"I might go to America. For a look."

He blushed. Max knew something had gone on between him and Lucy, something that would not be disclosed.

"Good idea." They ate silently for a while.

"I thought it might upset you."

"The gifts or your trip?"

"Both. I don't want to upset you."

Max was touched but saddened. The pack was breaking up.

"You should get out of here, Gia. Travel. You'll find nothing here. You're a young man; you can make your furniture anywhere. In Paris, London, anywhere. You'd thrive. What is this place for you? Empty winters and fucking the tourists in the summer. And Masha..." The meat stalled slightly on Gia's lips. It was finally out on Shota's tablecloth between them. "It doesn't matter. There's more to life than all that nonsense, Gia."

"I know."

There was no need to mention it again. Another silence swaddled them.

"So you never killed anybody?"

"Does that disappoint you?"

"You wouldn't lie to me?"

"No, I wouldn't Gia." And Gia's gaze held him for a few more seconds.

Max paused against the battering wind and looked for Gia's figure struggling up the hill to his house, but he, the hill, his house, workshop and the whole landscape beyond the thin reeds of streetlights standing along the shore path were consumed by the darkness. With all his youth and strength Gia would be buffeted like a tethered balloon on that exposed hillside. Below in the relative shelter under the woods Max reeled like a drunk against the violent gusts. He turned his back to the wind so he could breathe. It jostled and slapped him like a rioting crowd, stinging his coat collar against his cheek and he listened to the groans and wails of the battle above him between the wind and the thrashing branches. "Jesus!" called Max but his voice was whipped away before he could hear it. Boat's lights suddenly winked in the blackness at sea, and as suddenly were eclipsed by invisible waves. An engine bleated through the squalls and was cut dead.

In bed the sound of a boat engine fighting the waves briefly woke him. It faded behind the sea, then snapped at him again. Banshees wailed through the woods above the house.

Next morning

Max kept journals down the years. Fading and curling notebooks spattered with intermittent notes on things that happened, things that hadn't happened, people, memories, things that made him laugh, his moods and reflections, even the occasional joke, a rag-bag of Max's world committed to posterity in an illegible scrawl. Some journals were thick with entries, some practically empty, but the scribbles fixed events, reactions and opinions, episodes that had faded from his natural recall. They were his Proustian Madeleines, bringing back forgotten scenes from the comedy of high office to the pain of personal disappointments, and sometimes just everyday banalities, the stage backdrop to living. A journal always lay open on the desk, where it could wait months for a scribble.

When he rose the next morning he crossed to his desk with his coffee and wrote an opening paragraph:

To shave or not to shave? That is the question. Maybe a change is needed; the commission to translate Hunter S Thompson makes me a writer of sorts, so a hint of Hemingway might not be amiss. I should surrender to the stereotype. More work will come my way; if you look the part you get the job. The world thrives on cliché.

There was nothing more added, but he would remember the rest of that day second by second.

The storm was still strong in the morning; the sea thrashed the beach, grasses switched and flattened in the wind and the sky streamed over the first cracks of light. He loved the long limbed summer days, but he also loved the winter rages. The elements enticed him to layer himself in thermals, woolly sweater, woollen hat, and his big all-weather coat, and step out.

Screens of sea spray hid the village. Waves dashing along the harbour wall really looked like running horses, a phrase he would never use, as he was sure Hunter S Thompson would not deal in waves like running horses, on or off amyl nitrate. The wind cuffed him but he felt invigorated. Despite the great loss around Masha, this was his home, his stretch of earth. He was a cell in this place, part of its fabric, and after his death there would be some shadow of him left in memory. For a while. In three generations everyone is forgotten.

He padded as close to the thundering water's edge as he dare. A dark shape rolled in the tide, a tarpaulin he thought; something torn from a desperate fisher braving nature at her worst to keep up with inflation. Max hoped that the fisher made it back to wherever it was going; when the Black Sea turns rough man has no place on it. The tide rushed the thing over the swell, and a loose edge flipped like an arm beckoning, and it chilled him. Then a wave spewed it back into the shallows, fell away and momentarily beached it. This moment nailed itself into Max and would remain in him for the rest of his life.

The thing was not a fisher's tarpaulin but a naked male, his skin shot through with purples, raw whites and yellows; all the hideous colours death and a cold sea create. His face and genitals were missing; teeth grimaced through a butcher's pulp, the legs flayed around a cave of a wound. Max looked round desperately for help knowing there was none. The village was still asleep, ignorant of the nightmare that would start its day. It was impossible to comprehend this carcass; it was like something from hell's abattoir. There was one other wound, a small one on the back of the left hand in the fleshy part below the thumb and the forefinger. That was how

Max realized this dehumanized mess swilling about the shallows was Gia.

The sea scooped him up, and sucked him away till he rose in a wave twenty metres out, hanging like an exhibit behind milky glass, his jaw open and the lower teeth dropped in a demonic wail stretching a terrible accusation from the eternal lodgings of death. Then the wave broke, and battered him towards the shore.

The sea had stripped him of enough dignity. Max was calling don't worry as he waded out. He caught a flailing arm and Gia spun round him in the currents like he did through the air when Max swung him as a kid. A wave hit Max's back and he fell with Gia under the water and was caught in his thrashing limbs as the sea tried to drag him away, but Max held on and found his feet. The water seethed round his legs but he was blessed by some reserve of strength and got Gia up the beach, all the time trying to keep where his face had once been out of sight. He laid his big coat over him and wanted to run up the hill to his house and find him there, waking in a bad mood.

"I won't be long. I'll be back.'"

Shota was in the kitchen, half asleep, hair tufted up like a brush, feeding the baby. Max vomited against the window and Shota shouted. He assumed Max had been drinking.

When Masha opened her eyes, Max was soaking wet. Shota stood behind him like a scared kid.

"Masha, I have some terrible news."

His jaw muscle bunched. He was such a drama queen.

"Gia's dead."

She heard the bougainvillea scratching the glass roof and thought he can't be because he promised to cut it back.

What could they tell the cops? Gia had no enemies – apart from jealous husbands and discarded women. He had no connections to the hoods in the big dachas lining the roads into Tbilisi apart from selling them a few pieces of furniture. He wasn't involved in any kind of racket or favour trading, was never asked for protection, did nothing that could offend anyone. There was a Mercedes, four shadows and a pair of Slavic cheekbones and eyes. That was the mystery.

The cops dragged on their cigarettes. Gia wasn't to be moved until forensics arrived, so he stayed on the beach that except for trips to Tbilisi and one break in Paris, had been the circle of his life. Everyone stood vigil; he was part of everyone, they had murdered the village. Two men set off to Batumi to Gia's senile father, sister and drunken brother in law.

The wind fanned the black soutane as the priest crossed the beach. Kids desperate to see the corpse were driven back. Max lifted an edge of the tarpaulin and heard the priest mutter "Bastards." The grisly image obliterated memories of the living man and boy; his vivid awkwardness and good looks were reduced to a butcher's mess. Father Gregory knelt to administer the blessing and Max saw him take Gia's cold hand from under the tarpaulin and hold it.

Gia had lain on the beach for five hours before a police photographer arrived; a prime time drunk shuffling behind a vodka nose marked in the livery of a thousand bars. The camera trembled. His hat trembled. The lens trembled around the mount on the camera before it snapped into place. Max delivered another tirade about how they were letting poor Gia rot on the beach and where was this mythical ambulance? The cops lit cigarettes, made another trip to the radio in the car, and came back with the same thing. "It's on its way." So's peace in Chechnya, someone shouted.

The shakes threatened the drunkard's dignity the photographer was at pains to present. The flash vibrated in its shoe. "How can he photograph anything?" bawled Shota. A test flash went off like a silent shot. He nodded; the cops lifted the tarpaulin and exposed Gia. Villagers retched and cursed, cynical eyes filled, kids were beaten away again. The priest saw Gia's other wound and turned and walked to the sea and stared north.

Gia blanched under the flashes, and the white glow with the holes where his face and genitals should be burned into Max's retina. The photographer trembled round, winding on his film, checking his flash recharge, slowly shooting off a roll, and then the tarpaulin was finally lowered on Gia's humiliation.

"Does it get to you?" asked Max.

The photographer smiled as he chased the film in the back of his camera.

"Nothing gets to you if you've seen as much as I have."

"Then show some respect, you trembling cunt."

The purple face blackened: "I'm doing my job."

"Fuck you and your job. Do it away from me."

As he shuffled across the sand, struggling to get the film leader into the spindle, like a small vision Max saw the sadness that runs core deep and is unshaken till death; sadness at a self inwardly despised; sadness under the anger at how it's all shaken down so badly; the same sadness that persisted in Gia even though things were well for him in many ways. Success and sex could not extinguish it, only death. But a death of incomprehensible terror, screaming for mercy, for his mother, Max, Masha, God, for everyone who was not there for him. Guilt pitilessly lashed them all with the conviction that there must have been something they could have done. He could see it in the other villagers. The murder had made the place ashamed of itself.

When Father Gregory sloped up the beach and started whispering to a cop Max became paranoid that he was being fingered as a suspect. He was the last person seen with Gia; Gia was his ex-lover's lover. He found himself shaking his head, then everything disappeared and he bumped onto the sand.

They took him to Mrs. Arveladze who stuffed him with eggs and tea. He hadn't eaten all morning. Through the window Masha's house stood above the sea wall. Women were keeping her inside, filling her with vodka, but sooner or later he would have to give her the details. Behind her studio the hill climbed in smudges of winter colours and pale trees to Gia's cottage and barn, then up to rocks carbuncling the sky.

Two detectives arrived. One, barely out of boyhood was pale with shock. He had just seen Gia. Max went through it all again then demanded to know how long Gia was expected to lie naked under a tarpaulin.

"The ambulance is on its way, sir."

"A horse-drawn one?"

The dead eyes in the Merc were watching him everywhere. He had looked at Gia's killer and Gia's killer had looked back with the indifference of the omnipotent. After giving the description, Max realised he had probably put himself in danger and felt faint again.

She woke into bewilderment and slowly was drawn back into the maw of
grief. A small boat buffeted beyond the raft. She swallowed more vodka.
A thread of saliva linked her cheek to the pillow. Voices bubbled up from
her kitchen. She made some distracted noise into the air and one of the
women came up. "Get Max" was all she said, then they had to help her to
the bathroom to throw up.

Inside Gia's workshop everything was neat and ordered. Tools hung in
racks under a line of roof windows: lathes and band saws stood like shining
soldiers. The floor was spotless. Chair frames, unfinished drawers and
cabinets waited for completion like Gia's abandoned children. A table made
from dark wood had edges and corners so softly rounded and swept, that
it almost seemed moulded. The young detective pronounced it the work
of an exceptional craftsman and his senior, an undemonstrative man who
registered the positive by absenting a negative, did not disagree. Hopeless
in so many things, with wood Gia was touched by God. And in bed too, they
said, though perhaps not by God.

Max and the detectives moved through the silence and light under the
boiling sky and Max understood how wood drew the peace out in Gia. They
sifted through everything for clues and of course, there were none. It was an
impersonation of an investigation, but Max said nothing because it seemed
important to do something. In Gia's house there were no signs of struggle
or forced entry. The door was open but Gia always left the door open.
Forensics had been up and checked for prints, but as the lights weren't on it
was likely Gia had met his killers on the way home.

Max reluctantly handed over the spare keys in case they wanted to come
round and play at policemen again, and as they descended the hill towards
the village the young cop asked for his autograph. He had six hundred
in his collection, including a letter from Khrushchev to a woman in the
Ukraine requesting her walnuts. Max could find no reason to say no. Why
disappoint a young man who has to wade in the sewage of humanity with
no guarantee of salary at the month's end? He found himself writing 'good
luck' on this of all days.

"You're American, aren't you, sir?"

"Was."

"I've got a penfriend in the Tulsa police department, Oklahoma. He's

trying to get me Luke Skywalker and Princess Leia. Not much hope
though."

To the north the sky spewed pewter onto the sea and Max hoped the
young cop got his autographs.

Masha woke to music drifting quietly up the stairs from the radio below. It
was dark. She called and Max appeared. Gia had lain till two o'clock. When
the ambulance arrived the police had to threaten arrests to calm things. But
he was gone now.

"Please stay." She shut her eyes.

Downstairs the music of Satie trailed out of the radio like clattering
wine glasses. The previous night had run itself in Max's head in an endless
loop: the meal, Gia's enigmatic mood, the Mercedes, the terrifying eyes, the
hideousness of Gia's death. Did Gia know it was coming? He had strange
radar systems sensitive to atmospheres in people. Had he seen something
that had filled him with foreboding?

The morbidity of the day began to crush him. He had been rushing
about since dawn, racing past the grief before it could catch him, but now to
Satie's lonely notes he began to sink. The wind had calmed, the storm gone,
the day had blown itself out. No sounds interfered with the crystal phrases,
and Max began to feel the fact that Gia was not asleep up the hill and never
would be.

California – February 1999

She had left for her father fuelled by a child's optimism, and coasted back
drunk, Fuck-off neon burning on her forehead. He received a call from
the airport. Would he please come and pick her up? And the life slid out of
him like mud. She was waiting in a bare room under strip lighting sitting
at a metal table with a lesbo look cop. They were not taking her in this time
but...

Brief periods of sobriety were achieved, but collapsed into longer,
devastating drunks. Phobias sprang from her. Phone calls, the mailman,

mornings, daylight, people, noise – all had her wincing. She had a lifelong
fear of seagulls, but now they became terrorising Eumenides wheeling in
thermals of pollution that brought on panic attacks that brought on panic
attacks in Timmy. Her sickness was making him sick. She felt hopeless.
He felt hopeless. As a frustrated artist his way of coping was to transmute
everything into a comic strip in which a helpless female is hounded by the
gulls. If art couldn't weave some miracle into the universe that would heal
his wife, then at least he might make a buck or two out of it.

He would escort her to AA meetings and sit in parking lots praying
the miracle would happen inside the strip lit rooms where her tribe of
fuck-ups hung out. He could offer nothing else but long, lonely stares and
reassurances that she would be okay if she just kept trying. But loyalty, love
and the desire to be well were extinct in her. All she needed was oblivion
and the bizarre netherworld of the bottle.

Despite the nightmares she brought back from Georgia, in a last stand of
denial they had married at Christmas on the storm blasted Island of Maui.

She made the effort. She tried to stay sober but couldn't. By the hotel
pool bar on the morning before the wedding, her uncle Henry caught her
sneaking a drink when she thought the others were catching the rays or
shopping. She froze when he told the barman to put it on his room number.
Her childhood abandonment had always been a touchstone for Henry's
hatred of Max, and she had returned from him trailing death on her
marriage day. As the barman mixed her drink and shuttled in the ice, she
kept silent. There was nothing in the world to say. She could feel Henry's
desperation and was terrified he might ruffle her hair the way he did when
she was little. Aware of her psychotic sensitivity he settled for a quiet "God
bless you, honey" which she deflected with a dip of the head. The barman
put the drink on the coaster, and like a dog with a stolen steak, she carried
it off to the hotel shadows.

Nature added her insult by breaking the mother of all storms that day.
A garden ceremony to the sounds of the surf and the breezes soughing the
palms was rained off and a corner of the dining room under a ceramic Mahi
Mahi became the place of matrimony.

By the time her presence was requested under the china fish all her
human wiring had fused and she moved like an animal in a kaleidoscope of

half conscious images of her own nightmare. 'On This Our Wedding Day' crooning out of a Sony speaker on the salad bar coiled its joylessness round her, as Henry led her to her frightened fiancée. Beaming with joy and pride her uncle had told her it was a privilege to give her away and she wondered which fucking wedding he was in. Sweating vodka, all she wanted was to get married quick so she could get to another drink.

As the hotel engineer couldn't be found to switch off the muzak permeating all the spaces in and off the lobby including the dining room, the sacrament was celebrated to the Sounds of the Seventies, with an accompanying – or in the circumstances, competing – live Hawaiian ukulele duo. The bride's asides caught by the microphone the Fotophot Greg Toland had pinned on Timmy's tie, underscored the Papuan Minister's veneration of the spirit of Aloha in the sun, sea and rain, with a 1,000 decibel whisper that something had to be done about that fucking music.

Inevitably she stopped the ceremony till someone was found who knew how to switch off Mowtown. Heads turned to the civilizing force of the storm as the wedding manager set off to castrate the hotel engineer. Epileptic flower tips in her bouquet transmitted Georgia's shattered body rhythms. She asked for a glass of water and Nathan, Timmy's cousin and best man smiled sure and brought it. By the time the glass got to her lips half the contents were on her satin dress where they remained like an incontinence blemish. At that moment Timmy realized he was participating in an act of public cruelty.

Finally Martha and the Vandellas cut off. The sun blew a hole in the blackness, glittering the sea and edging the slopes of Molokai in gold, and the smiling Papuan minister invoked all the spirits of Aloha and wed Timmy and Lucy.

She skipped the feast in favour of the mini-bar in their room. Everyone except Timmy was grateful. He was ashamed of himself. "I'm only ever wise after the fucking event," he complained to his cousin. "You need to get fuckin' real" was Nathan's response.

Going back to the room was a nightmare. He never knew what to expect, but she was still there, glass in hand, *NYPD Blue* flickering across a soundless TV, angry that he was interrupting her vocation.

"I'm going to bed" was all he said and she wandered onto the balcony to keep him out of her way. Sometime in the night he woke to see her still standing there in the darkness, watching the sea. It struck him that she might be contemplating the jump; the waves of humiliation she had endured that day would be enough to sweep any normal person off to a welcome oblivion. But she had that oblivion in her glass. He watched her, willing the thought and that split second of utter hopelessness to combine in her so all the pain could be brought to a dramatic end. But she remained still as a statue with a mechanical arm rhythmically lifting the glass to the lips. What in God's name was going on inside that head, he thought, what was she seeing, feeling; would the mass of madness, drunkenness and confusion move her to the jumping off point? Surely anything was better than this? Did she need help? A slight push, a moment's struggle, a brief cry, all over. It would be an act of kindness; a dog would not be allowed to suffer like this. The curtains blew in the breeze and veiled her, half seen, a blurred shape. They shifted, a shadow limb moved. She seemed to disappear.

She did get into bed eventually. There was no question of the usual honeymoon formality. Eventually he fell into some kind of sleep. She spent some time staring at the night beyond the balcony before she fell into another oblivion.

At five he woke to something warm on his buttocks. She had wet the bed.

Somehow Timmy thought the marriage might fix her. But she was receiving instructions on another wavelength, and when they came back to Santa Monica, she began to float further out till one morning she just didn't come back.

California – March 1999

"Is she worth saving?"

Near the end of his graveyard shift ministering to the wrecks spilling into his E.R., the doctor is disappointed she is still alive and needing attention. He had come to this place with its socially marginalized because he had misgivings about the health insurance racket, but six months in the place has made the Hippocratic oath a little anorexic.

"Stinking like a distillery."

"There's this too," The nurse lifts her wrist. Rubies of congealed blood button her forearm.

His ophthalmoscope scours her retina. There have been no diagnostic tests, no witnesses, she was found in the street, so there is no way of knowing what she has shot into her arm, though he's pretty sure it isn't Gatorade. He straightens painfully. If his back gets worse, maybe he can get time off.

"Empty her."

Her upper teeth gouge skull feathers and the lower slide under a rough feathered crop. A beak touches her throat and she gags. Why are they forcing her to swallow a seagull? The great head hinges her jaw wider till the joints dislocate like a snake's and the thing shoves past her throat, down her gullet, the fat sleek bird stretching her lips to tearing point, stifling screams from vocal chords pressed flat against the front of her throat by the big feathered body. It scrambles deeper, dives into the sea in her stomach, plash! kicks for the fish, round and round, a rapacious bird shimmying after and no escape for the fish but to vomit up in a bunched shoal like a muscle pushing her open all the way up. She wants to cry to them to stop but she can't speak and fish don't talk.

Something pushed into her arm and she floated down again. She could hear Timmy sitting on the edge of the boat making Masha laugh and Gia asking if his skin was as soft as Timmy's. Joseph popped above her bed pleading with her to come round for a coffee and his big wife hit him with a tie-dyed cleaver. She was aware of Timmy sitting on the edge of a bench now, elbows on the table looking at her father, who has a Russian accent for some reason and is wearing a very bad toupee that is fashioned in a thick widow's peak, like a joke Dracula wig. He looks at Timmy and indicates Lucy and Mom with his eyes. "I vos a bad boy," he says confessionally and childishly in a cod Russian accent, and the eyebrows jerk up and Timmy says "That was a long time ago, man, c'mon..!" and she wants to murder both of them; boys against girls. Dada moves off with the silent young woman he is with and they stand at the end of the table in the sunshine rubbing noses. He has a ski-run nose, but as he noses his loved one's nose his nose seems to fold into a perfect little nose and he looks completely different.

"Who is that man?" says Mom.

"Dad!" incises out of Lucy in a lacerating whisper.

"I've never seen him before," says Mom and Lucy sighs hopelessly, but Timmy thinks he looks twenty, maybe thirty, years younger than Mom and is nearer the age of the young girl he's canoodling. Mom's a wrinkled old hag. He's not much older than Lucy. She knows he is thinking this.

"He looks like... that actor... you know," says Timmy

"Bill Holden," says Mom, "he used to when he was young."

"He *is* young, Mom," hisses Lucy again.

"Naw," says Timmy, "naw, not Bill Holden, that other actor... Although he's got the kinda Bill Holden-type nose till he shoves it in the babe's face, naw I mean... God, I can't think... Oh, you know..."

"No, I don't fucking know!" comes out of Lucy like compressed air. The pressure's building, building.

"I think he was a Brit. *Lost Weekend* guy. On TV. They show it on Classics on TV. What's his name?"

"Yeh!" cries Lucy, "I know. Oh, what's his name? He wore a toupee too... Oh God, yeah, he was a Brit..."

"You know," says Mom seriously, "You never get Half Moons in Ohio."

Lucy closed down for a while.

Fire broke out at the top of the lace curtain. She saw the Edwards fire alarm but her body was ten times its normal weight. The fire became sunlight, a mouth of brightness at the top of the curtains. Everything else was in shadow and she was swaddled at the bottom of the gloom. The room was bare and cheap, cheap green walls, cheap cream framed beds, cheap linoleum. On another cheap bed was a heap with a face pulled in pain, deep asleep in some awful place. A nurse came in.

"Well, Lucy! Welcome back."

Lucy looked at her blankly. "Is it rabies?"

"Rabies?"

"Is the kid dead?"

"What kid, Lucy?"

"I ruined my Birkenstocks for her."

"That's a shame."

"Tell the dog I'm sorry."

"What dog?"

Her eyes closed. As the light slid out of her world and she returned to the comfort of oblivion, the words "Ray Milland" softly floated to the nurse and she wondered if she had heard right.

April 1964

The concerns of fatherhood were never going to apply to me and the sense of connection a father might have to a new child, had to be smothered. But Nature does her thing at key moments, releases a new batch of chemical instructions to divert the mother's attention from father to child. Mom and the kid cosy up; dad is out. Oedipus arrives with the diapers. This little newborn thing had all Peg's attention. She possessed her mother and something very deep changed in Peg. It seemed to herald an ending for me.

The night of her birth was a haze. I used Jack Daniels as my own anaesthetic. I felt a complete fraud, joking with the other husbands, participating in their wonder at the miracle of birth, pretending to the nurses that I was washed out with emotion – which I was, but not with joy, with quite the opposite.

They took us to view our children in rows of cots behind glass screens, products of the baby factory, all lined up for us as if we were going to buy one. Mine was pointed out to me and for a moment something unexpected happened; a sense of attachment transcended everything. I felt a weird continuum, that I was part of a line coming from behind and stretching beyond me. This little heap of nerves and flesh was what I was handing on. It was fleeting and, in my condition, deeply disturbing.

Peg asked me to name her; that was the deal, I would name a girl, she would name a boy. I called her Lucy and took them home when she was a

week old. She wasn't born with Peg's white blonde hair but with a corona
of my hair colour that started shedding immediately. Where it went I never
knew; no cobwebs engraved the baby bath, no tangles fuzzed the soft brush
Peg used to groom and adore her; it seemed to dissolve in air.

I would look at her in bewilderment. All I saw was another weakness in
me. Around her sleeping head the gas chamber danced.

Peg's mother had moved in for the early weeks as I had to be at work and
Peg would need help. It was just another opportunity for her to interfere.
Normally I might have been grateful but because of the peculiarity of my
circumstance, her presence was a further strain. Peg could do nothing
around Lucy without her mother poking her nose in as if she were the only
woman ever to have a baby. But at least she would be there for support
when the news arrived with the official knock.

On Sunday the 26th of April, 1964, we took lunch in the garden. By
midnight the following Tuesday I would be crossing the border into
Canada under the name of Dr Greg Hanson. That Sunday was warm,
spring was charging through, and I set the table under a neighbour's tree
that conveniently spread its leaves and shade into our patch. My beloved
mother-in-law busied herself in the kitchen. Peg was with Lucy.

Lunch under the neighbour's tree was a success from certain
perspectives. Lucy slept on a little mattress at our feet in the shade. The
food was good, the conversation mindless and a few wines slowed me down
and I fell asleep. Looking at us over the garden fence we were just another
American family with a small but special reason for joy.

It was Lucy's wailing that woke me to the sight of a giant seagull
standing over her. The thing was picking up food that had fallen from the
table but to little Lucy it must have been her first vision of hell, a giant
yellow beak drilling down at her. I launched myself at it and picked her up,
but she bawled with such intensity that Peg and her mother came out from
the kitchen at a gallop.

"Something scared her, I think."

"What?"

Peg took her. Lucy was in a terrible state; that such a little creature could
make so much sound astonished me. The neighbours must have thought we
were barbecuing her.

"What scared her?"

"I don't know." I couldn't tell them I had fallen asleep on duty.

"What did you do?" asked my mother in law. I would be so glad never to see her again.

That night I took final orders from Yura. It was too late now for any deals. I was going across that Tuesday, the Twenty-eighth of April. Peter would give me the nod if plans had to be changed. When I returned home I did not know how to connect to Peg.

"You okay?" She asked.

"Yeah. How's Lucy?"

"She's asleep."

I crossed to the cot. She was doing what babies do best – resting from the strangeness of this new world; I remember being struck how the sleep of a child is so pure, so uncontaminated. I sat on the bed with my back to Peg; I just couldn't look at her. "Macbeth hath murdered sleep." It just slipped out, a vocalised thought.

"Why do you say that?"

Her face was hard, worried. She knew. At some level. She would tie all the loose ends up later in one blinding moment. I must have left clues all over the place.

"Nothing, naw, just... Quote, you know, school." I couldn't think of any other quotes about sleep.

"What's up, Max?"

"Nothing." Again it slipped out. I had no control left.

Georgia, April 1999

The bus terminus was among the run down high-rise blocks to the edge of Batumi. The driver gave him instructions how to get to the suburb.

"How long?"

"Twelve minutes." Impressed by his precision, Max got off with the huddle of women and their shopping, feral teenagers and sullen men carrying kids on whom the imprint of anxiety was already clear. Several pointed in the direction he should take, but other faces stared from the tower blocks with the unblinking, malign curiosity of those on the edges of survival. Across these vertical labyrinths all the marks of poverty were visible: broken windows, boarded up doors, detritus littering the stairwells and roads; bottles, plastic bags, smashed furniture, the roughly erected power lines playing out of the substation like long confusions of black spaghetti.

It was a long walk and hot. He had never ventured into these broken parts of Batumi; his territory had been the downtown and port bars, the parks and the grander avenues where a whiff of nineteenth century opulence still perfumed the evening air. Between the concrete warrens rising behind him were glimpses of the distant sea, and the banging in the docks punctuated the horns and traffic that thickened the air in downtown Batumi into a soup of sub tropical heat and pollution.

Looking back at the rags of sea beyond the apartment blocks, he indulged a feeling of detestation. Sometimes the earth and mankind disgusted him. He had fought hard and long to love humanity but had a suspicion he had done nothing but batten down a natural loathing with a synthetic ideal. He loathed authority, though he had held plenty in his time and loved it. And he loathed and loved the beaten masses with equal passion. "Moods. Just moods," he said to himself as he stumbled on the cracked road, "Today's a tough day, Maxie. You'll feel differently tomorrow."

He twice asked the way and received contradictory instructions but eventually found himself in the right suburb, a place that may have had a certain charm a hundred years before. The road was ridged with the cracks that latticed all roads across Georgia like branches of a national nervous system. The trees were peeling and depressed, but the houses were small villas with walls and large gates that were the badges of long lost bourgeois aspiration.

He found Irakli's house in a wide deserted avenue, far away from the noise of dockland Batumi and the hideousness of the tower blocks. A shabby peace lay on its dead elitism. No noises broke from the unkempt trees and bushes that hid the houses, and the tired bougainvillea that leaned against the broken stucco walls. Irakli's gates had once been splendid examples of art deco style, sweeping down from high pillars to fuse a symmetrical display of floral shapes. Now wisps of old barbed wire tangled the tops like stained lace on a low-cut dress, and metal sheets had been riveted onto the ironwork so no one could see through into the home behind. This was a neighbourhood whose citizens shut themselves away.

The bell brought no response. When he struck one of the gate's metal panels it rattled down the avenue like a thunder sheet and the only response it provoked was from some chickens somewhere behind the walls. In time he heard a rhythmic tramp of feet, then a break in the stride, a curse, and another chicken crescendo. The spy slot opened and a pair of long lashed eyes that Max found disarmingly beautiful stared at him, but before he could announce himself the slot shut and the gates were dragged open with a noise that would have wakened Hell.

"Mr Agnew," said the man.

Max stepped inside while Irakli set himself to closing the gates, a task which threatened to fail till Max lent his shoulder too. The gate issued metallic groans of resistance, but with a final iron wail and clang, the street was shut out. This achieved, Max stood, feeling his pulse climb to the red band and reflecting how the Scaean gates of Troy would have required little more effort to close. In blanks of stress he would often retreat to private streams of classicism and hide there.

Irakli's eyes were his best, indeed his only attractive feature. Several teeth had been left behind somewhere and his body had the gnarled toughness of a man who subsists on nicotine and willpower. Inside the walls of his little kingdom it looked like a peasant's farmyard. Anorexic chickens pecked around discarded engine parts. A car body was planted near the front door and weeds grew into the wheel arches. A kid's swing hung limply from a broken tree.

A walnut hand was offered and they shook. He smiled at Max as if awed by his guest's presence and Max became self-conscious as the handshake extended until he thought Irakli was holding him there for some sinister purpose and found himself scanning the sad, dust blown trees and the filthy windows for the shadow of a gunman. But it was just the overstated welcome of an overstated man and he was released and ushered to a conglomeration of metal chairs around an old wooden table covered with chicken shit. Max perched his bottom delicately on the edge to minimise the amount of guano that would press itself into the fabric of his trouser seat. A brown palm tree hung on to a thin trickle of life above them. Irakli plunked himself opposite and offered Max a cigarette. Max declined.

"I wish I didn't smoke. Started when I was eight."

"I'm lucky, I never started."

Smoke rose lazily in a blue cloud towards the palm fronds then turned sharply and fled over Irakli's walls. That smoke knows something I don't thought Max. The begging chickens were kicked away in a flurry of wings and clucks. They came back. Irakli kicked up another fountain of flapping chickens. A teenage girl appeared with a tray of coffee and small cakes and laid it on the table between them. The chickens gathered again by Max's feet.

"My daughter. This is Mr Agnew."

"Hello." She shook his hand and Max was unsure his identity should have been disclosed so casually. "Hello."

Delicate hands set out the coffee and poured. She was slim and gorgeous, rather aristocratic in looks, hardly the offspring one would expect from a sinewy branch like Irakli. But she had her father's eyes, glowing with intelligence and softened into feminine beauty. Max could feel her father's pride irradiate the chicken shit.

"Thank you," said Max. She smiled and left the men to their business lightly trailing a sense of grace and modesty across the trash.

"Sixteen and doing well at school. She'll make the university. Speaks German like a native."

"That's wonderful," said Max.

"If they've got the brains these days you have to set them on their way, eh? These days, huh? What a fucking mess they're making of it, huh? Excuse my language."

"That's fine."

"But what are they building for our kids, uh?"

"Yes, it's a responsibility," said Max, "I'm sometimes relieved I don't have children." It slipped out with an ease that took him aback, but he found no reason to correct himself.

"Ah, children are great."

"Yes."

"But there's no future for them here. That's why an education is important. To get out. With a good degree, they've got hope in Germany, or even your old country."

"Yes, I suppose so."

They sipped coffee and Irakli crushed a cake and threw it to the chickens.

"Can I ask what you need?"

Max lowered his voice; the neighbours were only a wall away. "I'm not specifically sure. You probably know better than I."

"Anything can be got."

"Whatever it is, it needs to be simple, reliable, easy to operate. I'm not an expert. Quite the opposite."

"What specifically is the problem?"

"I might just be suffering from paranoia..."

"Paranoia keeps us alive. The way things are these days."

"I suppose you're right."

"It's becoming like the Wild West."

"Yes, unfortunately."

"So, how would you define your problem?"

There was an impression of running, short calls, hard breathing from the other side of the wall. Max seized up, the openness of this whole transaction just inside a suburban wall among starving chickens struck him as casual to the point of carelessness. But he supposed Irakli knew what he was doing. The sound passed and they fell back into run down suburban peace.

"Sorry, I've never done anything like this."

"I know you haven't. That's why I'm asking the nature of your needs so I provide the right thing."

"I think someone is after me. Someone dangerous."

"Right. Self-protection."

"Yes." Max was relieved it was out.

"Something you can carry around with you at all times?"

"Probably best."

Irakli poured another coffee and stuffed a couple of small cakes into his mouth. His jaw worked with an erratic movement as it manipulated the cakes to the parts that still had teeth.

"Is it to do with that carpenter?"

Now Max felt the blow of mortality, and the sickening realisation that he had led himself into a trap. Every abominable scenario of destruction had glutted his imagination at some time, but death on a chicken run was never one.

"It happened in your village?"

"Yes."

"You witnessed it?'

His speechlessness declared it. He may as well hang a 'Shoot me' sign round his neck.

"The way they left him, huh?" Irakli insinuated a false sincerity into the exchange. Max coughed limply. "Calling card." The world focussed down to a single, tunnel view of Irakli's Adam's apple recoiling up and down his neck as he swallowed his cake. "That's the Russian way. The face and the tackle."

"Russian?"

"Russians."

"Russians?"

"From Moscow."

"From Moscow?"

"Yes."

"That doesn't make sense."

"He'd been horsing around with their women."

Suddenly huge breasts and a dark beauty drilling contempt down at him from a starless night, ghosted among the chickens and car wrecks. All the pieces fell into place. Something callous peeping beneath their gold bangled vulgarity had always disturbed him. Theirs was the over dressed trashiness of the horizontal escape from the Moscow gutter, their gaudy jewellery and cars coming to them courtesy of torture, murder and extortion. Why hadn't he thought of it before?

They had rented one of Shota's cottages and he would still have their details. Connections could be made. Identifying the killers would give him options. Among the chickens, in this sad and awful place, his life leaped again with purpose. The reaction was stuffed down; nothing was to be given away. He still wasn't sure he would see the other side of Irakli's ramshackle gate – so he stared at him as if all this news was meaningless.

"Moscow, eh?"

"Behind most of man's trouble is a woman."

Max smiled courteously. "How did you come by this information?"

Irakli smiled courteously back at him. Max felt a little foolish, "Of course I..." and it trailed off into the strutting and the clucks and the weight of an empty afternoon.

Irakli took another deep pull on his cigarette, and at the end of a long exhalation spat a dot of tobacco from his tongue tip. "I think I've got what you need," and Max was left staring at his feathered admirers, pecking round his shoes for crumbs.

"Those bitches" he said to them, then crushed the last cake over the guano earth. "Eat up, girls."

He had come to the chickens for protection and had found information, but the oddness of it left him shaky; he was paddling in a world in which he knew none of the rules. If Irakli knew about it, then the Georgian underworld knew about it and that put him in a very dangerous place. Irakli himself might pass on the information; despite the reasonable tone and gangster graciousness, he did not ply his trade under the terms and conditions of the equal opportunities scheme. Life was cheap; a contract could be taken out for a few Georgian units or American dollars.

All the edges of the world closed in and the struggles and concerns of his life were nothing more than a cavalcade of pointlessness. He was finished; the clock was ticking. What use was a gun? He could put a bullet in both those Slavic eyes and someone else would just come after him. Chance had condemned him. Time and place. Misfortune, bad serendipity. God. Fate. Flight was the only hope. But where and to what? Drink and suicide bustled forward as options. "Gia, you and your dick have got us all into trouble," he sighed to the pecking chickens and became jealous of their primitive state. "We've something in common. We're both waiting for the plucker," and he swept the last cake crumbs off the shit-spattered table.

Irakli reappeared with a gun in his hand and a lack of concern that suggested the moment of extinction for Max might have arrived, and the trip to this suburban garden had been a remarkable and clever set-up. But the quiet salesman mode switched on as soon as he reached the table. Max watched him like a hawk and picked over all the implications and hidden meanings in every nuance of everything he said, and every look in the big, soft eyes.

He laid the gun on the table with the reverence of a priest placing a relic in front of a believer. To Max it lay there like an execution, dull and scarred, well used and he wondered who had felt its awful indifference. "SR1 Gyurza. Classic. Range of fifty metres, and with these," he held up a clip of bullets, "it can pierce body armour and cars." Max remembered the Mercedes coasting up to him in the darkness. "Russian army pistol but the Federal Security Service uses it now, your old boys as they are now, eh? So that's a good endorsement, eh? I can really recommend this. It's a big grip, too big for me, but you've got big hands, try it for comfort", and he handed it to Max grip first. It felt reassuringly heavy, comfortable, balanced, although it was obviously old, the gunmetal blue worn on all edges to dull silver. This was a gun that had seen action and for some reason that now comforted him, as if he were linking up with a veteran. "It's simple, easy to strip and clean, you know about guns?"

"A little. Long time ago."

"If you want something smaller, I've got this'" and he produced another gun from his belt. "Makarov PM, classic self-defence pistola. Not much use beyond twenty metres and it doesn't have the penetration of the Gyurza but it's a little beauty."

"I remember this. It was standard Red Army issue."

"Yeah. Very reliable. Elegant little thing, uh?"

"Yes," said Max, taking a gun in each hand, turning both for balance, holding them up to the light, aiming along the sights as if he knew what he was doing, "Light. The Makarov. Very light. Compared to the other one."

"Too light? Some people like a bit of weight. Gives stability."

"This one will go through a car?" He held up the Gyurza.

"Like paper. It was part of the design specification."

"But the Makarov..." Dapples of sunlight fell across it and freckled his hand as the branches above him shifted and rustled, "easily concealed."

"If it's likely to be close stuff the Makarov's the deal."

"I might need a little more."

"Then I can't recommend the Gyurza highly enough."

Max placed both on the table, looked at one then the other. The chickens moved in the background. Irakli waited and smoked. The silence reminded Max of another silent suburb many years before. Nothing is as silent as a silent suburb.

"How much for both?"

Irakli paused. "I have to charge you for the Gyzura and the clip of armour piercing bullets, because they are expensive, but you can have the Makarov and two standard clips for each for nothing."

This kind of bargaining seemed misplaced around guns.

"No, no no..."

Irakli reached forward and put his hand on Max's arm. "You're a great man, sir, a person of substance."

Max laughed, "I wish... Not any more."

"No, you are sir, a great hero. Perhaps one day you can help Irakli."

"I really don't have any influence any more."

"Of course you do. You only think you have none, but you're a part of history and that counts for a lot here, a former hero. Maybe a word in someone's ear if ever Irakli gets himself in trouble, perhaps..."

"I really don't have..."

"A good word from the right person can go a long way. Or perhaps if my daughter – God forbid! – has a problem with the university, a man of education such as yourself may be able to help her."

"Well for your daughter, of course. Of course I'd be happy to do what I can, but I'm really not sure I..."

"You don't know yourself, sir. Please accept this from me as a token of my esteem for everything you have done."

He seemed an ally, an ear on the movements underground, an early warning perhaps. The old animosity between Georgians and Russians still existed. The Georgian underworld would not have been pleased by a couple of Muscovites coming down to create mayhem on their territory. So perhaps Irakli could be trusted.

Max stayed for a second tray of coffee, subtly probing as he regaled Irakli with a few stories from the old days. The chickens squabbled over more cake crumbs. Business and the afternoon drew to an amicable close. "If your daughter has problems, certainly... I can't guarantee anything, but I have friends who may have some influence at the University."

When the gate clanged behind him he felt a mix of relief to get away from Irakli's cloying esteem, but also a realisation that he had put himself into a world where conflicts were played out with violence and debts had to be paid. "What have you done, you old goat?" he muttered to himself as he slowly started trudging in the direction of the bus stop.

Back at the bus terminus on democracy's high-rise wasteland, he was conscious of the peculiar hang of his jacket, with two pistols and seventy clipped bullets distributed around his pockets. All secured for little more than the cost of a few of Irakli's chickens. But despite being fully armed, he was no less fearful of the haunted eyes watching him, or of the eyes that froze him on a black winter's night, and which still seemed to stare from across the sea. The world had turned upside down, and so had he.

Moscow – April 1999

"There's no need for you to know who the client is, but it's Max Agnew."

"My God."

"There's some money, loose change as an earnest of his good intentions to pay the rest and I've heard that for forty years, so if you have a problem, let me know and I'll screw it out of him."

"I heard he drank himself to death?"

"Work in progress." Alexei shook his head. "I gave up on him years ago but last week he phones and this arrives. It's a couple of women who were decorating the beach down where he lives. Just check out who they are, what they are, etc., etc. Credit card slips in there, and their addresses. I didn't think they were evolved enough for credit cards in Georgia."

"What's it about?"

"Max playing Sherlock Holmes. God knows. I think that waitress fancies you. Have you..?"

But Dimitri laughs. Business done they drink coffee and chatter. Alexei has little to fill his days except the exercise for the new hip, walking the old streets of new Moscow and watching the world make a mess of Yugoslavia. They discuss the occupation of Pristina airfield in Kosovo by the Russian army. Alexei doesn't think it unlikely the Yanks might have a pop; they are stupid enough. "Too much John Wayne and this shit" he nods at the interior of the Pizza Hut, "strips away the cortical layer of the brain. They're so rich they've lost the power of thought." He looks out the big window and lifts the cup to his lips and Dimitri sees the tremble. Despite the hip operation and the increased mobility, Alexei has gone through some gate of age. His skin is thinner and opalescent – yellows, blues reveal themselves mysteriously through its pale sheen – he has shrunk half a size, his chest heaves; the mischievous stage presence that charmed or terrified, has dimmed. Dimitri's fingertips lightly fall on the bill and draw it across the table.

"You know when he quit America he had a tiny daughter? New born."

"New born?"

"He never mentioned her, all the time we were talking to him. Whole bloody de-briefing he held out. I was intrigued, so I let it go then smacked him with it near the end. He went into a trance. Lost the power of speech. Anyway, last summer his newborn turns up on his doorstep. Unannounced."

Dimitri whistled. "How'd he handle that?"

"I would give my left testicle to have been there. Now it's of no bloody use to me. Goodlooking too, apparently. The daughter. Must have got it from her mother. The mother, yes, I wouldn't have kicked her out of bed."

"You wouldn't kick a female bed bug out of bed."

Dimitri smiles at the sexiness in the old bastard. Enhanced by the new pharmaceuticals, escort agencies and the new hip, there will be no stopping him.

"You know some over-dressed bitch in a Mercedes nearly ran me down in Tverskaya Street. Thirty years ago I could have had her thrown in the Gulag."

"Thirty years ago she wouldn't have had a Mercedes."

"Anyway, this commission – if we can invest a plea from Max with such a dignified description – ASAP."

"If its just ID stuff it won't take long. And it is for a Hero of the Soviet

Union."

"We were all bloody heroes. And for what?' he tossed a contemptuous look at the citizens of the new Moscow strutting past outside, "T-shirts, guns and fucking Givenchy."

Max expected photographs from Alexei, and had neither video player nor television. When Shota closed up he showed Max how to operate the video and left him in the bar to his solitary viewing. When he had finished Max sat for a while, then invited Shota to watch.

They found themselves staring at apartments that Max explained had once been a luxury block for Party officials in the middle of Moscow. Two women slid in and out of focus in street crowds, sped under the Kremlin walls in an open-top car, and lurked in café shadows and smoke; blurred actors in a drama of banal ordinariness. A department store struggled for sharpness before revealing a clear shot of them. One was tall, dark, beautiful and the other's breasts were bursting her dress. Both men recognised the tits.

The image moved into darkness and rainbow flare before the two girls materialised at a nightclub table laden with glasses. The Slavic cheekbones of the man smoking beside the huge breasts confirmed everything. Lizard eyes he had last seen scanning him from a dark Mercedes now scanned the lap dancers simulating ecstasy behind. He sat at his drinks with his pumped up woman, full of life in its debased, foulest forms, while Gia's mutilated corpse returned to earth. Irakli had been right. They had come for Gia all the way from Moscow. Gia had finally fucked himself to death.

Words were redundant; the tribe's divine rubric held the commands. The police were not worth a thought. Information need be passed to no one. Shota took the video out of the machine and they quietly bade each other goodnight.

The fire burnished the thuja and walnut trees. Max dropped in the video and sparks belched at the stars. Blue flame hissed from electronic bonds; tape curled, melted, and the girls and their murderers deliquesced from their magnetic gallery into plastic lava running into mouths of red embers. Then the Slavic eyes floated up from the embers and he automatically withdrew from the fire into the darkness of the trees, looked and listened.

The Makarov was in his pocket, but there was no one but a ghost in a melting video.

Max has a photograph of himself and Alexei, taken by Petra, Alexei's wife, in their apartment near the Bolshoi. They sit under a gallery of other photographs festooning the wall above them; a pictorial history of Alexei's socialist star life. There is the boy soldier with older comrades hoisting the red flag in war shattered Berlin: the young Party member being patted by a bloated Stalin in a high Kremlin room; laughing with Kruschev; standing with glum, badly tailored Members of the Comintern and a back-combed, uniformed dyke effulgent with her Order of the Red Banner of Labour Junior Class. There is one of Alexei and Max, both dark haired and content sitting with beers at a table in the Old Square Prague, and a young, startlingly handsome Alexei, Jimmy Dean narcissistic in coat and dangling cigarette against St Petersburg's classical townscape. A young wife with luminous beauty glows from an old photo above the samovar.

Max knows that the man who now sits under this gallery is frail as a bird and bearing no resemblance to the matinée idol in the photos above, that he spends a great deal of the day sleeping in an old chair brought back to him in the Fifties from the Selfridges store in London, that he takes walks to exercise the hip replacement that leave him wheezing and dribbling spit, that his flesh has thinned to parchment, his neck hawsers disappeared into a collar now several sizes too big, and that his wife now shuffles about in an exhaustion of remoteness and weight gain that reduces her to an inflated prettiness, the soft, doe-eyed and enigmatic beauty of her face squashed onto a body that has grown spherical over the years, a Da Vinci pumpkin. Their presence in each other's life passes almost unnoticed now, and the last time Max saw them he left sensing some longstanding complaint in Petra that she never articulates.

He listens to her voice down the phone as she shouts at Alexei to wake. "Phone! It's Max! Alexei! The phone! It's Max on the 'phone. Oh, I better go and make sure the old goat hasn't died, Max."

"Not yet!" he hears faintly and the familiar voice – aspirate yet rasping, with an attitude that had not faded with his physical vigour – comes on the phone. "Okay, get to the fucking point."

"And nice to speak to you, Alexei. I believe the lobotomy was successful?"

"Completely. I have no recollection of who you are."

The banter that was their team trademark in the old days sputtered then died when the subject of the call was reached. From Max's point of view it was a bitter lesson in the realities of the new Russia. He was trading on good will and years of collaboration from the old days, but Alexei adopted a tone that had about it a whiff of his old superior position, a cadence reserved for the subordinate who hasn't quite come up to scratch, and Max was informed that it was now a fee-paying culture. The days when an army of fixers could be sent out on the street to clear up a little inconvenience were gone.

"Well, how much are we actually talking about Alexei? Give me a figure."

"Including the women?"

They were talking in death sentences. Max felt calm, determined. "I suppose so."

Alexei plucked a figure from the air that had Max reeling. "No concession for old times' sake?"

"Max, money's still owed for the identification. Getting rid of the problem cannot be done till you pay that bill. With cash. Not promises. It's the market." Alexei had purloined the language of the entrepreneur and banker. "Strict conditions have to be observed in these transactions."

"I understand Alexei, but I really am in a very dangerous position. If I don't sort this problem out, it will sort me out."

"Get a bank loan."

"What?"

"For house improvement."

It was clear the conversation was to be ended.

"Max, this man, what's he called...? Tolya. Tolya Verkovensky. I don't want to alarm you, but he is a serious figure in certain circles."

"You've alarmed me."

"That's the point."

"You're not making this a very good day for me, Alexei."

"I'm not a fucking psychotherapist."

"What's his name again?"

"Tolya Verkovensky. Max, we can do this for you. But you must meet the fee."

"Well, that's just not possible, Alexei.'

"On the contrary, Max, I know it's possible."

"How?" asked Max.

"Because you always get what you want."

Shota was enraged by the refusal of an old friend to help and apoplectic at the price quoted.

"Muscovites! What's so fucking special about these bastards? They'll kill a man down here for the price of an orange."

"Maybe Masha will help."

"Max, you're grabbing at straws. She'll have nothing to do with this."

"What about you Shota? You must have a little spare cash."

"I spent everything on those two cottages and I haven't had the bookings. The whole tourist trade just hasn't..."

"Just a loan, Shota. I'm owed money on these translations I'm doing."

"If I could, I would."

The end of the line had been reached. There was no protection anywhere. "If I were a Christian, I suppose this is where I'd go and pray."

"Max," said Shota, "this isn't our kind of thing. We're not killers or mafiosi. This isn't our kind of contract. Your contracts are for translating, mine are for building and renting out holiday homes. This is beyond anything we... you know. We shouldn't be getting involved in this."

"It's my life, Shota."

"I don't think so, Max. If they ever arrest them – which they won't – just withdraw your statement."

"I don't like to give in to that kind of intimidation."

"You're no longer a big man Max. You're just one of us. Get real."

27 April 1964

The night before I defected, I was home late, reeking of drink, trying to hide what had been planned for the next day. Peg had been picking up on things, it was slipping out in little seeps and spills and, as usual, she would look at me as if it was all her fault. I wanted to hold her and reassure that everything was okay and nothing was her fault. Of course, it wasn't okay, but I couldn't tell her a thing. I suffered in silence and she suffered in ignorance.

Memories of that last night are very sketchy. I was back late but she was up with the baby. Little Lucy, full of milk, slept unaware of her father's fingers stroking the disappearing fluff on her head. Peg reassured me her hair would grow back, and probably blonde. I remember saying I wasn't sure I could take two Jean Harlows in the house and I remember her saying "Jean Harlow was from a bottle." I'm sure we said many things later but that was the last fragment of conversation I recall having with Peg.

In bed, Lucy was lying on Peg, who gently burped her. With her eyes closed she looked like a little blind animal, a human puppy with a limited repertoire of movements, a head stretch, an arching of the back, a soft smacking of little lips and the pure talent of the tiny for undisturbed sleep. Peg's sleeping positions were a perfect complement for little Lucy. Usually she slept on her side, her face buried under her arms, but with Lucy balanced on her chest, she acquired a Zen stillness, even her head remained absolutely statuesque and her breathing was as soft as a moth's, puffing up into the darkness above her. Her thick, blonde eyelashes lay on her sleep like soft guardians, and with the helpless little puppy daughter on her chest, they were life in its entire curious miracle, unaware of the disaster that waited next day. I didn't sleep, but watched them all night and as Lucy rose and sank gently on her mother's chest, I resolved yet again not to go over but to take my chance with the authorities. I argued through the night against the certainty that this path would lead to the chair or the gallows and I would lose them that way. But I had been round these delusions many times, and inevitably they vanished. My boats were burned and I knew it.

Lucy woke at five thirty demanding breakfast. My hangover was punching hard. I assumed the role of an actor playing the ordinary morning routine, got ready for work, left, then the performance collapsed and I re-emerged in front of Peg and Lucy, briefcase clasped tightly, and hovered, staring at them. Lucy slipped off the breast and her piggy little eyes turned up at something beyond me. I wondered if she knew who and what I was, if I were a visual imprint and a smell that meant something to her. Peg looked at me and said "Yes?" there was a pause and I said "Nothing." Then her mother came into the bedroom and pushed me out. Milky breasts and husbands should not mix. That "Yes?" was the last thing I heard Peg say.

Black Sea – April 1999

One gun stays in the house, the other goes with him everywhere. He pines for the days when thugs walked in fear of party members. Now he is condemned to paranoia waiting for the Slav face and the knives. Every dark Merc passing through the village bottles his diaphragm. The police, of course, have done nothing and he is grateful for that. Shota is right: being called as a witness would be certain death.

Masha has emerged from her long solitude and they spend parts of days together, keeping some fragment of Gia suspended between them, mainly in silence. The sea is their sound, its different tones changing their feelings like key shifts. On warm days it marauds the beach and falls on it resonant and full voiced. On white days it slips ashore in a quiet hiss.

"I find it difficult to grieve him properly because of this damned anxiety."

She says nothing. She has no response to anything. She moves through the days like an injured cat.

Waves tickle the horizon with spume. Their coffees under Shota's magnolia have long gone cold. They sit huddled against the world. Max struggles with his desire to ask for financial help for a set of killings. It gnaws at him, barely under control but he must assess the best time. Her mental condition must at least be a little more in tune than it has been, but her native unpredictability makes such assessments almost impossible. No one knows how Masha is at any given time, least of all Masha.

"I've had to buy a couple of guns."

"I may borrow one."

He refuses to rise to it. He must make his point.

"We know who killed Gia."

Her eyes do not flicker from the horizon. Her reaction to a lover's infidelity had always been savage. But she must have known about Gia and the Moscow tarts. Everyone knew everything about Gia. Even his name would raise a laugh.

"I don't want to think about that." It was crisp and clear as the chill on the wind, and the cue for Max to drop the subject, but he was advocating for his life.

"There is a solution."

She stirred not an eyelid, a turn of the head, but seemed to drop into stone, fixed on an unseen place beyond the horizon.

"It would be relatively expensive. I have some money, but not enough."

"Solution! What a ridiculous word."

He was down to the final pitch: the last fragment of anything that had ever existed between them had to be thrown in the ring.

"My life is in danger. There's no doubt about that. Does that mean anything to you?"

"At the moment: no."

It whispered away from him leaving no rage or disappointment, just a numbness creeping slowly over his old skinny limbs. They sat in another of their silences, one that Max felt he could break like a biscuit and scatter on the cold waves, waves that had brought back Gia to him.

One night he suffers a compulsion to ring his daughter. He doesn't know why and resists for a while then the phone finds its way into his hand and before he has another rational thought he's through to California speaking briefly to someone who he learns is her husband. The late twentieth century Californian accent is something he has difficulty following. The word 'like' litters the sentences. He also has difficulty dredging up his own rusty American English. The husband seems guarded, and claims she is not at home. Max assumes his call is unwelcome and that Lucy has refused to speak to him, which is entirely understandable and a great relief. He leaves no message because he has no idea what to say and has no idea what he would have said if she had come on. The whole thing seems mad and afterwards he feels he has got away with something. But he wakes the next morning to an indefinable sense of regret.

Some days are too much. He can rotate three hundred and sixty degrees and see nothing but flatness and emptiness. He cannot reveal these feelings to Shota; certain things are not disclosed to other males. There is only Masha; some days she is less remote, but there is little give and take. He has to listen on the days when she chooses to talk and is there with the shoulder for her tears, but there are never any tears for or interest in his torments. But he tells her, because there is no one else to tell. He tells her that he feels there is nothing round him, that he is nothing in the middle of nothing and she responds that he is being abstract and arty smarty. Apart from the shared grief of Gia's death it is clear there is now no other connection between them. Everything has gone as if it never existed.

"I rang my daughter."

Nothing came back, nothing reflected in the cold surface.

"I started letters to her. Several. But I threw them away."

She laughed and it jagged him with anger.

"Gia gave me her number and address."

His veiled reminder of what they got up to on her last night in Tbilisi had no effect.

"You're just filling the vacuum left by him." It was said without emotion. "Have you any idea what that girl was like? I know your daughter better than you do. You didn't even have the decency to give her an afternoon of your time. To show her the town. "

"This isn't about me and my daughter. It's about your childlessness."

It was days before she would speak to him after that.

She had lost weight since Gia's death and he wanted to tell her how much it suited her but now these simple compliments would be impertinent. He can't remember the last time he made love to this woman who had given his life a kind of crazy basis. Nor can he remember the first time. Making love seems strange and alien now. Nature packed it away years ago. He can't even remember whom the last person was he made love to.

"You should paint."

"No."

"The translation I'm doing is saving me. I don't like it, but it gets me out of bed in the morning."

The translation depresses him. He recognises Thompson has a unique brilliance, but of a kind that bores then depresses him, and, particularly for someone grieving a murder his obsession with weapons seems sick and infantile. Under the baroque defiance there is something of the loser in him too, which touches Max's contempt. Each day he gets through slightly less. It is a chore that increasingly fails to distract from his problems.

"I don't want to paint."

However, he begins to feel the slow seismic change in her. Life takes root like weeds. A leaden normality returns, she is seen more and more about the village. Bursts of anger decorate the cold, nerveless surface she has shown since Gia's funeral. The resonance of death lowing round her gives way and she begins to look to life after Gia, and talks to Max of spending time in Paris. Good idea, Max thinks, and wishes he were free to make such trips. She rages over problems the idiot lawyer in Batumi is gumming up Gia's estate with, leaving her to chase outstanding invoices, cancel commissions, gather Gia's receipts for the bloody tax authorities, do all the work so the sister and her drunk of a husband can inherit everything and let it rot. Anger is life to Masha. When she begins to berate him he will know she is recovered. But the thought of even a few weeks without her touches his desolation, and he begins to think of Paris the way a man begins to suspect someone is his wife's lover.

California – Spring 1999

On some days, if she had a little cash, she killed the pain with another drink, and the wheel rolled on. Being sober was unendurable, oblivion the only remedy. The looks of others stoned her a thousand times a day. But over the weeks her orbit pulled her closer to AA meetings simply because she had nowhere else to go. Arriving after they started, hiding at the back by the door and escaping before anyone spoke to her, she sought only the meetings where she was not known and never returned to them. In many meetings no one knew she was there and that suited her.

These bleak rooms in hospitals, community centres and churches, with their uncomfortable chairs, blank walls, slogan cards saying 'Keep it Simple' or 'Stick with the Winners', and bad coffee, were the chambers where she had once found hope and the weird current of power that kept her sober. But she found out that there is no lonelier place than the outsider's among the insiders. That power still buzzed around but she was untouched by it, and sat on the edge, separate, different, dreaming of bars.

Over time a small voice started nagging her to open her mouth. Meetings are for listening and saying. She barely listened and never said. But meeting after meeting passed and the mouth stayed stubbornly shut. Quakers sit till they quake with the urge to speak, and she quaked her way from Newport to Venice Beach and back. The quakes would start and the need to speak swell her gorge, but the mouth produced not a squeak, and she left each meeting beaten by her own cowardice.

"I'm Lucy and I'm an alcoholic."

It just popped out one day and surprised her.

"Hi, Lucy," the backs in front of her mumbled, but she took so long to find the next word that faces turned and read her like an open book. She scanned the shoe sole smudges on the floor for inspiration.

"I'm sitting here behind you all because I don't want anyone to look at me."

The faces turned away.

"I don't look at myself. If I like catch my reflection in a window, you know?"

Another silence stretched patience. The clock on the wall swept away a minute.

"I'm back after a relapse."

No shit, Sherlock.

"I was found in the street. I don't remember. I woke up in hospital. And I had a sexually transmitted disease... I sometimes feel it would be better if I had died in that street."

Sunlight glowed on the leather waistcoat and ten-gallon hat of a black dude under a window, nodding in rhythm on a stack of tables that hiked him high enough to display his rhinestone cowboy style. He knew what she meant.

"I had four years of sobriety then I had an encounter with my father

and... I suppose I was just looking for an excuse. I remember someone
saying when you first get sober the universe is like a benign, friendly place?
That's how it was with me first time. Maybe it was like benign hysteria."
A couple of people let out soft laughs of identification. An old man craned
round. Flesh-coloured hearing aids filled his ear cavities. He wanted to lip-
read her share. She flicked her head back to the floor.

"Tooth fairy stuff, but... But this person said when you go out again
and try to get back, the universe is just that little bit colder. I can vouch for
that. It's frozen out there." Another couple of heads nodded in the corner
of her averted eye; as her share proceeded she was becoming less original.
"I got married and then, like, took off. I used to live with him before and
make coffee in the morning and stuff? Ordinary stuff. Deciding what to eat.
Which movie to see? It's like it happened to someone else."

The old man was eyes front again and there was that eerie silence she
had known in the rooms when someone was bringing a warning from the
doors of death. This time she was the trailer for everyone if they ever lifted
a drink: the state that comes with a nod to a barman or the clang of a liquor
store door.

"My father is..." A couple of faces flicked back at her in the pause, but
she had curtained herself off with her thick hair. "My father is an American
scandal. He's Max Agnew. The traitor. He defected when I was three weeks
old. I suppose some of you old-timers will remember him. I remember
nothing. I don't give a flying fuck about your politics by, the way. I'm telling
you this because I've spent my whole life not telling it to anybody. That's all.
With good reason, you know: there's a lot of jerks out there just looking for
another excuse to hate someone. But also, of course, because... well, how do
you say it? So I haven't said it. Till now. "

She had to pause and release a huge sigh that was threatening to choke
her. A couple of deep breaths punched into her and blew themselves
straight back out at a square of floor in front of her scuffed shoes. The rest
of the meeting waited patiently for her to continue, all the backs, fat necks
bulging from collars, long hair and short, broad, bulky shoulders and the
bony T-shirts of the thin ones, barely moving, all faces dutifully turned
away from her.

"I suppose if you have to keep something from people all that time, it becomes second nature. You kinda have problems with trust. I trust nothing. I hear a lot about God in these rooms. I don't think he can find his ass with both hands." Defiance had a narcotic effect on her; once started its sweetness could race her off to disaster. She felt the rush – there were always a few Holy Joes in a meeting and she liked to have a dig – but suddenly her mood swung the other way and made her afraid she had pissed people off.

"I always had wild dreams as a kid and my drinking just brought on the wild dreams wilder. But this Fellowship gave me a life below my wildest dreams – little, ordinary things, you know, but precious. I know I can get them back. I know that I could walk down the street and look people in the eye without burning up with shame and wanting to fucken die, you know? Or look at myself in the mirror. If I just get sober. Simple. But what I really want right now, more than anything else in the world, is another drink." Lucy trudged from Venice to Newport, from meeting to meeting and AA members inflicted themselves on her till she began to subside into days without drinking. Nights were insomniac but fused into mornings of catnaps. Coordination of hand and eye returned. Her skin regained a glow.

They were tumbled out of the Mission first thing and not allowed back till evening. She padded the streets, head down, away from the contempt in strangers' eyes, but one day on the Newport sidewalk she caught a look from a young dude in a surfer headscarf that suggested she was not as far down the food chain as she thought. She noticed traces of interest in other men's glances; the normality of life began to get at her, and slowly the unthinkable issue of her husband insinuated into context. Timmy rented her conscience till she shared about him at a meeting and a woman flipped open a cell phone and offered it. "No time like the present. Just dial." Her evasions were swept aside by a fusillade of reassurances. She made the call knowing he would be out and left a message on the answer machine. But the heads grinned at that old dodge, and suggested she try his work, where a hard-voiced bitch made fetching him sound like the relief of Iwo Jima.

When his diffident voice came on the line, she felt the scale of her loneliness. The group around her discreetly distanced itself and Lucy and Timmy wrestled with the awful prospect of finding the next sentence.

A week later she rang again and Timmy suggested they meet just to talk. She had no desire to be hauled from the lovely limbo of being rubble beyond the world's call towards the obligations of life. Nor had she any intentions of asking Timmy to take her back; it was too complex. In her present state she could only think minutes ahead. The amends would be made and she would leave. But when she made it to his apartment she was confronted by two wedding presents from Georgia that sucked the air out of the room. Gia's chest of drawers fashioned from pale, speckled wood and subtle curves that seemed to breed each other filled the place with her transgression. An oil-sketch of a hideous woman and child, hung in a beautiful hardwood frame above it.

"It's Jesus and Mary, believe it or not."

Mary's terrified eyes drilled accusations at Lucy and the Holy Child screamed from his mother's shrunken paps.

"It's morbid."

"I think the Pope's with you on that," said Timmy.

The day's burden had to be addressed, the sooner the better. But she didn't know how to start; the insult was too big. Maybe the best way was to stay out of his life. An apology for ladling so much crap on him stammered into the sunny room with an undertaking to make it up to him if she could – how, she had no idea..

"It's okay," was his response and she thought 'Okay'? As if she had been talking about spilling Sprite on his shorts. She had been spending weeks in the abattoir of the human spirit, going down on strangers for another JD and he lacked the imagination to see that facing this might be painful for her. The decency of his reaction infuriated her; it was false and fearful.

"Slate's clean. You owe me nothing. Just stay sober. Let's not mention it again."

She chewed on it and let it pass.

Coffee was made. Silences bruised them. He kept drifting back to Masha and Gia. She felt under fire from the other side of the world with Timmy as artillery guide.

"So, who are they to send presents?"

"I suppose they feel like they're in-laws or something."

She explained the complexities of the so-called Georgian family of Max, Masha and their surrogate son/lover, keeping it as vague as she could.

Timmy was impressed by Gia's skill but the present's material value was
so obviously high that it triggered suspicion. On long lonely nights he had
brooded on all the scenarios.

"Kinda weirdly generous."

"Georgians are generous."

"Kinda weird though."

She watched dust float up from a hot oblong of sunlight on the laminate
floor. She wanted the afternoon to end. Should she tell him everything?
Traditionally the AA programme advocated scrupulous honesty except
when disclosure would cause someone else harm or pain, and telling him
would certainly do that. She contemplated her desire to hurt him.

"Tell me about your dad. You didn't talk about him before."

An old defence against her mother's rants or the cheap jibes at school
was to erase the tapes as they recorded, and call up a trance nothing
could penetrate. This had triggered in the fifteen minutes she spent with
her father leaving the tumour in his hair and his stale smell as her only
memories.

"You know, I just can't remember. And maybe that's best."

But she remembered how Gia was driven that night to do what he
clearly would regret, and how urgently she helped him on, and how he left
disgusted with his own weakness and shocked at her drunkenness. All the
things he failed to say to her he had said in wood. They were as clear as if he
had carved them in perfect English. His guilt and decency were waxed into
the gorgeous surface. The human spirit glowed through the grain. She ran
her hand over his chest of drawers. "This is kind of beautiful."

Something shifted. It was clear where the afternoon was now pointing.
Athletes pacing the lanes behind the starting line, shaking their muscles
and warming up, rather than come forward to the blocks that led to the
long space they had to run. Time measured itself in pauses. He touched
her arm; she dipped her head, communication reduced to a semaphore of
physical moves. Right hands landed lightly on left forearms. Sunlight flared
the blond hairs on her skin. They came a half pace closer and the awkward
dance steps with the arms and shoulders began. Her head brushed his
cheek and left her in a maidenly nervousness. He kissed her hair, and
eventually, under Gia's drawers and Masha's Madonna of pain, they got in

the blocks and the pistol fired. He tried a couple of new techniques and she realized he hadn't been wasting his time while she sucked the dream pipe.

A seagull landed on his balcony. He felt her stiffen. He could have chased it off, but lay listening to it padding about, flapping a wing, feeling her panic rise. When it flew off she relaxed. The moment of cruelty felt good. He asked if she wanted to move back in. This had not been the plan; he had spent the morning steeling himself to a strategy that was the complete opposite.

"Okay" she said because she couldn't think of anything else to say. It was settled. He would go with the flow. She was blank. "When?"

"Whenever."

The words had come and gone. A fly wandered across the ceiling.

"Your friend? Masha?"

"She's not my friend."

'Well. Whatever. She rang. Twice. First to check we'd got the gifts. Then again." Progressively he saw more and more as comic strip: people in cafes, the homeless round trash bins, sex, loneliness, couples struggling with each other – they were just drawings in a cheap story. He imagined himself and his estranged wife from the fly's viewpoint; two bodies side by side but not touching, staring up, resigned, a storyboard frame enclosing their intimate separateness.

"The guy who made the drawers?"

"Gia."

"Yuh." He slipped in a little pause. "He was murdered."

The fly rubbed its front limbs together.

"Murdered as in dead?"

"Brown bread."

He waited for some reaction, monitored the pause, analysed her body tension and voice quality.

"You mean really murdered?"

"Totally. No more."

There was nothing more, no request for details, not a flicker. He still couldn't be sure.

"That was a while back. A message. I didn't ring back. What would I say? But Man, she was upset."

"I bet she was." She watched the fly. "They were lovers."

"Who?"

"Gia and Masha."

"I thought they were..?"

"Yeah. But they were lovers too."

He watched the fly.

"It's a Georgian thing."

How many other 'Georgian things' had she learned? She used up all the emotion in the relationship. He wondered if he could take it again.

"There was another call. More recent."

"Yeh?"

"From your father." He felt her stiffen again. "Just saying 'hello'. What could I say? You weren't around."

The neighbours said hello when Lucy passed on the stairs. The artist had moved in his girl friend, and when they discovered the girl friend was a wife Lucy experienced approval. The marriage certificate possessed a runic power, even among women younger than she, who by her logic should be spending their evenings topless on bars littered with vodka slammers. Respectability in the young seemed neurotic.

Strong urges to drink still hit her; each day was knotted with struggles against flying to the nearest bar. It exhausted her. She forced herself to meetings though they were the last place she wanted to be, and in some desperate moments prayed to a God she no longer believed in to help her stay sober, and in others philosophically mused that if she drank again, it made no difference. Maybe she just hadn't quite had enough this time round. The mental hospitals, stomach pumps, sleaze balls with diseased dicks, and suicidal longings didn't seem too bad on days when the booze called. Sobriety, a roof over her head, a little money to buy sale price shoes, and the capacity to remember what she did the night before, were poor substitutes for a return to the ninety per cent proof that left dry vomit in her purse.

Between these crises life rumbled along in an outwardly normal way. Timmy went to work and she nursed him through the little depressions and failed ambitions he brought back with him. In the evening they would eat, watch television, go to movies, or she would borrow his car and drive to a meeting. He talked of a future that seemed to be from someone else's life; of possible things she might want to do, of college courses and re-training while she could think no further than the next Weight Watchers recipe or how the fuck she was going to get a drink before she went mad.

At times the episode surrounding her father overwhelmed her. It would hit her in the street and deflect her eyes from any human face. In AA they urged her to get on the programme or that shame would whip her back to the bars and death or madness. When she got sober first time round she had indulged an idea that she was safe, that sobriety brought insulation from the world's harshness, and had sustained this naïve delusion with a conviction that now astonished her. It had died in Tbilisi's bullet-pocked streets. If nothing else, her father had given her a sharp dose of reality.

Sobriety also brought exhaustion and insomnia. While Timmy worked, she went to daytime meetings, walked on the beach till the seagulls drove her off, toppled asleep in the most inappropriate places to wake over cold coffees or attached to magazines by strings of saliva. But then night came and switched her awake.

She wandered the apartment, read a little, tried not to eat, absorbed the scorn and sadism in her head, and fought against hitting the streets like one of the un-dead cruising for the next high. When she got sober in Palo Alto first time round, she used the insomnia to go on long night drives and turned her life into a nocturnal road movie, cruising coastal routes under the stars or past the little buildings and parked Beetles of Silicon Valley, where the dot-com boys, Heroes of the new mythology, hauled in the infinite numbers of the universe in Pentium nets, and Hermes, the winged messenger was finally grounded by snowboarders with the Information. Everything seemed possible then, but now? Even if I get properly sober, what can I do with this raw material that is me, she asked a deaf universe. What little marks would she leave? The mortgage, the child with the learning disorder, the final face-lift? For her – so they kept assuring – ordinariness was an achievement. Keep it simple.

The night-bred thoughts of her father and the yellow brick road to brutality in Tbilisi was picked over incessantly. The killing of a weakness in her, the death of romance, she thought, the snuffing out of a childhood comfort, was it such a bad thing? Hadn't the dreams just led to a thousand gutters and beds of strangers? In the bedroom, a murdered man's dreams held her panties and bras and her husband's socks.

She quietly opened the glass door onto the balcony and sat by its edge. Stars were visible above the milky fade of light from the city. Everything under the same sky she thought: all the problems, all the good stuff, all the shit; her mother asleep in an exclusive estate in Arizona beside her millionaire husband, her father god knows where, Gia in a grave or wherever they put the dead in Georgia, and Masha now going without it. Without her older man, without her younger man. Without. The Madonna and Child watched her from the shadows. Their eyes were portals for all the misery and darkness she had touched. She kept staring at them and they kept staring back till she became afraid of ghosts. "Come to us. We are hideous, we are frightened. Embrace us. Love us," they whispered to her.

"Okay, okay. Get off my fuckin' back," she replied.

She took a number from the message board in the kitchen area, lifted the phone and returned to the window. In AA they suggested she write to Masha to thank her for the gifts. "Don't phone," someone had said. "And if the gifts disturb you, get rid of them," another had added. She looked back, and allowed the Holy Pair to disturb her again.

It would be daytime, she was sure of that. Seagulls hung over the palms in the sodium light. She dialled Masha's number. The answer machine clicked on.

'Masha, it's Lucy. Hi. I'm sorry I haven't got back in so long; I've been off the rails. Gia. I don't know what to say; I was really shaken when I heard. His work is so beautiful. I don't know if beauty is the right word for your work; powerful? Haunting, certainly. I'm no expert, you know, the only culture round here is live yoghurt but certainly you are so talented and I am very moved by your kindness. And Gia's... God... There's a little bit of both of you in Santa Monica. It's four in the morning. Insomnia's good for the time difference..'

Masha observed her arm extend and lift the phone.

"It was the theme from *Solaris.*"

They picked up as if they were still in the dining room in Tbilisi but with all the weight time had loaded on them. Lucy was aware of the eerie calm

in Masha's voice as she was given the details of Gia's emasculation. "Fuck!"
trailed out of American night into Georgian day. No one knew why he was
murdered, but in Masha's vendetta-ridden country murder was almost a
sacred tradition. Her grief bridged east and west in an uninhibited arc of
pain. God had taken away someone who was as near as she had to a son –
albeit with an Œdipal complication – and with him had gone the tattered
illusions of a future. No detail was spared in the description of how Max
found him or the depth of his devastation. Masha knew Max's love for Gia
might by rights have been for Lucy, but what Gia and she had got up to that
last night in Tbilisi was as clear as if she'd stitched a thank-you note in his
underwear. The deliberate insensitivity flattened Lucy but she saw how
fighting for her own flimsy self-esteem over Gia's broken body would be
beyond churlishness, so they sat with it ten thousand miles apart in a truce
girdling half the Earth, letting the light and the dark coalesce.

Eventually the conversation stumbled on to the Maui wedding. Lucy
gave it the stand-up treatment and had them both laughing, Bloated with
symbolism and sentimentality, Timmy was insisting on a second marriage
in Santa Monica. "A symbolic new start, as if for God's sake... Oh, maybe,
maybe I shouldn't be so damned cynical. Who knows?" Lucy stepped onto
the balcony, her eyes fixed on the circling seagulls. "Why don't you come?
There must be cheap flights. See California. Shop, eat too much. The light's
great for painting" Turning up the intimacy she confessed the whole kit
and caboodle about her alcoholism. Masha declared that was another thing
Lucy could blame her father for.

28 April 1964

I am paranoid. Every car is following, every person watching, every call
monitored. Nothing matters or has any impact except the problem which
grinds me smaller every second.

A low barrelling sky squats above me. Pressure is high; it has been
a day of headaches and calls for Advil throughout the office. We need a
thunderstorm to clear the air. Way in the distance the rain is charging in

like rampaging locusts. In the baby store parking lot I have a strong desire
to turn myself in but grab my hat and spring cheerily into the store.

"Hi. How are they?"

"Good. Real good, thank you. Hey, could I use your men's room?"

"Men's room?"

"I must adjust my maternity girdle."

She laughs her bridgework at me and wonderful breasts balloon the
'Happy Stork' logo on her work coat.

The john window frames backyard America: a Hopper Hopper never
painted. An alley runs the length of the stores and beyond it are roofs of
single storey houses over wooden fences, cat's cradles of phone and power
wires, loneliness in a familiar landscape. That alley is my Rubicon, lined
with broken pallets, trashcans and Happy Stork Babygrow boxes. Agents
hunt me down in cheap suits and Ray-Bans on this side; my legions wait on
the other in cheap suits and fake Ray-Bans.

I unlock the rear door, walk to the fence and scan the alley. Nothing
but a heavy sky, and the noise of banging blood in my ears. A sweat drop
spreads into a tiny flower shape in the dirt and fades, breezes whine in bare
trees. A gate stands twenty yards down the other side of the alley, but the
twenty yard stroll is open ground where men will swarm out of yards and
young wives watch over meat loaf mixes as my rights are read by hats and
horn rims. This is the crucial moment in my life, knee deep in diaper boxes.

The pull to do nothing is almost irresistible then I am walking down
the alley and in through the gate, along the side of a house, past a small
kidney shaped pool with a candy wrapper marooned in breeze patterns in
the middle. Then I am on a front lawn in a street of front lawns, then on
the sidewalk. The street is empty but for a green pick up. Nothing seems as
quiet as the silence in a suburb.

Then the green pick up hacks into life and cruises over to me. The
driver is swarthy. He says "Hi, bud." The cabin stinks with blue collar
smells of metal and grease and is littered with cigarette packs, grubby work
manifestos, chewed pencils and gum wrappers. My feet slide on oily rags.
We drive off, each second putting distance between me and the baby shop
and everything. Wintry lawns slide past. A woman in a headscarf smokes
in a window. I look down and see my hands knuckle white round the keys

to the Chevrolet Impala. Peg needs them; there are no spares. I curse at my thoughtlessness.

My watch reads 6.38pm and rain begins to drum the roof.

Georgia – Spring 1999

About ten-thirty in the morning he saw a dark blue Mercedes parked a hundred metres on the road towards the village, roughly where he had walked into the killers on the night of Gia's death. The other passengers had gone, leaving the driver looking down at something below the dashboard. Suddenly he got out and the movement startled Max to the guns. He moved without thinking, beautifully controlled by adrenaline. The Gyurza materialised from the drawer in his writing desk and the Makarov was retrieved from under his pillow. The man was leaning against the Merc door by now, smoking and looking at the sea, keeping an eye out. Max loaded the Gyurza with the armour-piercing clip. Slav Eyes and his thugs would be on their way to the house, picking their way through the woods no doubt.

"Get out of any building. Don't be caught somewhere" snaked down to him from the Marine who took them through basic weapons training in the late Fifties. He ducked his way from shadow to shadow, looking long-range through windows. The obvious place for their approach was through the woods tumbling down the hill to his house at the back. Peeping through the edge of the bedroom curtains he saw no movement in the trees, but they were so dense they would hide a rabbit. The Slav Eyes could be in there watching him already. There could be four of them, but more likely to be three. Overwhelming, but never mind, the whistle had gone, the game was on; Max felt okay.

There was a brief gap in cover from his window to the trees and if they were waiting for him he wouldn't last a second. However he knew his house was not a defence but a trap; he had to get out, to make his stand. But the few open yards from his sill to the woods seemed as wide as a prairie.

He would take his chance. If this was the moment he was to follow Gia, he prayed it would be with a well-aimed bullet and not the knife and their amusement. He could use a bullet on himself. He would go down whatever path fate had beaten out for him.

He quietly opened his window, poked the gun out to give himself some sort of sightless cover and clambered and fell and was across the gap with an agility and speed that surprised him. Facing death was taking years off him. He was in the wood, climbing as quietly as he could, keeping the breath from his aching chest under control, watching for movement between trees, stopping to listen, moving from trunk to trunk, a geriatric veteran of a thousand TV westerns.

Could he kill a man? He had no idea, but suspected he would betray himself with that moment's hesitation. He will fall like an actor. Think of it that way. You are in a scene. Play it to the hilt. Point and shoot. Bang! You're dead – a kid's game. He could feel no hatred for them, nor did he feel fear, only a strange, exhilarating nervousness. Remember what they did to Gia; remember what those last minutes of his life must have been like. But it had no effect; his body was in an altered state impervious to everything.

He found a gap on the wooded slope that gave him a view of his house and the man by the Mercedes. Breath wanted to burst from him; he fought to regulate its exits and intakes and sat against a tree and waited, both guns pointed downhill at the ready. His pulse was beating so hard the guns in his hands twitched with each heartbeat. My God he thought; would the guns have a kick? Do you aim low or has the bullet left the gun by the time it kicks?

His bedroom window was wide open. They would see it and perhaps that would attract them. Or they would deduce exactly what he had done and break silently into the woods for him. If they went for the window was he too far away for an effective shot? Irakli had said fifty metres for the Gyurza, but he was well out of the Makarov's range. He tucked the Makarov into his belt and clasped the Gyurza with both hands, resting them on his knees for support, pushing his back against the tree trunk for purchase for the kick. He wasn't sure this was an ideal combat position.

Nothing happened; there was no movement in the woods, no one approached the window, or the house. Small noises interrupted the calm, but he was able to distinguish the difference in noise a human would make to the wood's natural inhabitants. He had a perfect view of the kitchen door and a clear view through some foliage of his bedroom window. The man at the Mercedes seemed uninterested in anything that might be happening around Max's house. He smoked and stared out at the sea, watched some kids play way to his left in the distance then exhaled a long geyser of smoke, flicked his cigarette onto the beach in a fast, twisting arc, got into the car and drove off.

It hit him like a wave. He began to shake violently. His chest seemed ready to rip out of him. Heart attack, I'm dying of a heart attack. I'm dying of fear. Stupidity. His panic slowly coalesced into relief, then foolishness, then shame, not just for this ridiculous armed sortie into the woods, but for an inchoate mass of everything. The kids playing at the water's edge were watched by an old man under a tree with two loaded pistols in his hands, one of them containing armour piercing bullets. For a businessman, or a taxi driver stopping for a moment's peace. The episode rushed him towards tears. Even Gia's death, with all its shattering emotions, had not brought tears; he had stopped up tears for so long that he seemed to have dehydrated his humanity.

The kids' voices came to him in high snaps of sound. Birds landed in trees, took off, the Mercedes disappeared over the top of the hill leading out of the village. Life was untouched by his crisis. The Slav eyes didn't need to kill him; the fear would finish him off in a moment like this or when an incomprehensible sound wakes him at night. Alexei had the answer; all he lacked was the price. He would persist with Masha that very day, while the nerves were rattling round the old bones. He had to make her see how much danger he was in. He could repay her – or at least part of it – once the further instalments for the translation came in. "Make it business. Simply a business transaction" he muttered to his trembling gun.

He drew up a financial plan and gathered letters from the publisher itemising his fee for the translations and when the instalments on each book would be paid. He rang her and set off for the coffee under Shota's old Magnolia.

She seemed softer, reflective. He felt hopeful. They joked a little with Gia's niece Shorena when she brought the coffee. Then it landed.

"I'm thinking of basing myself in Paris," was the first thing she said, "I can't take this place any more. Or this country. Time to move on."

A few words above the beach and part of a lifetime draws to a close. So many things want to be said but he sits, nodding and saying nothing. Perhaps there is some natural progression in this he thinks, that everything in my life has been stripped away for a reason: my old world with its beliefs and principles, Gia, now Masha, that even the visit of my daughter has some part in a sequence of fate that is separating me from everything.

The herd is moving on and he is the old one left behind for the predator. He looks out at the raft to which he can no longer swim. Perhaps he should make one long, last attempt. That might be the way to go. The financial plan stays in his pocket.

"Georgia will be empty without you. So, I've lost two in such a short time. I suppose that's often how it happens."

He sees her eyes following the kids on the beach.

"I spoke to Lucy."

Nothing but a sigh is left for Max.

"They're getting married again. A fresh start."

"Sounds typically Californian."

"They've invited me."

Max wonders how long he will have to pay the price for that blunder in a basement corridor one day in Tbilisi. He is tempted to lose himself in Moscow for a while.

"You should go, Max."

"I'd be arrested."

She smiled at him. "You've always got an excuse."

Something had flown out of him and he didn't care what she said any more.

"Did you know she's an alcoholic?"

"Lucy?"

"Apples don't fall far from the tree."

"I am not responsible for my daughter's social habits."

The word shocked him; it always shocked him when it was used about him, usually in his opinion by some puritan desperate to put him in his place. Americans, however, seem to regard it as a character asset, as if they had been led to a state of grace simply because they'd stopped vomiting on their shoes.

"They turn everything into a new religious sect: holy drinkers who have found the Way. The world has too many idiots who have found the Way. The Way should be banned."

"You found it, didn't you?" she riposted languidly and with a lazy look that told him that whatever she once had for him had emptied itself from her. She rises, says nothing, leaves some coins for the coffee, goes home and he is left thinking of her grotesque Mother and Child and how deliberately and brilliantly repulsive it is. The holy pair, cratered with marine crustaceans matted into the paint are physically composed of death and decay. Christ clings in terror to his despairing mother and they look up as if they are the damned, not the serene pair pedalled by the church and her tame artists. He knows she modelled them on photographs of the starving in the Ukraine under Stalin's programme of depopulation. But there is some other quality in the picture that wails at him from the mental asylums she was locked in, and sets him thinking about the brutal side of the quest for grace.

The kids are still on the beach, running pell-mell to the water with their buckets as if the sea will leave if they don't hurry. Kids need tension in their games. Life or death. The little girl is always several metres behind. She holds her hand over her bucket and comes back up the beach in a fast waddle. Her bikini knickers have flounces. It'll take them all afternoon to fill the trench.

Next morning Max was once again pondering the thuja tree and the dark Circassian walnut, wondering whose lives before his had been lived out in this little house to the sea's eternal counterpoint. On the veranda with his fruit he watched the beach umbrellas, spades and buckets slowly emerge in the dawn. The village had changed for him overnight. He had good companions like Shota there, people he was fond of but the real connections were gone or going. If he sold up what did he face? Increasing difficulties climbing the stairs to his apartment in Tbilisi? Would he be safer there? Possibly. Would he miss this place? No doubt.

In mid-morning, the beach heated to a wonderful descant of the kids' trebles and the waves' baritone, and Max digressed from the translation to write a letter to Lucy, explaining that, although he could understand her curiosity, and accepting that he had no rights over any correspondence with Masha, he felt it was improper and unhelpful to everyone. He redrafted the letter twice then tore it up and returned to the translation. An hour later he wrote another letter and posted it.

When Shota heard what he had written he told Max he was offering up his throat, and predictably, Max regretted mailing it.

Dear Lucy,

Masha tells me you are marrying again. The institution of marriage must agree with you if you are to celebrate it twice. I tried it three times. If you and your husband are proposing a second honeymoon, may I suggest you have it here, by the Black Sea? I will pay your air flights. Accommodation may be Spartan by American standards, but it is pleasant, warm and, as yet, relatively unspoiled. Just a wild idea – if you were to consider having this second marriage over here, I dare say we could arrange something with a Georgian flavour. Despite the parlous state of things, people here are gracious and they love a good wedding.

I appreciate that you may find this offer offensive. Whatever, I wish you and your new husband well.

Best wishes, Max.

Russia – 1960s

When an agent defects, the possibility of his being a 'double' has to be ruled out. So when I arrived in Russia in the early Sixties, I was squirrelled away and underwent what is politely known as debriefing, a process not necessarily conducted with courtesy and warmth for the new guest. One of my interrogators was particularly brilliant and quickly took me to a point where I didn't know if I were coming or going, a state where even an agent trained in resisting interrogation would find it impossible to hide anything. This state was induced with wit, charm and, when needed, a scalpel-like threat. At times I wondered if I might end up in some gulag or be despatched with a bullet in an anonymous yard.

I shall call this man Alexei – it's not his real name. He is small, is now old and with a bad hip, but was then wearyingly energetic, blessed with glittering film star good looks, and, it was said, despite having a very beautiful wife, possessed the sexual appetite of an alpha baboon. He was chief puppeteer in the various wooded retreats and windswept places I found myself in for clearance and re-education, and delighted in leading me a merry dance.

One night he decided to take me for a walk, a suggestion that made me instantly wary. Was I going to be despatched in the woods with a sniper's rifle, the way of Sydney Reilly and, no doubt, many other agents who had outlived their usefulness? I was very unsure of my position and suffered from the recurrent idea that I needed to confess to something and get the whole torture over and done with, although I actually had nothing to confess. I was legitimate, on their side, but at times, under the incessant questioning and switches in technique, it was difficult to keep a grasp of this.

I don't know which region we were in, or even which country, but after a few careful steps from the compound, we found ourselves in a broad clearing between woods. We may even have been standing on a frozen lake. It was a full moon and the low lines of fir trees were purple in the moonlight. The snow crunched under our feet and the stars were sprayed crystals. The night was like some magic, white precipitate held in a suspension of indigo. We paused and Alexei lit a cigarette. I sank into that wonderful muffled silence of snow with the cold on my cheeks and for some reason no longer felt afraid, I was just a smudge on a winter miracle. We stood wordless for a while, Alexei quietly smoking, my waiting for some statement from him, some word to disturb the harmony of this winter night. When it arrived, it was, as usual, unexpected.

"What do you feel about your wife and baby?"

I couldn't find an answer anywhere. The night flew off and peeped back through the wrong end of a telescope. A low level tinnitus broke out in my hearing and Alexei spoke to me through my own white noise.

"She'll be three months now. The little one." He dragged slowly on his cigarette. "Lucy." Another long slow drag expanded the point of ruby light at the end of his cigarette. "She'll have changed."

I imagined this was how a boxer felt when he'd taken a hard punch to the head, and lost the connection, leaning against the ropes not sure what was going on, what was next, what the noise was, seeing shapes and movements that he knew he once understood, but which were now meaningless.

"Do you want us to get a message to them?"

"Saying what? 'Sorry'?"

His breath blasted the smoke round his cigarette tip. His face glowed against dark fir trees. He was watching me, reading me, filing me. The blue eyes were black and still under the Communist moon.

"There can be no weakness, Max, in any of us. You understand?"

I nodded.

"Begin forgetting." The ruby cigarette tip vaulted into the night and died in the snow with a weak hiss.

Needless to say, once I was given the all clear, Alexei became my case officer, the one who could most easily trip me up, keep me on my toes and make my life anything but relaxed. But in all his capriciousness and tricks, I could see there was fondness for me, and he became a good friend.

In my second summer in Russia, now well clear of debriefings and interrogations but still under surveillance, Alexei took me to his home village about fifteen kilometres outside Moscow. After sturgeon in aspic and pork with beer under a hand-tinted portrait of Stalin, we left his wife Petra to his garrulous mother and disappeared into the woods.

Every insect in the wood took a liking to my face and I slapped myself till archipelagos of their tiny corpses smudged my cheeks. We found old paths and strolled through tunnels of luminous leaves, and the glades where Alexei and prepubescent village girls discovered the difference.

The thick foliage gave way to a dusty road running by a high wooden wall. Above the wall, strings of barbed wire diminished like an endless musical stave to the horizon. Sweat scattered down my sides and buttocks as we followed the razor-wire. We passed a short door in a solid gate.

"Knock, but no one will hear."

"What's over there?"

"Old military zone. Absolutely *verboten*."

In this country with its Byzantine imagination, it is easy to feel even the wind dare not trespass. Alexei picked up the pace.

"You're wheezing."

"Booze in the middle of the day. And the heat."

"There's no point in coming to this country if you don't drink."

The wall gave way to a chain link fence. Alexei scuttled along, scuffing his English brogues through the grass till he found a tear in the fence and pulled it open.

"Enter."

Resigned, I folded my jacket, threw it over, got down and striped my shirt with grass stains. Alexei slithered through without removing his jacket or picking up any stains. He stood, smacked the back of one hand into the other's palm and took off through the woods.

We continued under a mixture of trees, some of which were still in flower. It was restful and beautiful, green and soft and quiet. In a wide clearing he stopped and lay down in long, shadowed grass on the edge of the trees. When he spoke his voice had an intimacy I had never heard. His seriousness sanctified the place; something beyond the briefs that constituted our official relationship was being offered.

"They say to a kid 'don't go in the woods', so you go in the woods. We had our little arses whipped if they found out. They were shit scared."

"Who?"

"The parents." The breeze raised a chorus in the leaves. "It was thick with fruit and berries but nobody came in to pick them. Except us. Till our little guts ached." Some old fruit memory amused him for a while. "We'd lie here and wait for the lorries. Straight past, flat out, into the military zone. From Moscow. A lone lorry would have two cars. Then we'd wait for the next bit. Sometimes we'd turn chicken and get out. It was a test – a kid's dare. You'd be worried your mother would guess where you'd been, but you'd wait, and then you'd hear them." He nodded at where the clearing turned into the afternoon sun and disappeared. American landscapes are huge but the Russian landscape has a quality of infinity. The clearing would run into a secret country within the country.

"Single shots. We'd count them. Twenty. Forty. Whatever. It would go on all day sometimes." His gaze was fixed where the clearing bent from sight through the trees. I suggested we go for a look, but he shook his head. He had never dared beyond this point, and still wouldn't. I had found the minotaur at the centre of his labyrinth, a forest clearing dripping with beauty and mythic fear. He was showing me his limit. His high office was the Ariadne thread that led him to safety, his calling to search in the fear of his victim for the reflection of the fear he discovered under these quiet trees. This wordless confession came to me obliquely. I was privileged; it was an act of love in some corkscrewed way.

The stutter of a distant tractor blew among the rustling leaves. "In the first year of the purges, they brought two thousand here. We heard some of them being done from this very spot. Under this old tree. Hi, my friend!" he waved to the tree above us. "It was never mentioned in the village, even when the wind was right and everyone heard the shots.

"I looked it up in the archives. Their best day was the twenty-eighth of February nineteen thirty-eight. They got through five hundred and sixty two. That's a day's work. I would have been at school. I was thirteen. What were you doing in nineteen thirty-eight? The Mickey Mouse Club?"

I asked about the bodies.

"'Under the green sod.' I could smell the thick grasses, the wild flower; feel the ground on my belly.

"Drop in the ocean. Nobody was safe. I'm surprised Stalin didn't have himself shot. Two of my mother's brothers died building the Volga Moscow canal. Probably in the concrete in one of the locks, waste not, want not."

I remembered tinted Stalin smiling fatly over his Mother's table.

"And my father's cousin, Olga, died building Norilsk. Don't bother with Norilsk. Two thousand miles northeast, a ten-month winter. Hell isn't hot: it's cold, and it's Norilsk. Clouds of smoke from its big chimneys, filthy white on filthy white, yellow sky from the chemicals, slush and smoke and darkness and stink. The prisoners designed it, built it; nickel mines, roads, houses, power stations, mills, brick factories. Cousin Olga was one of them. She was young. She was a metallurgist. An economic necessity."

He watched a tiny spider crawl hyperactively over his knuckles. "They would let the male prisoners rape the women. Organized, en masse gang bangs. Queues of them with their hard-ons. Some of the weaker women were literally fucked to death. Olga might have gone that way. It's how I'm trying to go." He put the little spider back on a stalk of grass. "Would you fuck Petra?"

"What?"

"Would you fuck my gorgeous wife?" I stared at him in the long grass of his morbid childhood. "If you were in a camp and Petra was there, would you fuck her?" His blue eyes drilled up over his irritating film star smile. "You would." He nodded at the bright green clearing and the oak and elder, aspen and birch, rippling in the sunlight. "This is idealism's terminus."

Spring 1999

Max's letter was a crisis for everyone. Thirty years of sediment shook up and Henry called his whole daft life into question. Peg was incandescent with indignation, and Arnold – Peg's ancient and very rich third husband – worried for Lucy. Timmy was so terrified Lucy would drink he bought her a cell phone and checked up every hour till she left it switched off. Curiously for Lucy, the trauma blew away the craving for drink and left her motoring along in a stunned haze. Within AA, her opinion became that of the last person she spoke to. Many were emphatic she should not go, but the siren voice from the east started its sales pitch: the arguments for and against dizzied her. Then one morning she woke to a state of clarity.

"I'm not going. It would be madness. I'm getting on top of this shit and I need to carry on."

Timmy joyfully rang Henry at his publishing house who interrupted a meeting with an important author just to take the call. When Timmy told him Lucy's decision, the brightness in Henry's voice dulled. "Yes, well, I suppose she's being sensible."

"I am just so relieved."

"Yes it's the wise decision I suppose. I have to go now Timmy. Give her my love."

However when Timmy got home she had mailed a letter to her father saying she would come to Georgia, but only if her mother, uncle Henry and Arnold could come too. He freaked.

"Relax. He'll never agree to those conditions."

"Then why give him the fucking choice?" She had never seen him as angry. "What about me? What if I don't wanna go?"

"Don't be ridiculous."

Lucy's challenge gave Shota his best laugh for a long time.

"It's her way of saying 'no'. She's just passing the buck." Max grasped desperately for an escape.

"Why?"

"Oh come on, she knows these are impossible conditions. She knows I can't possibly accept them."

"Why not?"

"Don't be ridiculous."

They would beat him with the conviction that everything on their side was right and everything on his wrong.

"You made your bed. Now lie in it," said Masha.

But there was no question of the rest of the family being invited. A letter was drafted graciously declining Lucy's conditions.

"Why?" said Shota.

"Don't be ridiculous."

"What they going to do to you? Cut your balls off? They're no use now anyway."

"My ex-wife Shota, my ex-wife? I still have her car keys."

"Time to give them back."

"Very funny."

"She can't chew your balls because Henry will have cut them off."

"Ah Henry.. yes, Henry. No, no that. Once CIA always CIA."

"Not you though."

The village wanted the wedding. Max had ignited something and it was clear the response to his daughter's conditions would determine his position in the village as respected elder, or mouse. The bluff of a gesturist was being called. "Jesus," he said in a desperate moment, "where's that bastard with the Slav eyes now I need him? Tolya, I'm ready for you."

The sea washed in and out. How reassuring to be a wave shifting endlessly across the globe, to be unthinking, unfeeling, just a motion without senses.

Dear Lucy,
Of course the family is welcome. But please be aware that this is not
Florida. I shall send a driver to pick you up in Tbilisi. I haven't driven for
years and I shall have to hold the helm here.
    Look forward to seeing you all.
    Max.

One other place in the village sold alcohol but stopped serving Max when
Poland became free and Shota made it clear he would not serve him. Max
was shocked his drinking was a public concern. A few nights in police cells,
a brief break in the Tbilisi asylum, and a certain amnesia about what might
have happened or been said several-nights-befores hardly amounted to
a problem. When things seemed to go a little too far, he would stop for
lengthy periods. It was nothing to worry about, but the village had him
on probation; the marriage was a gleam of international brightness after
Gia's murder and years of poverty, and the locals were not going to let Max
urinate in his daughter's trousseau. Some spirit was abroad, frail as a new
born calf and they were fighting to give it life.

    Curiously, Max was reassured; if the wedding belonged to the villagers
as much as to him they might draw flak and absorb the impact of the
family. Only Masha remained aloof, and this was an irony too far for Max;
it was her invitation to California that provoked his incomprehensible offer,
and importantly, she was the one person in the village able to provide a
healthy cash injection, but it was too late for that.

    "Its going to clean me out, Shota."

    "To hell with the money, Max. The important thing is we do it good. All
of us."

    The idea that the wedding should be held in the church with full
Georgian trimmings gained ground. The devout were reassured there
was no offence as the couple were already married and this was to be a
symbolic ceremony. As an atheist, Max was deemed unfit to approach the
eccentric Father Gregory, but Masha had his inner ear. However, she cried
blasphemy.

"Of course it's jealousy," maintained Shota. "You're reclaiming your line into the future, your posterity, Max. She has no one."

"My daughter is simply a biological fact."

"You're a biological fact ahead of her."

Nevertheless, Shota told her she was taking things a little far, and that her resentments found little sympathy in the village; this was something to celebrate, not regret.

He and Max approached Father Gregory with all the wiles in their repertoire. Gregory was initially suspicious that two of the unfaithful – one a well known atheist – had arrived on the church's doorstep with enough charm to float a musical, and was appalled when the reason for their unexpected visit was revealed. The church was not a theatre to be hired out and he was not an actor. However, that evening something about the idea of a lost child returning caught him in the silence of the church and persuaded him to rethink. Even the atheist must never be turned away from Christ's door, so over a large Ukrainian brandy that Shota told him was French, he agreed. Max raised his Pepsi, Shota poured himself a real Scotch, glasses clinked and the church became Lucy's. As long as the Bishop didn't find out.

Now the adventure had an attractively heretical quality, things were falling into place, but as the days crept closer to the event, Max began to be horrified. A terror he had not felt since the months leading up to his defection rose in the morning and stumbled through the day with him into bleak stretches of insomnia. He raged against his insanity in bringing it all back on himself and lay in bed feeding the night with schemes to call the whole thing off, but could never find the wherewithal to do it. The village had preparations in full swing and their anticipation trapped him. The tension wound into increasingly irresistible compulsions to drink.

"When sorrows come, they come not single spies. But in battalions." Shakespeare's phrase came to him when he put down the phone. Fate or God added a spicy ingredient into this mix of fear and regret that his moment of irrational generosity had produced. He took a call from Irakli. There had been some talk around the drinking dives in Batumi of a 'witness', a leak from the Batumi police; nothing specific, nothing heard of any plan to deal with the witness or who he was, and certainly no news of anyone beating a fast path from Moscow. They were just asking out

of interest more than anything else who the witness was. "Curiosity, Mr
Agnew, that's all, bar chat. Don't worry; nothing's going to happen. Not
from any of us anyway. Us Georgians. It's nobody's beef down here, but
I suggest you keep an eye out. If anything specific was happening, we'd
probably have heard."

"Probably?"

"I'm sure you'll be okay."

"If it's a leak from the police, surely the police could leak my identity?

"There's all sorts of shit happening with the police at the moment –
'scuse my language, Mr Agnew – accusations of corruption, that sort of
thing. So nobody's going to be leaking anything for a while. How are the
guns?"

"The guns are fine. How's your daughter?"

"Thank you for asking. She's done well in her exams. Especially in
German and physics."

"Congratulations to her. And thank you for the warning."

"It's an honour to do business with you. If I hear anything more, I'll let
you know. Don't worry, Mr Agnew, don't worry."

And that, of course, was the thing Max did till it put him in a trance.
Days passed in contemplation of the guns; one bullet would avoid
everything; the simple squeezing of a trigger and the family filled with
vengeance, the slit-eyed killer and his loneliness would all disappear. A
magic trick: now you see them – worrying you, making you conscious
only of your shortcomings, keeping you awake at night – now you don't.
Disappeared. "He who dies pays all debts." Shakespeare again. All solutions
to be had in a finger movement. "You won't even hear the gun go off, or
feel a thing. The last thing you'll hear and see will be the waves. It'll be
like switching off a television." He scrutinised the hair fine scratches on
the chamber of the Makarov and wondered what had made them: where
had this gun been, who wielded it, who suffered it? Matchless designs and
engineering, dedicated to the extinction of human life. What a curious and
skilled occupation. And yet necessary, given the lizards who stalked the
earth in human form.

He loaded the Makarov and sat with it in his hand. There were twelve
bullets in the clip: eleven of them unnecessary. He could have bought one

gun and one bullet.

With a drink inside him he could probably do it.

The Batumi bus disgorged him at a drinking den that had his elbow imprints on the bar. No one greeted him; no one greeted anyone in this place. He saw the hunched bodies and vacant faces staring over half empty glasses, tables sticky with beer and loaded ashtrays, watched the beer dribble from tall, swan neck spigots into thick glasses with the sound of an enlarged prostrate piss slowly filling a toilet bowl, scrutinised the huge barman in his chef's whites and turban looking at him blankly, again scanned the drinkers from the shabby wreck in the corner with a hole in his ancient suit to the gaggle of businessmen laughing over a bottle of cheap local champagne, heard some nutter bark obscenities at nothing. Max turned and walked out.

In a tiny store he found himself hanging around the drinks shelf. A small bottle of liqueur with an ornate yellow label attached itself to his hand. It was a rather pathetic drink but the bottle was flat and would lie in his jacket without being conspicuous. It was also small enough to avoid a major drunk, just enough to relax him. But would it be enough to get him to that point where the impossible was possible? Anything short of complete inebriation might leave need for a little courage and he couldn't be sure of finding that. Too much and he knew the brake would go off and the bogey would run to the end of the line, which was always unconsciousness. He would wake with an unfired gun in his hand and a hangover. "Or you might miss," he said to himself and laughed. The storeowner looked at him with the weariness of a man sick of the defects crawling into his store with the dramas in their heads.

"Couple of drinks will be nice, though." He muttered to himself on the bus home, and as the landscape of his adopted home slipped past he experienced a warm sense of relief. The Americans would be rich; they would witness how shabby his life was and judge him on that. He had passed out at Harvard *summa cum laude* and ended up with a couple of pianos, two guns and an unfinished translation of *Fear and loathing in Las Vegas*. It was always about superiority with Americans, and he had nothing to fight them back with. His hand pressed his jacket to stop the bottle continually clinking against the gun.

Shota was waiting when he got back and hung around sniffing for traces of booze. By now Max wasn't absolutely certain he wanted to kill himself, but a little time off from this sense of approaching doom would be nice, a brief holiday in the bottle. His past was relentless; it would overtake him sober, drunk or dead. It was merely the manner of the last inch or so that was at issue.

Back home he stared at the bottle and at the Makarov. The Ukrainian irregulars who were used by the Nazis to exterminate Jews in their villages were fed on vodka. Daily drinks were dispensed to concentration camp guards like pharmacy prescriptions. Bottle and gun. One facilitated the other, a partnership of oblivion where the unthinkable was easy. He held the gun in one hand: the cold, mechanical object that produced so much feeling in the human race: grief, fear, the elation of the victorious, the dark satisfaction of the natural killer. In the other was the bottle, the magic potion that made order out of disorder and sense out of nonsense and vice-voluptuous-versa.

"Not today."

Today he wouldn't kill himself. Nor would he drink. With a supreme effort he cleared space among the cleaning chemicals in a kitchen cupboard, tucked the bottle away at the back unopened, then wondered why he was hiding the drink and who the hell he was hiding it from.

The next few days introduced a fresh headache courtesy of the local press who heard the whispers that a former People's Hero and holder of the Order of Lenin First Class was to be giving away his American daughter in marriage. Several phone calls were fielded and all the old skills of diplomacy and evasion leaped into play as Max fought for a square inch of anonymity. But it was clear such a thing was impossible, so he tacked with the wind and explored the best way of minimising the damage this publicity might bring to his safety. This involved a certain degree of accommodation with the pencil chewers. In exchange for some compromise over discretion he was prepared to offer a limited amount of information. A couple of journalists were permitted into his house and despite a ban on photographs a camera hack crept in on their coat tails as if butter wouldn't melt in his mouth. With as much good humour as he could muster, Max made it clear that questions would only be answered if he remained photograph free. He didn't want Tolya Verkovensky picking up a newspaper over his morning eggs and saying "When's the next flight to Tbilisi?" The photographer was abandoned on the sofa in a funk till he took his cameras onto the beach to amuse himself with the solitary beach girl and a couple of kids who were happy to pose for him.

Events were painting him into a philosophical corner. He had no control. Sometimes he was able to shrug and surrender to this, sometimes it flew him in a panic to stroke his Gyurza and its armour piercing bullets and to dream of the yellow labelled bottle among the cleaning fluids.

The press of course, got round their arrangement by printing an old shot of Max in the local paper.

"None of them expects me to get through the wedding sober."

The Communist and God's representative had to meet to prepare things. Father Gregory declared the marriage a healing of a sundered family and of past and present, and as such it would be churlish to stand back and do nothing. As long as the Bishop didn't find out, again: "I must stress that". He insisted on learning part of the ceremony in English and took instruction from Max and over the course of the English lessons, Max, who had spent his life deriding the superstition of religion became aware of a warmth and an openness infusing their exchanges. It occurred without effort, as if by stealth, and he soon found himself disclosing things to Father Gregory that he would deny ten minutes. Curiously, Max who had spent his life deriding the superstition of religion, found himself willing to disclose things to the priest that he would deny ten minutes later to anyone else.

"I don't want to get drunk in front my family, my former family. It would be what they expect. But the fear of making a fool of myself drives me to the thing that's guaranteed to make a fool of me. Nature is perverse."

"God has a reason for giving you this problem. I know you don't believe, but interpret it your way. This wedding is an opportunity, a key moment for you, Max. Sometimes in our greatest challenges we find our greatest resource. For me, it's God. For you, perhaps you will discover just what that great resource is, some grace that will help you. Kindness, for example; just

being kind even if they're setting your arse on fire. Anyway, I shall pray for
your sobriety."

"Thank you."

"Your daughter must love you, of course."

"No. She never knew me."

"Love is fixed in us, but we can't choose who or what we love." Max felt
Masha's shadow cross him. "You offered, she accepted. There is some tiny
nut of love in there."

"I don't think it's love, Father. Curiosity, perhaps. Maybe even
vengeance."

"And on your part?"

"I wish I knew."

"Perhaps it will just be nice to see the old folks again."

At the headland summit, a sea breeze suddenly warmed them. Through
the heat haze oil tankers lay like slugs on a shaky sea. Both were short of
breath.

"Masha talked of the depth of your daughter's disappointment when you
walked away. She described it as quite shocking in its intensity, she said it
was like sitting with someone who had been touched by death."

"Masha is melodramatic."

"Why not act as if you love her? That's an act of love in itself. You've
offered this wedding, arranged the church, involved me, are preparing a
feast. Don't bale out half way, Max. Follow through."

All the disappointment Max had caused down the years resonated in the
priest's adult encouragement. A million fingers wagged from the past.

"Masha says she has problems? Your daughter."

"Problems?"

"Like yours."

"Mine?"

"So, is it genetic?"

"Is what genetic?"

"Well, anyway, she's one of those for whom Christ came to earth. And
you can help her. An atheist can do Christ's work."

"Can he?"

"You're not aware of the power you've been granted, Max. You can help her. As long as you stay away from the bottle yourself, of course."

Max recalled HG Wells refusing to drive in France for fear the temptation to run down a priest might be too great.

"She has come to find out something."

"She'll certainly do that."

"Don't make it about yourself, Max. Make it about her."

"For some of the guests it will be about me."

"To hell with them. It's about Lucy. And Jimmy."

"Timmy."

"They are the heart of the sacrament. They have come to you for grace."

"Oh come on, Father Gregory. Biologically, yes, she's my daughter; but in every other way, there is no connection."

"'There is no time scale on it, no matter what has gone on. She is your flesh and blood, your line. She has been brought by the guiding hand of God. Even if she doesn't believe. Some things are best not questioned."

Max laughed. There seemed no argument with that. They stood for a while and absorbed the blue heat of the day. "Look, Father Gregory, I have nothing for her but a wedding gift. If I'm honest, I still don't know why I did this. If I had a reason I've forgotten it."

"You are an atheist doing God's will. Of course it's confusing. We don't know why we do certain things, but we discover how to help as we go along, but you have to be there when the chance reveals itself. You know Goethe?"

"I've read a little."

"He said, 'The power is in the starting.' Or words to that effect. I haven't actually read him; a parishioner gave me the quote when we were discussing the church roof."

Georgia – September 1999

The fear of her flying back to the bottle edged the trip with a nervous vigilance. The journey began to settle into looks and glances at the main player to see if there were signs of preoccupation or moodiness, and Lucy assumed the gravitational pull of a black hole, sucking the family in till they disappeared.

On a stopover in Vienna, Henry asked if she missed it. She realised she was under surveillance and cravings that had been dormant in the recent weeks erupted again and her hard chip started computing how she might shake them off and get to a hidden bar. The more she smelled their fear the more she wanted to drink to spite them.

But the cravings were real; they ambushed and held her hostage for long sections of the day, obliterating everything to the lurid dream, knotting her stomach and clamping her throat. Every second ticked past in a tussle with the aches of her body for its medicine, and she thought it would never end even though she knew it would.

"He drinks like a Georgian," a Brit from the embassy in Moscow had said. What if her father and she got drunk together? They might find their relationship in drunkenness, the family outcasts bonding in the bottle. She might, however, see the shock in his eyes she had seen in countless others when the depth of her alcoholism was perceived. She made other drunks feel good about their drinking; she was the one whose capacity to continue into some psychosis of intoxication reassured them. "I'm not as bad as her," they would say and order another. "You make me feel good about my drinking" was the line of gratitude she heard most in her life. Death in one of its forms waited in another drink: suicide, asphyxiation, varices haemorrhage, traffic accident, liver collapse, extinction through self-disgust; she didn't have another recovery in her. She had made the long haul back and could now walk down the street and look in another's eye without melting, she had left the other drunks, druggies and wrecks behind and was treated with respect by others outside the family, but these things were worthless beside the infinite beauty of another drink. "There is no mental defence against the next drink" the old timers would say, "Stick close to the programme." When Timmy asked if there were meetings in Tbilisi, he got his ass bitten for his concern, but somewhere in those streets the programme waited for her. However, she had no intention of finding it. She had no time for meetings, too much to do, she was getting married. Again. And then, she was going to have a drink. Afterwards. Somewhere, sometime. She just knew it.

In the Midnight Bar where she met Gia, Henry poured out his anxieties about Lucy to Timmy. There was an agenda in Henry that was slightly off-message. Lurking behind the concern something had Timmy wondering what Henry was really up to and what other reason he had for the trip.

"Personally I don't know how I'm gonna react when I see him. There's so much wound up in it all." confessed Henry, "There was a time when I would quite happily have shot him."

"You and two hundred million others."

"With me, it was personal."

"Everything's personal."

"I was family. That was enough. I wasn't fired, just demoted to a position so menial it was guaranteed to have me walk. All of us who were close to him were regarded as security risks. Classic ass covering. Fire someone else."

"You weren't fired. You walked."

"As good as."

"If you stayed you might be running the Agency."

"I don't think so." Henry had no time for banter. Timmy could see he was onto another problem, "Maybe we shouldn't have coerced Peg into coming. Life's been tough enough for her."

"She's okay now with Arnold."

"What affects her will affect him too." He pushed his glass out of the sunlight that bisected the table. "I'm quite anxious that Peg might do something crazy."

"Like go back to him?" It was meant as a joke but Henry wasn't having humour. Timmy's reactions were an irrelevance; he was just a presence who saved Henry the embarrassment of talking to himself.

"Maybe we're sticking our heads in the lion's mouth. Or certainly sticking Lucy's in. Maybe we shouldn't have forced the issue."

"I didn't force the issue. It was you and Lucy who were so fuckin' keen."

"Yes, I suppose she would have come anyway."

When she had emerged from her relapse a place called Kosovo was on television more often than Sunset Beach, but in Tbilisi little marked the year that had passed. The dog garden haunted the street; Joseph's car sat where it was when the child's screams sucked her into the garden as if time

moved nothing and her fall to an LA gutter was a dream. The constancy
soothed her, but Joseph's spurned invitation from the previous visit nipped
her refurbished conscience. It wasn't much of an offence compared to what
she put her family through, but an offence against a stranger sits more
awkwardly than one against the family. In this country where courtesy
flowered strongly despite the corruption and violence, it was an insult of
some proportion, and any opportunity to practise the amends step of her
AA programme might diminish the urges to have a drink.

Joseph's big hairdresser wife, looming in the hall shadow like a cigar
store Indian, answered the door. At first she was unable to recognise her
visitor, but when Georgia recalled the day of the dog, she seemed to buckle
slightly, and made way for the American guest.

In the front room Sony badges and Chinese electronics gleamed
under tinted photos of men in red caps and solemn women staring out at
unimaginable futures from washed green backgrounds. Eight-inch busts
of Lenin peeped between displays of patterned plates in a glass corner
cupboard. The several ages of Joseph gleamed across a Yamaha upright
piano in silver frames, tracing him from the young Frank Zappa tribute
in a white wedding suit and cascades of black hair, through the receding
years to the cropped version with his son under the Ferris wheel in Stalin
Park, the pale amber of his eyes burning in the low winter light. The skinny
woman beside them was the sapling into which the current mighty oak had
grown.

The photographic collection was complete. Joseph was dead. She
had kept her promise, but a year too late, and her shock was tinged with
predictable self-reproof. The dog's weight twisting the fork out of her
hands, the cloud like a foot treading above them, briefly reclaimed her. She
had killed a dog with an enemy whose decomposing body was found with
five Russian mercenaries in a Kosovo village. The widow blamed NATO and
western arrogance. She had raged at American and English businessmen in
the street and at Joseph for making a widow of her.

"Why do you support people like that?"

Lenin's gimlet eyes drilled into Lucy. She had no opinion. History didn't
happen in Santa Monica.

"They treated Serbs the way you treat your blacks." A small motorbike whined past. "You think the world is your schoolyard; you bomb Belgrade and Baghdad but send senators to the Irish."

It wasn't the time to defend her country or deconstruct Milosovic and his ethnic cleansing as insatiable ego needs and unresolved childhood issues, so she sat and took it, and tried to give Joseph's death meaning, but it had none. He had dramatically entered her life one morning then died doing what males love doing. The fall out of this masculine obsession scattered from the silent valleys of Kosovo to the classrooms of Denver, while on prime time they kept pushing the product – increases in defence budgets, NRA rationalisations, the Hollywood love affair with the handgun as penis substitute. Hunched across a table was what the soap opera boiled down to: a weeping hairdresser.

Lucy was not surprised by man's inhumanity to man; she was surprised there wasn't more of it. What surprised her was decency. Higher Powers and God and all the quasi Christian AA spiritual propaganda had withered on the back streets of Venice CA. She no longer believed in the natural goodness of man any more than the absurdity of original sin. She knew that nothing is more selfish and uncivilised than a baby, and in the pain of her recent disillusionment had learned the hard way how nurturing is a process of saving humanity from itself.

Joseph's gift to her was a brief sense of the authentic; they had no time to develop the nonsense between them; for a morning things were uncontaminated by her wayward nature and the world's bullshit, and she cherished him for that, and thanked him in his own front room, in a small, silent prayer between his widow's diatribes.

Small things in the room booked space in her memory: a burn on the carpet, dust on the television screen, and no photos of the son beyond childhood. It was not the time to ask if the widow had lost both males in her life. Her grief was palpable, pressing its great weight down on the room, so Lucy sat in silence wondering where Joseph's Kalashnikov was. Kosovo? Decommissioned by NATO? In the kitchen?

When the wedding was mentioned, the widow became the marriage fairy; matrimony was a joy to her, a sacred blessing on the human condition, and Lucy wondered if her enthusiasm stemmed from happy years fattening up with Joseph and watching his hair thin, or if it were

another example of the human propensity to value something only when it
has gone.

As for the couple next door it had all been much ado about nothing. The
dog had been dead for a year but mother and daughter survived. "Rabies?"
snorted the widow. "It was just a bad dog." In the street Lucy stared at the
new garden gate and felt cheated.

A feeling of universal insignificance sometimes descended on her and
she saw humanity scrambling for dignity against the odds, insects with
philosophy and insurance. God put lemmings on Earth as an example, not
as role models. Alone in the tea bar, on the banquette she had shared with
her father, the reason for the trip suddenly seemed false, and as far as Peg
was concerned, unnecessarily cruel. An important part of the exercise was
the pain she knew it would cause her mother. The thought shocked her.
At a corner shelf over a tawny tea, a man flaunted a brocade waistcoat and
yesterday's *Wall Street Journal*, obviously gay in a sedate, Georgian way.

"Where's the Cossack doorman?" she asked a young waiter.

"His brother's place. In Nice." The waiter added "France" because she
was American.

"Is he a real Cossack?"

"He was a cavalryman. He fought Hitler on a horse and got seven years
in the Gulag for it."

On the road from Tbilisi, trucks and cars hurtled over the ruts and potholes
without regard for life and released a torrent of demands from Peg to slow
down; she didn't come to this backwater to die. The tattered upholstery in
the old minibus-taxi infected Peg's sensibility with the stink of nicotine and
the sweat of a thousand peasants. They stopped for a break in an ancient
place with buildings older than Christ, and their driver swelled with pride
at his penurious country's rich heritage. But as far as Peg was concerned
medieval ruins did not excuse medieval bathroom facilities.

Gradually changes distracted her: a stretch had a look of California,
another a twist of Colorado. A large bird floated down a valley beside them.
Sheep scattered on slopes, goats shuffled along gullies, domed churches
slipped past. Passing landscapes hypnotised her, and a bright flare on

Lucy's hair lifted away time. One of Peg's tail-chasers, long decayed into a decayed past, had christened Lucy 'light-bulb' because her hair was so bright. But her baby hair had been a corona of Max's colour that started shedding immediately.

She remembered more about her mother the morning Max defected than she did about the husband who was in the process of abandoning her. But her mother always made sure she was the one everyone remembered. Peg heard Max mumble angrily in the lobby as he left and those last, indistinct sounds haunted her for years. As soon as he was gone she was subjected to her mother's dissertation on the reprehensible trend towards breast-feeding. "You were brought up on a bottle" was one way of daring her daughter to say she was wrong.

She had got up and gone to the kitchen. Lucy wanted more and Peg reconnected her. The kitchen sank into silence and she had sat in it content, not knowing his absence had begun to insert itself between her giving nipple and her child's sucking mouth.

They pulled up for a hitching peasant, granddaughter and dog. Arnold and Henry calmed her objections; in these parts transport arrived with the kindness of strangers. She turned away from the walnut face and the dog flat on the floor in submission to American aid, but with the loquacity of the socially unaware the old man embarked on an explanation of the tea fields slipping past, and ribbed them about the American aversion to his crop and its subtle flavours. If every American drank one cup a week, the Georgia tea economy would boom and he could travel by taxi. Arnold declared he would drink a cup of tea a day forthwith. Henry apologised that he just couldn't get into the stuff. Peg sat dizzied by the peasant babble and the double translation into Russian then English, and dreamed of the ease of the hometown mall; the rest of the world was such an effort. But the little one's eyes stayed fixed on the gloriously made up old face; a nut brown sun child locked onto an old exhibit preserved in air conditioning, and finally talks were brokered by the Jar Jar Binks T-shirt tucked into the child's burgundy shorts. Yes, she had seen Episode One. Yes, Jar Jar Binks was her favourite. No, she had not seen the original *Star Wars* films.

"They're better." declared Peg. "Do they have videos in this country?"

"Mom, for Christ's sake!"

"I'm only telling her she should see the original trilogy."

"She's right," said Henry, "Episode One sucks."

The day Max left passed in the usual blandness of the suburbs. She remembered nothing of it till the night, when she finally got Lucy down and went to bed, exhausted but unable to sleep because Max was late again, and her mother, an iceberg of resentments, floated round the kitchen doing her bit to wind up the stress. She lay awake listening for him and wondering if he really drank alone or if the drink was always decorated with a skirt. Approaching cars sucked up her hope then spat it back as they passed. Way after midnight she rang Henry. He suggested Max was in a drinking ring and would get back in the wee small hours. But Henry made some calls. The awful possibility snapped everyone awake. In several bedrooms across Washington, lights burned and state employees in pyjamas grasped that the unthinkable might have happened.

About two am Lucy was playing arpeggios with her tiny fingers then shaking as if something above puzzled her. This was a pattern marking her discovery of the world around her. Peg gathered her up, shuffled into the kitchen and 'phoned the police. When she was told a call on Max's car was already out she knew something serious had happened. Bars have broads but this had eternity edging it. She remembered his haunted dumbness, hovering above her bed that morning. Numbed with fear, she sat with her shaking baby under the only light in the neighbourhood.

"How much further?" asked Peg.

"Forty minutes" translated the shaking baby. Thirty-five years ticked down to thirty-five minutes. The tea planter, Jar Jar Binks fan and dog were gone. Lucy had no grandfathers to flag down passing rides, only a small knot of women squeezing a short length childhood: a traumatised mother, one grandmother shrill and impossible, the other institutionalised. No men inhabited her landscape beyond the stray lovers drawn to Peg's depressed beauty, and the distant Henry; no pets were allowed but goldfish. Somewhere down the pike Peg had grown into her own mother.

When Henry and the posse arrived in the morning it was obvious
something serious had happened. The car had been found by the baby shop,
condemning her to wonder if it were a last regret mailed in code. She had
known all night that he was gone for good; deep down all the messages are
there to be unscrambled by anyone with a mind to.

It was explained that Max had been under investigation but no
conclusions had been reached, and until they knew what happened his
salary would be paid into the family account. If anyone asked, she should
say he was away on a project. Had anyone suspicious called? Had he
ever acted in a way that made her suspicious? Only about the women she
smelled on him among the cocktail vapours. She was shocked and couldn't
grasp the information about his treachery, but when she asked if he had
gone to Russia, their evasiveness poured into her like concrete.

The next night found her back in the kitchen, baby at breast; alone
with the night voices insisting she and her child weren't worth staying for.
There were interrogations, shocking questions, long empty days. Her milk
stopped.

"The only good thing is it's got the little one on the bottle!" crowed her
mother, happy that she had been proved right. "I always knew there was
something wrong with him."

A year after his disappearance, the Kremlin announced he was in
Moscow and his salary stopped.

No one had spoken for miles. The bus was filled with stage fright. She
looked at her watch. Twenty minutes.

Black Sea

The driver drew their focus from the two bare bodies on the beach to a
middle-aged man in polo shirt, shorts and sandals walking from the sea.

There are no instructions for the epic that wraps itself in ordinariness,
no clues on how to cope with the next few ticks of a clock or heart that lead

to a dreaded moment. Sliding his toes through the sand towards them, Max clung to the thought that they too would be reeling under the hammer of the next few seconds. He worried that he would sound archaic, use phrases and words that faded with the sixties, sound foolish. What would he say anyway? What might they say? What is the formal language that bridges the unbridgeable? What will he say if Henry suggests they have a drink? That was the easiest route for most; the stiffness melting, the laughter after the second glass, the ease, the natural inclination to fondness of everyone, all in a few mouthfuls he daren't take.

He pushed on past the happy kids and the topless Germans, towards the mini bus that had brought the judge and jury to his house. Notions of mending fences had been washed away by the sheer absurdity that there were any fences left to mend; they had been atomised decades ago. He had visualised Peg a thousand times in the past few days and had come up with no stratagem to deal with the awful prospect of seeing her again. Now he drew close enough to recognise the silhouetted head in the minibus, but a drag of skin from chin to neck shocked him. The same broad head bulked up beside her. Henry was occupying more space these days and Max supposed his own roughened edges would shock them. They had been such glorious young creatures. The sun suddenly caught Lucy's blonde head at the passenger window, staring at him like an onlooker at an auto accident.

He left the sand and crossed the road easily, as if he were sauntering back from the john after the ruckus at the hotel, put his hands on the sill by Lucy, and nodded.

"Hi."

"Hi."

Peg, the hundred-metre freestyle champion in the Eisenhower years was now a painted, bejewelled *grande dame* of the Biltmores Arizona. Tucked away in the shadow at the back of the minibus, she had a dreadful Dorian Grey impact on Max.

"You made it."

"Yeah." Lucy broke the American paralysis. Shock buzzed the minibus as she introduced Timmy and Arnold. "You know the others."

Time had disarmed them. The great division that straddled the twentieth century and split the shadows in the minibus and the old man leaning against it was nothing more than memorabilia in a collectibles market; history had moved backwards to raise the ravenous gods of the old religions and beach these Cold War refugees as out-of-date modernities. Everything was neutralised in a lacuna of self-consciousness, wordlessness and inactivity, but the driver wanted to get home and he shifted the historical stasis, opening doors, unloading suitcases and ushering them out. Max led to the little house with apologies for its simplicity, and they followed like sheep into a male nest where nothing matched, and everything was marked with the imprint of unaltered habits.

Coffee was offered, the bathroom pointed out. Brief outbursts of chatter rebounded in the silences. The little house thrummed to the strain of verbal constipation. Non-sequiturs bounced from free university places for Georgians in Germany to the beautiful dolphinarium in Batumi, and whether the accordion was the national instrument. But the personal disintegration that accompanied the long swan song also hit them. Max ripped them from youth to age in one leap. Lucy was a decade and a half older than Peg had been when the rheumy face replete with evasion currently making coffee in the kitchen, first caught her eye.

As Max produced coffee aromas in the kitchen, there were things to be taken in: books, ornaments, caps of a kind once found on men with ponytails in San Francisco. The first sprays of evening pink dusting the headland treetops prompted clichés on charm and beauty. Everyone was drawn to but didn't mention the three topless Germans bringing their Teutonic exhibitionism to a little place that like their American guests was still easily shocked.

Henry found refuge at the piano and to his adagio vamping they took turns for the bathroom and observed the differences in this small house from those of their homeland: the appalling absence of television; the sense of time layered into the walls; the kilims, seat covers and cushions with their alien patterns, the wild flower and grasses dumped in cheap jugs: shapes and smells from an incomprehensibly different civilisation, and Gia's smooth desk supporting stacks of papers, a thumbed copy of *Fear and Loathing in Las Vegas*, and an old Soviet typewriter which drew Arnold to its antique mechanics like a wasp to honey. It was a home laden with strange traps for them. In the bathroom vases of flower mottled the white walls and a few local luxury products softened the Spartan functionalism.

Lucy was the first to notice the absence of alcohol, and wondered where he had hidden it. With his reputation it would be around somewhere. The others also noticed, discreetly. Nevertheless, Henry could do with a stiff one. Later. A glass of local wine perhaps, under a vine, with his feet dangling in the Black Sea and the strains of a distant accordion on the evening breeze. Peg stayed fixed on the horror of the nipples on the beach. Timmy slid to the stained glass panes in the sidewall window and pretended to be scrutinising them and the view of the headland at the end of the beach. Lucy joined him; nodded back at the girls on the beach and bustled up her own tits and they smirked.

Max brought in a tray of small cakes and tiny cups and disappeared again when Henry made the first blunder by suggesting to Peg that he looked good. This propelled Arnold to a window to itemise the trees in Max's garden: orange trees, magnolia, possibly a walnut, and some coniferous that had him beat.

"Thujas." carried clearly from the kitchen; the spy was listening, "African, originally. Sometimes known as the *arbor vitæ*."

The light through the coloured panes turned the grey varnish on Lucy's nails brown. The headland forming the west horn of the bay burned bright and hot and the houses in its blue shadow seemed cool. It was a little paradise, worn at the edges. She could see why her father had ended up here. Timmy talked quietly about the peoples who had passed by, Greeks, Romans, Persians and the Mongol armies of Genghis Khan.

"The Romans called it Iberia, like Spain."

"Couldn't they think of something else?"

"Georgian wine was big in Ancient Rome." He wondered if he should have mentioned alcohol.

"Been reading up?"

"On the 'Net. You're dad's on the 'Net."

"I know."

The coffee tray entered in Max's uneasy hands, the cups trembling as they were brought to the table. The act of pouring became ceremonial, conferring a respect as if these simple actions transcended regret and treason. Keep pouring the coffee, each seemed to say – nothing can happen

while the coffee is being poured. For Lucy, the little black connection
between jug and cup released a wisp of steam and recalled a cabinet of
pastries in an ex-communist café under the Popeye forearms of the solid
ladies of a solid past. Arnold could feel the stupidity of the grin he had fixed
on his face and as the coffee aromas reached him tried to remember when
he last trimmed his nose hair. Henry had never been short of conversation;
discussions, anecdotes and words were the material of his income and
influence, but watching the coffee hit and jump in the little cups, the topics,
jokes, openers, and points that made him such a smart guy abandoned him.
And behind them Medusa stared, daring each to look directly at her and be
turned to stone.

They sipped and nibbled tiny cakes. Mumbled compliments progressed
to nothing; reservoirs of small talk quickly baked dry, so Max swung to the
practical. He was staying with Shota; the happy couple had the run of his
house. After coffee they would be taken to Masha's, where Peg and Arnold
had a room in the house and Henry a bed in the studio gallery under the
stars. Masha would be back from Batumi soon, they had after all, arrived a
little early.

"You're a little late," reminded Peg.

The shot across the bows pulled everyone into line. The venom that
Henry reserved for Max had been a comfort down the years, but Peg could
see it evaporating on Max's piano stool. An old drinking friendship where
they could lean on the bar comparing beach tits and mourn the passing of
exaggerated virility threatened to resurrect itself. She felt the flinty edge of
everyone's disregard, as if the pain that drove her from pillar to post were
too distasteful to be acknowledged. Decades of humiliation and poverty
were passed over for peace with the criminal currently dispensing coffee
like glass beads to the Indians. Nothing that happened had any meaning.
She sat facing their backs as the villain explained they were invited to a
meal at Shota's after the wedding rehearsal at which there would be an
exchange of greetings with the locals and, no doubt, the loaves and fishes
of forgiveness would multiply and the swords be beaten into ploughshares.
But the healing power of time was not going to remove the old knife
twisting in Peg's gut. They knew they sat with a suicide bomber fingering
the detonator.

Max ploughed on: "At an Orthodox wedding, there is a crowning ceremony in which the family participates."

"Crowns?" said Timmy, "Like Queen of England crowns?"

Peg had never thought of this son-in-law: the extent of his existence was a temporary addition to the Christmas card list. She realised she could pass him in the street and wonder where she knew him from.

"Yes. We'll be shown what this entails at the rehearsal. It's not too complicated. Also the tradition of the bride being given away by the father? In light of the circumstances, it might be more appropriate if Henry...."

"You do it." fell like a guillotine from the abandoned wife, reminding everyone that punishment was part of the itinerary. Max looked at his daughter for veto.

"No. That's okay. Let's stick with tradition," Lucy said as casually as she could, and Peg hissed at the window.

"I think in Georgian," said Max, "Am I making sense?"

"Sounds like you've never been away." Henry's second gaffe filled the room.

"Something interesting out there, Mom?" A storm brewed in Lucy's voice, but Arnold suggested a swim might wash the journey out of them and the thunder rolled away. Max couldn't find a reason why they shouldn't swim, as long as they weren't too long.

"Mom, did you bring your bathing things?"

"Don't be stupid."

Max bore a straight course through the rest of the evening by guiding them with inexhaustible charm and patience through the rehearsal at the church, a process hardly enhanced by Masha's sullen presence, although she and his daughter did flicker into sporadic conversation. Peg's disapproval of this native trophy woman with her earthy fashion, her ethnic beauty and her unadorned but hot womanliness filling the recesses of the church with a sexual waveband was as fixed as a mask. Thereafter every nook and cranny of the evening, the place and the local customs was picked over for disapproval. Max could never remember her like this; she could slip into a certain indifference when she was young, but the change to this hardened state had required years of assiduous application. Glimpses of Henry's old jokey self peeped through the general anxiety that seemed to be his characteristic now. Arnold, Peg's third, or was it fourth husband, was utterly charming, a peacemaker and an example of that particular type of unassuming American for whom Max had always had a great deal of time. The long road down the years seemed to have wrung profound changes; it was like seeing only the first and final acts of a stage play. How much of this was due to his impact and how much to the usual ravages of time could not be ascertained, but there was enough in this little church to keep a whole faculty of therapists going for years.

Timmy was interested in the icons and Max was happy to translate his questions and father Gregory's enthusiastic answers. Lucy seemed quite mischievous, as if this powder keg they were sitting on would give her a good laugh when it went off.

Shota's meal was a roaring success. Several locals had been invited and, with the exception of Lucy, the Americans were introduced to the secrets of the Tamada, the Georgian ritual of talking and toasting, and creating the right ambience for conviviality, in this case conducted by Shota with enough restraint to protect their guests from undesirable alcoholic excess. In fact, the stream of Shota's wit and some of the local wines whose viniculture he explained in fine detail, carried the guests into a very relaxed state. Even Peg was able to smile a couple of times and shift momentarily from her aloofness into the current of the evening. Lucy and Max were served a whole range of squeezed fruit juices, cherry, orange, grape, pomegranate, which they discussed as if they were great wines, defining the nose and the aftertaste. There was no lack of wit in his daughter; she could sustain a length of humour farther than he could and to a much more absurdist place. But Max sensed the dark history lurking behind the sociability, the sleeping dragon around which everyone but Peg quietly tip-toed.

"Best way to handle it," said Shota after everyone had retired to bed, "get them half-cut. Shame you can't do it. You'd look less like a trapped rabbit. You're not going to die tomorrow, Max."

That was Max's conviction. Tomorrow would be the day of reckoning. But it would not come from the family; they would provide the torture; the *coup de grâce* would come from a Moscow hood. His fears and neuroses were coalescing into a conviction that his daughter's wedding was the day

selected by fate for his death. Despite his best efforts, the reunion of the
former Soviet Hero and his family had not only made it to the local press
and television but had also been sold to Russian news by some ambitious
editor. Tolya might well have seen him over his breakfast eggs; he would
certainly have to be some kind of idiot not to now know who Max was and
where and when he could be found. And if he missed the information in the
newspapers, there was a brief mention at the end of the Moscow evening
news.

"Max, this is completely insane. I can understand that you're under a bit
of strain, but don't go mad with it," said Shota.

"Shota, they know for certain I'm going to be at my daughter's wedding.
Time, place, opportunity."

"Max, they probably missed it. You know, these people tend not to be big
readers and news watchers. And with due respect, you aren't exactly front-
page stuff."

"I might be the day after the wedding."

But the rational convictions were backed up by something subtler. Life
carried a weight of irony that would be rejected in the average script and
the law of probability indicated that there should be no surprise when
apparently unlikely things happened or strange coincidences collided. They
were within perfectly normal sequences of logic. The wedding, far from
being an unlikely setting for his murder had a peculiar appropriateness
to it. Press would be sniffing around the edges for scandal or stories. It
would be easy for a hood to blend in with them and wait for his moment.
Psychopaths such as those who had dispatched Gia in such gruesome
fashion would derive a further kick of satisfaction from such criminal
boldness. It was part of it all, the high of the risk, the hit of the hit. They
were like addicts and would no more be able to stop themselves than Max
could stop himself all those years before from betraying the people who
were the wedding guests next day.

"Max, don't you have enough problems without worrying about being
shot?" asked Shota, "If things go as bad as you think, it might be a relief."

Max had placed himself at the heart of darkness and madness. Now this
great mass would move and there was little he could do except move with
it and be vigilant. He never thought he would bring himself to this point,

where he was throwing himself upon the mercy of his family and offering his throat to an unknown killer. All in a celebration that in itself would become historic in the village, even without the morbid events he felt sure would occur.

He could find no relief from these convictions, but felt lost in a vortex that was rushing him to destruction. He spent the night before his daughter's wedding with the Makarov under his pillow. Shota's spare room was a condemned cell and the scatter of stars he saw through the window, his last, nervy meditation on life.

Wedding day

Shota was all Georgian humour and earthiness around Lucy, gently denouncing her father as a run-down intellectual adrift in a land of peasants. Timmy was ignored and breakfast on his second wedding morning became another tranche of small humiliations. The priest asked him a couple of questions and he called Max to translate, while his bride, dazzled with Shota's Old World masculinity, was ushered under the magnolia to look over the table arrangements for the feast.

A bottle of five-star French brandy was produced, and even though it was early, there seemed no argument against having it. "I shouldn't really."

"Come on, how often do you get married?" grinned Shota from his Nietzchean moustache, and Timmy watched her transfixed by the bronze liquid gurgling into the glasses and knew there was nothing he could say or do.

"Let's go round the other side of the tree," she whispered in Russian to Shota. "They'll just have a hissy fit." And they touched glasses and as it burned over her throat a great sigh of relief bubbled up from her through the magnolia leaves.

Light smeared the room and the sea fell in the silence. Her place in the bed was empty. Timmy rose and rushed to the bathroom door, "Lucy?" In the front room he lay like a fly against the window. She was missing again. The village was barely discernible in the dawn gloom, then he saw a dim shape moving parallel to the beach in an easy crawl. As his eyes adjusted and saw it was Lucy, he realised it had been a dream. She often had dreams in which she drank; all alcoholics had them, she said. He just had one of her drinking dreams. That was taking co-dependency too far.

He watched her in the huge space of the sea, at home in all that grand loneliness. Some people seemed so at odds with humanity. Out on the waves, she was fine. He turned back to bed for a couple of hours before another attempt at marriage, lay there and tried to invest the occasion with some significant thought, but found nothing.

The dawn turned up the bay. Jet lag woke her on her wedding morning to swim in no more light than a tear in the sky, face down, arms lazy and rhythmic, a slow dip and stretch she could keep up for hours, held on the kissing lips of the big sea.

It was a peace she could never find anywhere else, the sea, the sky, her body and the rest of the world a shore length away. Back home, she often swam way out beyond the jetskis seeking the distant stretch of peace away from it all. Cursed by many of her parents' demons, she had been blessed with their ease in water. The internal and external clamours faded and gave way to a rising and sinking rhythm, and the complete harmony of her tiny body on the huge seas. But she became aware of her private Idaho being invaded. The stranger bore out in a fast crawl then slipped into an easy breaststroke. A gasp skimmed against rocks quarter of a mile off. Then came the sense of commonality; the wave between two climbers on opposite rocks, the joggers' nod as they wheeze past each other, and she realised her companion in solitude was her father. They were alone, the thing she wanted and dreaded. They would have to talk. All her questions, banked over the years, deleted themselves. He waved, she waved back; he called, "Lovely, isn't it?" She called back "Yeah" and suddenly there seemed no need for anything more; they swam around, never closer than fifty yards, and luxuriated in the emptiness, the sea and the growing light.

Max noticed three gulls cruising for surface food and heard the fracas as they hit the surface. Wings flapped and they squabbled over something, but through the racket he heard her coughing and kicking up and automatically sped towards her. She was in trouble, swallowing gouts of the Black Sea, all her co-ordination gone, as if she suddenly had forgotten how to swim. She didn't notice him till he touched her arm.

"Seagulls," she gurgled by way of explanation and he understood and remembered a giant gull over her tiny body in an American garden and thought all that Freudian shit is true, then.

She felt calmer with his swimming between her and the gulls, near enough if she got into trouble, far enough to let her be until they hit the surf and walked onto the beach. A child's giraffe rubber ring watched Max shake sand from her towel. He felt her tense when he draped it round her shoulders and withdrew his hands, but she remained transfixed by the squabbling gulls out at sea. They picked their way between abandoned buckets and spades, wind brakes and loungers.

The solitariness of the early light drew Max and the sea was his sanctuary. But another swimmer was trespassing and when he saw it was his daughter he had turned back for Shota's. Then he recalled the priest's counsel to act as if, and waded out. But he couldn't tell her this. He wanted to hide his distance from her. It was her wedding day. He was at war with his nature.

"Mom used to say I was a water baby. I guess I got that from you.'"

"Her too. She could swim real good."

"Really?"

"Schoolgirl champion."

"God." Her mother was an unknown space, gated and fenced off. The thought of her swimming, having an enthusiasm for a talent, seemed impossible. Lucy couldn't imagine her in a white cap grinning, maybe even raising an arm in happy triumph at winning a race, being congratulated by friends, pulling herself out of the water and walking to the victor's podium and the handshakes. The cheers of her classmates, the smiles and the waves, the small moments of pride; a young girl happy with her body. But it had happened. All buried now. She had never seen her mother swim, could not recollect ever seeing her in a bathing costume.

"Strange to think of her being remotely athletic."

"Yes. Tempus really fugits."

"Shit!" Her nails dug into his bicep as a gull landed by the abandoned bucket and spades and opened its wings. "They're following us!" He turned her up the beach between the giraffe and a canvas chair. She explained how she didn't know where this fear came from or why it started, that she kept thinking she was over it. But Max recalled waking under that neighbour's tree to her tiny wails and the huge gull flapping its wings above her. She had shaken like a puppy in his arms afterwards. It seemed too intimate to disclose, as if telling her would open a relationship for which he was not yet ready, or admit to something he didn't want to be known. All he could do was agree they were horrible birds. As they crossed the sand, other things to say crowded in both but neither found an opener. The night before, he'd kept it formal at the wedding rehearsal and at Shota's afterwards loosened a little, but when things threatened to get too familiar he found ways to keep distance, translating, and distracting himself with a host's duties.

The silence tightened round them and neither could break it, all the way to his little house. Max left her at the door.

"Well, it's a big day."

"Yeah. Thanks for..."

He nodded and smiled. "See you later." He turned for Shota's.

She roughed her hair with the towel and crossed to the small side window. Through the orange pane, she saw a distortion of his figure on the road to the village pour and flit from flaw to flaw in the glass. She cursed and her eyes unconsciously scanned the shelves where the drink might have stood.

When the sun pitched up, a few elegant smocks, sleeveless coats and embroidered slippers shifted among the suits and summer dresses. Peg dismissed them as ethnic Disney, but to Arnold they were the hospitality of legends. Since his commitment to this family adventure, his wife's hysteria and glimpses of her past induced a sense that everything between them was bogus. Peg never mentioned her history; the mysterious first husband was referred to as a civil servant. Only when he proposed did she reveal the cold war fall out, and this made him grateful that a life that had become routine but contented, now had a little infamy and colour, albeit, second hand. She was beautiful, and low maintenance. She ran the marriage the way she ran the house, formally and to rules from which there could be no deviation and that was fine by him; he liked the quiet life. One day she mentioned casually that her daughter had a drink problem. When Lucy phoned to say she had been clean and sober for six months and was in AA, Peg shrugged and said yes for how long, but Arnold shut himself in a bathroom and wept.

Two men in beautiful Georgian shirts waved when they saw him at the window. The sky was clear; the blue was urgent with heat. It was a fine day.

The magnolia lights snapped wanly in the brilliant morning.

"We have power for the wedding. So far," said one of Shota's girls. In the kitchen Shota and Max were arguing.

"You cannot take a gun to your daughter's wedding!"

Max was marooned somewhere the other side of rational thought.

"Max, leave the gun. You might drop it in the church."

He handed it over. "I wish Gia was here."

Shota looked up. "Why? He'd only try to dip his wick."

Lucy's wedding

Timmy and Lucy's wedding began in the open air with their betrothal in the church porch. Max who had brought and given Lucy away, stood back with Masha to translate and guide them through the ceremony. The sun slanted between tall cedars and warmed their backs. The dome above was missing huge patches of gilt as if it suffered a skin condition.

Max instructed them quietly as the rings were exchanged then asked them to hold out their hands to Father Gregory, who bound their wrists with his stole and carefully drew them out of the sunlight into the church. The night before, its bleakness had torpedoed Lucy's spirit. Cheap lamps dumped pools of dim light on chipped pillars and broken flagstones, missing windowpanes and patches of filler on grimy walls. But a few ancient effects worked a magical transformation. Candles glowed through clouds of incense, and through the smoke, gold burned on walls panelled with icons. Into this mix, the harmonies and cadences of Eastern chorale poured from a choir hidden in a gallery over the door, and the intensity of image, smell and sound, all the more powerful for being conducted in a language

neither understood, shook their New World sensibilities. Here Christ was
the holy source of the long river of faith that flowed through centuries, and
not a regular guy in Tommy Hilfiger to be crooned to. Barry Manilow with
scripture it was not.

As Father Gregory drew them along the threadbare carpet from the door
to a wooden altar in the middle of the church, the family fell in behind:
Max behind Lucy, and Peg behind Max, Masha behind Timmy, and Henry
behind Masha. Shota and Arnold made up the rear. Kids wandered, older
faces peered from spindly chairs by the pillars, everyone else stood. "Where
are the pews?" Peg had asked with contempt at the rehearsal, but this was a
nation that prayed on its feet. Saints shone above candle clusters on shrines
fastened to pillars or standing free in the body of the church. Necklaces
of candle flame snaked into recesses and a tall screen of saints on cream
panels rose up in the honey shadows beyond the altar.

This panoply of celebration of which she was the focus, fermented the
contradictions in Lucy. Self consciousness at the attention and feelings of
fraudulence were contrasted by a sublime sensation of being touched by
something that bored through Time, a long spine of religious constancy
from which history hung its flux and madness. The irony struck her that
she was being physically dragged to her wedding, physically bound to her
husband and being physically pulled to confront a previous indiscretion.
The altar towards which Gregory gently drew them was obviously Gia's.
Timmy too recognised the style, unmistakeable as a signature, and the
chiliastic power of two millennia of Christ and the Church of Byzantium
that had filled him with wonder the moment he stepped into the church
ebbed away. In the Master of Heaven's house, the Dark Angel settled on
him as a flock of his wife's adulteries, and as they stopped in front of the
offending altar, he saw Gregory give Lucy a salacious wink, confirming that
she was a local item by injection and he was the outsider and clown.

The Yanks were as overdressed as Oscar nominees in K-Mart. Her
mother in blue was a sapphire on fire; the men wore dance band white
jackets, cummerbunds with silver paisley waistcoats and under an inflation
of LA hair, Lucy strained her shiny Hawaiian wedding dress, gathered in
over ambitiously for these thinner sober days.

Gregory sent the long litany through the incense in a mahogany baritone. Her inner litany was that the choir above them, the glowing saints, the crowns on the altar, the smiling villagers, and the ritual were nothing but her father's stage management for keeping his distance. Father Gregory winked again at Lucy, then at Timmy; perhaps he suffered a little in translation but he seemed odd and over attentive at times even to their Californian sensibilities. "Mad as a brush" was Shota's assessment. His intonations prayed for the happiness of the couple, for fidelity until death. The night before when Max translated the final prayer that the marriage bed be not defiled, Peg pin-balled a "Tut" round the pillars. Today that Byzantine earthiness would be lost to her in the streams of Gregory's Georgian.

Praying that the couple have children and see their children's children, Gregory smiled at Peg, the woman the young Max loved, but decades of unhappiness remained set hard and he perceived the colossus of her disappointment.

"The servant of God, Timmy, is crowned to the handmaiden of God, Lucy, in the name of the Father and of the Son and of the Holy Ghost." The rings were exchanged, symbolising that the strength of one would compensate for the weakness of the other, and the imperfections of one be balanced by the other, an ideal honoured in their home more in the omission than the practice. Harmonies pushed to a crescendo and as the betrothal ended and the marriage began, they joined right hands and held a candle in their left hands.

Gregory beseeched the Lord to join these his servants and unite them in one mind and one flesh. A crown like a giant garlic bulb sank Timmy slightly then Masha's craggy hands lightened the load. Lucy's pearl and ruby garlic bulb was raised into the stream of notes. It sat on her easily and she realised her father's hands were taking the weight. Gregory continued with a prayer in Georgian, and lifted a small cup purportedly of wine from which they were to drink three times, but he was aware of the bride's difficulty around this and had spent part of the morning straining raspberry and sour blackcurrant to match the deep colour of local wines. He chanted the blessing in Georgian, then proudly in his new American English: "You drink from this common cub to show that togedder you share the sweedness and the bidderness which is marruge."

A bible the size of a small table was lifted onto Gregory's shoulder and he
turned his back on them to symbolise that it is the Gospel that makes a
Christian home and they should follow it.

"Go." Max's whisper brushed across her and she felt him lead her
lightly with the crown. They followed the giant bible perched on Gregory's
shoulder in a circle round the cross on the altar, her father's hands
synchronising perfectly with the sway of her movement, the hands of a
musician floating the heavy crown perfectly, letting her feel its firmness but
not its weight, slipstreaming the Gospel under billows of harmony, and the
numinous intoxication the sacrament was designed to charge.

A child stared up from his mother's skirt, a constellation of candles
reflecting in huge, dark eyes. Villagers smiled, cried, but those with little
respect for themselves cannot accept it from others, even the divine, and
in the piety and immanence, burned an acid presence in the stones of the
church stripping away Lucy's defences and probing something tender.
They would find she was a fake. The ancient ceremony and their generosity
oppressed her. Her father's hands were crowning her, a choir was singing
and a priest had learned English for her; "How much do you fucking want?"
she screamed silently at her self, "This is what you fucking want!" But she
wished she were back in Santa Monica hiding from seagulls.

The hands on her crown changed, Mom took over and their second
procession round the altar began a little less confidently. The crown started
to dip, then left Lucy in a long slide over her forehead. She shoved it back
before it took off for Saint Paul's lap. They were in ceremonial crisis when
a small miracle happened: other hands helped Peg stabilise the crown; her
father and mother were helping her together. This moment of parental
concern after three and a half decades dizzied her with a narcotic rush. Her
mother's hands dropped, the others remained on the crown for the final
circuit and she realised they were not her father's but Shota's. She fell into
the familiar pit of disappointment, but by the end of the short, holy circuit
she settled for acceptance and felt calm.

That small emotional shift was what she really understood by miracles:
modest things levering a soul from delusion to reality, from anger to calm,
the epiphany that switches off the voices in the head. The odours and

beauty of sanctity, the continuity of religion from the catacombs and the crucifixion, the Christian constancy through centuries that raged with change, resolved as nothing more than a wonderful piece of theatre which she would remember one day and cherish. She no longer believed in God, but as she and Timmy came to a halt in front of the altar, she thanked Him, because at that moment she felt the need to thank someone or something.

Everything was saturated in a painter's light. On Shota's low, white walls tubs of flower stained the sea with blues, reds and yellows. Emerald waves drenched the rocks. Citrus trees mottled the headland with orange, and above them delicate trees climbed so lightly they seemed nothing more than green air. She waited with the wedding photographer for her parents to dance into this brochure composition but they clung to the far side of the magnolia. Way off Shota's property, a barrage of other long lenses and video cameras followed her father's every movement, occasionally breaking to focus on her under a forest of waving arms and cries of 'Loosea'.

Max had disarmed everyone by dancing with his daughter then asking Peg to a waltz. This cued the village to wade into the Americans and get them all up. Arnold swayed with a willowy lass with a charming moustache and Henry beamed through sweat screens at his partner, a little younger but a couple of weight divisions above him and ahead on points. At a table Timmy and Masha were queens in a swarm of children demanding cartoon after cartoon.

These moments expanded in Lucy like the first hit of a favourite cocktail. She found the photographer, pushed him under the magnolia and pointed out her parents and he waited for the perfect composition on the long lens when her mother said something that drained everything out of Max. Suddenly they were staring past each other, marking time till the end of the music, and it was in this alienation, that they drifted into frame. The photographer looked at Lucy and she nodded as if nothing had happened and the auto-wind buzzed off shots of the cold reality and not the warm hokey fantasy of a few seconds before.

The celebration babbled under the wide magnolia and the sea provided its rhythmic harmonic, but what had passed between her parents set her sniffing every nuance of the main players for hidden meaning. Her mother's eyes now swept the horizons above her new dance partner, Menteshashvilli, the short fisherman, who had enticed her for another waltz which he invested with the ham passions of an Argentinean tango while she retained her stiff American correctness. Max and Masha slid coldly along the horizon together. Despite the evening in the hotel and the insomniac phone calls to Lucy, Masha hovered silently on the edges, daring anyone to speak to her. Peg brushed past again and the battle-hardened face gave away nothing.

Every morning Lucy woke to the thought of drink. Whether she actually drank or not was down to fate or whether her laces broke. This unpredictability was fathomless. She had no idea what the Heisenberg Uncertainty Principle was, but she knew what it felt like. Under a Georgian sun, blessed by an ancient church her radar began scanning for the drink opportunity. Some last fragment of pride prevented her from lifting a glass in front of the family and her hosts, but she knew she would find a way to a drink. In all other parts of her life she had no faith, but in the pursuit of this great love she possessed a gift that functioned without her bidding. She luxuriated in this certainty, watching everyone ease into a second glass. They had gone through a celebration in which she was top of the bill, but the show was now over; hosting was on rest mode, to be switched on only when the bride or groom came near. For all their warmth and generosity, they were her father's people, separated from her by an abundance of courtesy. Lightened by the knowledge that she was near to her next drink, she cut a path through the wedding guests to her father, who greeted her with a gentle smile.

"The village will remember this for years. Thank you for coming."

"Thanks for inviting us."

"You drive a hard bargain." He raised one eyebrow at Peg and Henry back under the tree.

"You seem to be bearing up."

He smiled. "And you? Are you bearing up? These occasions can be overwhelming. Particularly in a strange place."

"Most places are strange places to me."

He laughed up into the magnolia. She pointed up the hill at a cottage and barn among the scrub and trees. "Is that Gia's place?"

"Yes. His sister rents it out to tourists now."

"He made the barn doors, huh?"

"Yes."

"There's a kind of shape that runs through his stuff. A curve."

"His motif. It bored him, but it's what people wanted."

"He seemed shy."

"Yes, he was shy."

It was almost fascinating watching him keep everything buried about Gia.

"You must miss him a lot."

"It is strange. His not being here."

She would have been a presence, even in this remote village, in the last months between Max and Gia, a subtle contamination. How peculiar, she thought, that we can exist as a force in others' lives on the opposite ends of the earth, and it struck her how in the pain of that dreadful night in Tbilisi, sleeping with Gia was an instinctive way of hitting back that seemed to have worked. Beneath Max's wedding suit, she had made a little wound that was still painful.

Had Gia been alive she would not have been able to come to her wedding. Or would she? Adultery on her wedding night would have set the family off for years. May as well be hanged for a sheep as a lamb. With a drink inside her anything was possible. But even Gia would probably have resisted; not everyone was afflicted by the same urge to self-abort. She was sometimes driven to push herself through every boundary and taboo in the book, to go further than anyone else and shock the unshockable. Why? Just to prove she could. Life had often been an experiment in going further and the few minutes with her father triggered that recklessness. Had Gia been there she would have blatantly gone to him and shaken everyone. The Moscow assassins had probably done her a favour.

During the exchange with Lucy, Max's attention slipstreamed a Mercedes with four men in T-shirts cruising slowly past. It disappeared then, the T-shirts arrived and stood off behind the gaggle of press photographers, smoking, talking and watching. One had eyes that vanished in deep shadow. As soon as Lucy had gone Max called across to the prettiest of Shota's girls. "Shorena, see those men? Find out who they are and what they're doing here."

"How?"

"Just stand near them as if you're taking a break. They'll talk to you – you're pretty."

"Suppose they don't?"

"For Christ's sake, Shorena, just do it! Please!"

"Okay, Max, keep your shirt on."

"Sorry, Shorena. Say something. Tell them I'm having kittens."

"Kittens? What are you talking about?"

"Anything, just find out what they are."

"What is it with these guys?"

"Nothing. Just please do it. I'll explain later."

"Max, what's the matter?"

"Nothing, Shorena. What's the fucking problem? Just do it! Please."

"Alright. Keep your hair on."

Casually making her way off Shota's patio onto the road, taking out a cigarette and feigning having no light, Shorena made straight for the men with the subtlety of a flying mallet. "Jesus Christ, girl, disguise it a bit," muttered Max from the cover of the great magnolia trunk. As she asked one of the men for a light, a tap on his shoulder made him jump with fright, before turning on a smile and a moment's pretence of joy with old Georgi the house painter as he complimented Lucy's grace and beauty. Max felt sweat soak the front of his shirt and kept the men in the edge of his vision as he exchanged pleasantries till old Georgi left on an unsteady path to the drinks table.

Max observed a cold indifference to Shorena from the men, which, given her bonny face and manner, was suspicious. There seemed a glint of cruelty about them. Around him, the wedding heaved in motion, music and noise that clashed with the terror isolating him from everything. He imagined the great crowd of guests and family scattering as the first shots exploded. His attention was drawn to Menteshashvilli asking Peg for another dance and he saw something sinking in Arnold. A little unspoken drama was unfolding in front of him and he had no connection to it; he was marked down for death while they would live on with their petty and increasingly decrepit lives, waltzing backwards to a second childhood of decay and silliness. He knew that his life would end in absolute fear.

In front of him Peg declined, but Menteshavilli, as usual wouldn't take no for an answer. Max felt the urge to be close to bodies, lost in the density of the crowd, out of the men's sight.

"I think the lady needs a little rest," he suggested in Georgian to Menteshashvlli.

"Fuck off!" was the response. A whiff of fish defied his cologne. Menteshashvilli extricated himself from Max's grip and bestowed a flamboyant bow on his American guests before disappearing into the dancers. Max was on the point of sitting with Arnold and Peg for a couple of minutes to hide and exchange pleasantries in the hoarse shout that the noise was demanding in anyone wishing to be heard, but Peg looked up at him and for a second there was a shadow of some old look, an appealing look, not the hostile Medusa glares that had whipped everyone so far, but a trace of something they had once shared. It faded almost as soon as it appeared, but Max's nerve failed and he spread his arms in a burlesque explanation of Menteshashvilli's over enthusiasm and retreated. To his left he saw the T-shirted men walk off and disappear behind the headland again and the drumming in his chest accelerated.

When Shorena returned, he had trouble hearing her over the music. The men wouldn't say who they were. "They gave me the creeps. Weirdoes."

"Were they Russian?"

"Two of them didn't speak. The other two were Georgians. They offered me ten American dollars to get them into the party."

"Shit," said Max. He had no idea where to go or what to do. He was trapped. The men were now nowhere to be seen. They were biding their time.

When it was time for the consummation Lucy and Timmy left in a pony and cart under a blizzard of rose petals. Her mood had dipped dramatically. On the road to Max's, the marital act squatted between them like a toad. He knew consummation was a custom too far, but desperate for some sense of inclusion, grazed the beach breasts for inspiration. However, she left him staring through Max's windows at the kids stroking the pony while she changed into beach casuals in the bedroom and raged. She wanted rid of him so she could ransack her father's house for a bottle.

He was kneeling for his deck shoes under Max's sofa when he became aware of her legs. The whispers in her head had thrown her from the sublime to the ridiculous: she was now violated; her life burgled, her wedding a diversionary exercise. She stared through her freshly re-married husband and quietly stated "I can't continue calling you Timmy." then retreated into the bathroom, leaving him shocked and diminished, feeling a cut of agoraphobia in a strange room on a foreign shore.

"Timothy. I can call you Timothy" floated from the bathroom and she followed the statement in a new mood, her contrite head quickly nuzzling his chest. But something had given way in him and he was cold as ice. She baled off him in anger and went back into the bathroom.

When they had changed, they headed back to the wedding crowd under a single nimbus cloud, loaded with magenta rain. The stone terrace caught the sky's pinks, and under the magnolia conversation buzzed and lowed between flushed faces. Everything had wine slowed.

But there were no Americans. The remaining guests lolled on the wall watching kids dive off the headland into a sea that was now dark and loud and there were stares at the couple where earlier there had been smiles. Slowly, in broken English, came the tale of how Menteshashvili, who always got a little tedious when he'd had a couple, had tagged on to Peg and Arnold. There had been some tension, the American lady also had a little to drink and later it was noticed they were missing.

Lucy whimpered something Timmy didn't catch; he was lifting high into the twilight spaces, training his painter's eye on the unpolluted shades of purple dipping to lilac and then to a rose horizon. His breathing took on the rhythm of the sea. The bulbs from the magnolia warmed his neck and he sensed the moon waiting to glide onstage for the last act of the comedy in which he was bit-part fall guy.

Peg's laugh boomeranged from somewhere in the trees on the headland. Lucy fired off in its direction and he didn't care; mother and daughter deserved each other.

Max appeared with Pepsis and flipped open a bottle opener from a red knife. "Is that a Swiss Army knife?" asked Timmy.

"It's a Russian Swiss Army knife. You are currently in a parallel
universe." As he drank, the reflected magnolia lights slipped over the bottle
like fireflies. Timmy's flat beach dude tones fascinated Max. In his day
everyone tried to sound like Walter Cronkite. "When were you born?"

"Three years after you defected. Sixty-seven, summer of. Named after
Timothy Leary. You heard of him? My parents were into all that Sixties
drop out and tune in stuff, you know – screw convention, let's get real? Like
their contribution to reality was being able to play 'Mr Tambourine Man' in
three keys."

"Are they still dropped out and tuned in?"

"No. Now my dad's like a transport manager for a trucking firm in
Albuquerque and my mom teaches pre-school in Point Reyes California?
My brother's in a law firm in Seattle. Man, in the old days lawyers made
them blow chunks, but they love him now."

"I had a law degree once. Never practised." Max sipped his Pepsi. "And
you're an artist."

"I ink the pencil drawings of cartoon strips," corrected Timmy. "Not an
artist. At my launch exhibition in a Long Beach fish warehouse I didn't sell
one picture."

"Van Gogh only sold two pictures in his life."

"Thank you Max, I appreciate that but..."

"I have no artistic talent at all. Apart from music. I play a little."

"Proper music, you mean?

"Classical."

"Was your family musical? Because your daughter has a tin ear."

"No, there was no music in my family."

"No art in mine, despite the hippy bullshit." Timmy turned up at the
stars. "Hippies aren't artistic. They're just decorators. Bad ones."

"All those candles and spangles?"

"Kid's stuff. I didn't feel at home, you know? Living in a commune. Being
encouraged to run naked and piss where I stood. Hang loose and relax ,
Timmy. Just made me more uptight. I was like the odd kid, cruising around
like some little IRS clerk lost in the Velvet Underground." Light littered
the waves. The moon was waiting to escape. Timmy nodded up at the sky.
"But old Leary's still keeping the faith, up there now, turnin' on in space,

knockin' on Heaven's door." They absorbed the big, wide night together.
"Do you mind if I ask you a question?"

"Go ahead."

"All that espionage and stuff, you know: have any of them like actually
mentioned it?"

"It's a bit out-of-date now."

"You hope." Where everyone had studiously danced round the subject,
Timmy, the stranger had spoken out. It was almost breaking the rules, but
Timmy was an artist of sorts: it was in his gift to break the rules. However,
the moment in Max's room when his name had been dismissed had planted
and germinated in Timmy. Beached thousands of miles from his own turf,
his identity stripped away for loneliness and whisker biscuit, he was an
extra in this family's opera and he didn't give a damn what he said to the
other outsider. All the bullshit in his life was rising in his gorge and choking
him and he could no longer play the game. In the sourness of his feelings
there was also the sweetness of some kind of freedom.

"You know, sir, your daughter is a very difficult woman."

"Is she? I'm sorry." Max noticed the twigs on his jacket and busied
himself brushing them off.

When Peg went missing, Henry, Masha, Shota and Arnold had set off in
the wrong direction. Max saw Peg and Menteshashvilli disappear into the
headland woods, but said nothing. He checked that there was still no sign of
the T-shirted men, waited till the others disappeared then followed alone,
feeling for noiseless footholds, replacing bending branches quietly, climbing
till a kind of nothingness stopped him with the soundless sensation of two
people trying to be quiet.

Menteshashvilli's cigarette mingled with pine and sea scents; the moon
was lifting behind the headland, quiet conversation from wedding guests
burbled up through the magnolia way below. From somewhere in the trees
a slight rustle of repositioning, or hitching up of clothing conjured the
grotesque thought of his ex-wife skipping the light fandango with a fish
killer. No other sound percolated through the tide and cicada. The sweat
was sticking Max's shirt to the base of his back; he was a spinning-top of
second hand jealousy, yet Peg was a horror, Baby Jane with rough trade in

the bushes. Then her laugh descended on him free and young, unshackled from the battened down warrior he had seen in the last two days, and its independence shocked him. It transcended age and held him on a long line back to the young beauty he had to enslave then lose only after he had ruined her for others. "Menteshashvilli. Go home," he said in Georgian. The strong smell of bark sucked into him as he listened.

"He's not my husband." Peg's voice was clear and defiant.

He hid his shock in the darkness and their sounds snapped and scattered past him, geriatrics tottering back from Paradise Un-regained. Eventually Menteshashvilli's outline edged into the light spill from Shota's and wandered off, a cool thief attracting no attention. Peg was hanging back so they wouldn't be witnessed together. He stood till he saw her stagger towards Masha's. She was very drunk, and that shocked him too.

Henry's voice carried through the thick foliage. The posse was coming. Max descended quietly, picked up the Pepsis and found Timmy, staring up at the night sky in some sort of rapture and wondered if he had taken a drug. While Timmy was retelling tales of his hippy infancy, Menteshashvilli's squat figure made a reappearance, waltzing to his jacket on the chair beside Peg's where he found his spectacles and placed them carefully in his inside pocket. Then he wrapped his tie round his fist and deposited it in a side pocket, drained his glass of wine, wiped the wet moustache, found his cigarettes, lit one, lifted his jacket, turned and left without so much as a how do you do.

"That the guy?"

Max nodded.

"George Clooney he ain't."

Peg's truck-stop profanities burst through the darkness in Masha's house, stopping Lucy dead at the foot of the stairs. This was something she had never heard in her mother; she had never seen her anywhere near drunk, never mind in this blue-collar coarseness. Arnold's voice climbed rapidly to restrain the obscenities. Lucy called. The invective switched off. Then the word 'fuck' floated through the darkness. Lucy half saw Arnold's pale face looming at the door, then it disappeared and she heard the snick of the lock.

The intensity of her mother's rage and the obscenity of her language

left her trembling. From Masha's front door she watched the magnolia
lights burn above the remnants of her wedding. The greatest day of her
life had degenerated into madness. Her husband stood with her father,
drinking Pepsi. Behind them locals drank and amused each other. A couple
danced unsteadily. She stood watching them, breathing softly and loathing
everyone. The thought arrived casually, an innocent suggestion from a
patient opportunist. If her father were the drunk they said he was, some
would be hidden away, and as a fellow worshipper, she would know where
to look. The clichés, mantras and slogans of the AA rooms turned to dust
and were buried a million miles away beside her dead wedding. She left the
shadow of Masha's door and jogged onto the road to Max's. A Mercedes
swerved past her and four men in t-shirts looked at her as if she were an as
yet unclassified species.

Pools of moonlight patterned Max's floors and walls; ivory keys glowed on
the piano, the red velvet stool looked purple. She pressed a key and the note
filled the room like liquid silver, smothering the sounds of the beach and
the last exhalations of her wedding. She tried another, then another. There
was a beautiful independence in the sounds, a single note could penetrate
any remoteness and set it shivering. She looked at the dots and tails on the
staves, at another code her father and Masha understood but she would
never break. Everyone knew something she didn't.
     She kept the lights off and methodically searched all the likely places,
then moved to the unlikely. Through a small kitchen window the hill behind
the house was luminous, an amphitheatre of moonlit trees witnessing how
quickly the calm she experienced in the ceremony had evaporated. Others
were caught by occasional madness, then returned to calm. Her home
base was madness from which there was occasional relief. Some unknown
process had produced marriage; she had no idea how. She opened a
cupboard and saw bottles of cleaning fluids.

From the day Max defected Henry had driven with the brakes on. Over
the years, long stretches would pass when he could forget. Then it would
smack him out of a clear sky and leave him toxic for days. Curiosity sent
him to Max's mother in a public mental ward reeking of piss and run by

staff stressed to within an inch of sadism. A sallow, wafer of oblivion didn't recognise her son's name, and he left with nothing but pity and fear of the future.

Even when Max and his tribe were reduced to Berlin rubble, it didn't stop. He experienced no sense of vindication or victory, only depression when the wall came down and the Big Game was over. It had been a game in which his own side engaged enthusiastically and he had been a player, run by a nation defined by the enemy, his life handed over to a construct.

His little sister withdrew into a shell. Equipped for nothing but Baccarat crystal in the suburbs, she floundered in streams of martyrdom and enraged him with her helplessness. Then Arnold picked up the pieces and glued back some dignity. But under the moonlit magnolia Arnold had become a new victim; Max had made them all mad again. Peg's insanity with the scummy little fisherman had shaken Henry badly, and the scramble through woods against stinging branches to find her before she made a complete idiot of herself left him sore, breathless and furious.

When she was discovered raving at Masha's he had to withdraw somewhere quiet and stuff back tears. Then the anger boiled up and he advanced on Max, positioned with Timmy as his shield, sharing a Pepsi and light wedding banter. Could Max just say something to Peg at some point, that didn't keep her out in the cold, that let her squeeze a little of the poison, it wouldn't kill him for Christ's sake? But all he got was the Cyclopean gaze bricking up the distances between them, and the Cold War relaunched.

Henry never really got over being betrayed. In some sense, the politics were irrelevant. It was the act itself. Something fundamental was destroyed swiftly and brutally and for months after the defection he moved around as a mass of cells, flesh, bone and nerves, reduced to the primal level of food, shelter, excretion and little else. He observed human behaviour from a distance that seemed unbridgeable. Inch by painful inch he crossed back over. But it took a long time and any serious trauma or disappointment could yank him back to that distant outsider position, as if he were attached by elastic. When the KGB files were opened in the early Nineties and he discovered it was Peter who had tipped the wink to Max, he lay winded and broken again, and felt he had known nothing about his own life. That was what treachery did; it stole your life. He opened the exchange that had been festering for three and a half decades by talking about Peter, someone they had both loved for different reasons.

"He played golf with Bob Hope."

"Yes. He was a good golfer," said Max.

"Peter was dead when they opened the KGB files, so the press hounded his sons and daughter. One was a Hollywood movie producer who had licked a cocaine habit."

"Really? Cocaine?"

Everything glanced off Max; nailing him was like grabbing a shadow, and when Henry's voice bounced back from the stone terrace it sounded weak and full of self-pity. The anger that glowed down the decades vanished and left him sweating with self-consciousness. He was aware everyone was watching and lost all idea of where to take things. He could see Max, gloves up with no intention of fighting and simultaneously felt something weaken in his own resolve. He knew both of them were riding losers; it was obvious debate was pointless, how could they sort out stuff that happened so long ago? They might as well debate the Indian Wars. However he had to have a tilt, he owed it to his sister, to the niece who could be on a vodka aphrodisiac behind a bush lifting her wedding dress for a stranger, to lists of names in unmarked graves, to history, to something.

The morning after he left the Service he thought what now and wondered if Max had woken to the same chasm in the Moscow morning. How had he dealt with Hungary, the Prague Spring, delaying puberty in gymnasts?

Max didn't recall Henry questioning any of the scams they got up to out of Langley. "The clasping of mafia hands to get Fidel? The assassination of the fascist Trujillo in case, in case, he provoked a Communist revolution? Did you question those? I wouldn't have, if I held your position. I just saw it from another side. But please don't play the 'we were the good guys and you were the Evil Empire' cliché." A litany of American transgressions was trotted out, from the drug runs for Vietnamese warlords and right-wing Central American terrorists that inflated addiction in black communities across America that were given the wink by the 'office', to the programmes of destabilisation in Uruguay, Persia, Chile, Vietnam, Central America. "Did you question any of that? Of course not. You kept your nose clean. I kept mine clean here."

"Most of that stuff was long after us."

"And if you'd been there you would have made a difference?"

"We didn't kill millions in gulags."

"That was long before me, and you think my coming here was an approval of that?"

"If you'd been there, would you have made a difference?"

"If you had been born later, Max," offered Timmy, "you mighta gone hippy. You know, like parleyed your politics into a Hopi candle trade on the Big Sur."

The voice of youth pulled them up. Jagger pouted from the music system. Shota muttered something to Max and Max reassured him all was fine. Masha jiggled Shota's granddaughter till she gave a gummy grin at the blurring light bulbs in the magnolia. To Timmy, the two old men shaking up the sediment of their past, were ridiculous. His wedding day was not the ground for history's dead battles. McCarthy and the Cuban missile crisis were nostalgia trips for unemployed National Guardsmen. The jibe of youth reminded Max and Henry that the rest of the world gave not one damn about their historical principles. Their language was as dead as Latin or Assyrian. Only for Henry, a faint notion that he had to set a few things straight remained, but Max insisted that if he had come for revenge or explanations he had no idea how to provide them.

"How often you get asked the big one Max?"

"What's that Timmy?"

"Do you still believe?"

Timmy offered shelter from Henry's prosecution. "Do you believe in anything Timmy?"

"I don't think we need those big beliefs anymore. In fact, I think they get in the way."

"In the way of what?"

"Aah, just in the way."

The Cold War vets stared at a young face replete with a life collected at the checkout, unsure if he were dumb or a lot smarter than they.

"Has anyone seen Lucy?" Timmy asked.

Henry shook his head. "What..? Is she...?"

"This is a tradition on her wedding night."

"What tradition?" asked Max.

"Going missing."

"Is there any booze in your place, Max?" whispered Henry.

"There may be a little somewhere."

"Shit," said Henry, and Timmy's silence endorsed the concern. Max thought of his precious liqueur among the cleaning chemicals, and prayed Lucy missed it, not for her sake, but for his. He was shaken up and a drink would settle him. "I'll go back and check."

"Leave it Max," said Timmy, "It's probably too late or we're up our asses over nothing. I'm staying put." He shook his head at ship lights, far out to sea. "I wonder where he's going."

"Maybe Max should go back and..."

"Forget it, Henry. I can't go chasing this all my life. Get back to treason."

But the wind was out of their sails. Max's problem with the stuff was another secret distancing them. A long silence left both men hopelessly self conscious, and to sow peace and lower the siren calls from his cleaning cupboard, Max slipped into nostalgia, and Henry grudgingly joined him, as former enemies do in a time that has no regard for their old differences. Timmy became audience to a double act from a History Channel trailer.

"Somebody says Castro dives for deep-sea clams. So we rig dozens of clams with high explosive and fix them in the beds, so when Fidel cuts them free, they blow him to Kingdom Come."

"And...?" asked Timmy.

"He never dived for them."

Henry asked if Max remembered the poison they used in the diving suit.

"Madura fungus and tubercle bacilli."

"They impregnated a diving suit with this stuff. Somehow they got it to him. As soon as he put it on it would kill him."

"What happened?"

"He didn't put it on."

"If I proposed this to my boss as an idea for a strip she'd say get outa here poisoned diving suits and exploding clams, get real."

A scuffle from the bar turned everyone. A glass fell. Shota shouted something in Georgian.

"Is that a fight?" asked Timmy.

"Probably," said Max.

"I better check my wife hasn't started it." And they watched Timmy disappear into the bar.

"Poor sonofabitch." Henry scanned the headland and the hills. "Where the hell could she have got to?"

"It is a problem then?"

"Beyond comprehension," answered Henry. But he was less concerned with his foolish niece than the corpses over Central and South America, the Caribbean, Vientiane, nagging him from unknown graves. Max would claim there were no widows at his door; the dead were anonymous files closed when the shit hit the fan, and that was true; that was how they operated. But voices of the dead mumbled round the luminous sea.

"Henry, we were all killers by proxy; a memo here, locals with a bent for torture, promotions won over anonymous corpses. If that's what the boss wanted, that's what we gave him. If he liked the middle way, everyone became enlightened. Mostly what the struggle led to was another pension payment."

"You gave names, Max. And a lot of those names found a bullet or a garrotte. Kids were left with no fathers. Or mothers. Sometimes whole families."

"What do you want me to do, Henry?"

"Just admit it. Have the guts to say 'yes, I did that'."

Max laughed, "What? You were right and we were wrong?"

Henry shook his head. "I'm not interested in that crap. It's just about you, Max, just about you."

A tiny insect crawled over a leaf. Plates on its back lifted, transparent wings extended and it took off. A bonfire burst up way down the beach.

"And all the corpses with Uncle Sam stamped on their ass? How do you feel about those, Henry?"

"I have no blood on my hands."

"I seem to recall you worked on the Bay of Pigs fiasco."

"Over a minor, specific issue. Purely administrative. I was nothing more than a clerk..."

"We're all clerks on Judgement Day." Max moved into theory. "At the end of the day, espionage is simply an alternative negotiation."

"You could make the same argument for genocide."

"No one died in vain. We've had peace for fifty years."

"Thank you."

"That was not an admission, Henry," Max became agitated. Then the energy seeped out of him. The whole thing was too big, too complex and full of too many traps.

"Peg and Lucy?"

"I regret that."

Henry laughed bitterly. "And me?"

"I regret that too."

"What did you feel? When you went through with it?"

"Fear. Numbness."

"What was behind it though? Who were you getting back?"

"No one. It was balance in a world of fanatics."

"Oh come on, Max, get off that shit."

"There was a guy called Freddie Ancellotti drove the school bus in the town where I'm from: nice guy, loved the kids, we loved him – he was funny. He joined a truck regiment in the war, no hero, but did his bit, and came back set against segregation; blacks had died for America, why couldn't they have a cup of coffee where they wanted? Freddie was no more a Communist than Frank Sinatra, but he believed in unions and had opinions. He wasn't trying to undermine anything or change anything other than a few ugly old prejudices and a couple of unreasonable working conditions. But when the McCarthy circus came through town my father fingered Freddie and he lost his job, his wife, his kids, and the whole town turned its back on him. Even the school kids he used to drive wouldn't speak to him. He was completely isolated in his own neighbourhood. There was a breaker's yard called Bruno's had one of those small cranes ran on rails, you know? Freddie hanged himself on it with an old pair of his wife's stockings. It was the best day of my father's life. Not one voice raised in sympathy for Freddie. Not even a kid's. That was the scary bit. The kids said he deserved it."

Henry looked up and saw the word 'bullshit' neon-blinking round the moon. The Rolling Stones whined from the music stack and the horizon was a strip of Jagger's silver Lurex. Way beyond lay the shore of the country whose malign influence had given his life a point. "So you went to Russia and lived happily ever after."

Stars blistered the sky and the unknown dead stayed unknown dead. The moon was older. Henry had run out of steam. Max thought of his father translating the pain of his life into history and self-righteousness.

"Max, it was just you, what you were. If you had been born Russian, somewhere down the line you would have become one of our guys."

There would be no end to it, so Max let it go. The sea washed in and around their old unresolved differences and the huge night quietly called time. Both men were shaking. Moonlight jigged a path down the waves.

"One thing more.' said Henry. Max sighed, and wearily braced himself for the final jab. "I want to offer you a book deal."

Timmy opened the door to Max's house and waded lightly through draughts of moonlight. He listened for her breathing and any tell tale sounds of drunkenness, then let his nose lead him through the air streams and smells in the house. Old wood, musty cushions and flowers crowded his nasal passages to the bedroom, where she lay as a sculpture of bedclothes in the shadows. The nose hovered then dipped towards the mouth and settled in the quiet exhalations. There was no smell of alcohol. He could have shouted for joy. Maybe there was trouble storing up for the future, but she had got through this day without necking a bottle. He stared at her, safe in her father's house, and felt grateful. In the corner of his eye he caught the lights on the magnolia going out.

Shota had left them with a candle, floating Henry's face and the leaf clusters above them in a faint gloss of light. Behind him, Max could see the silhouette of the hill where Gia's house stood edged against the sky. The girls had cleared away most of the wedding feast, and Shota himself wandered about looking for empty glasses that had found their way into odd places.

"I had sent out a sackful of applications," continued Henry, "and received sweet Fanny Adams. 'Don't touch this man' seemed to be the word – because of you Max, because of you, no doubt about it; but then Phil called me in because of you. He was a senior manager. He only called me in because he was at Harvard with you and curious about you and I was curious about what he knew about you at college. I was still chewed up bad."

The night was weary; the only energy was from Henry's voice ricocheting among the cicada and sea hisses like a stone. It was so loud in its full frontal American way that Max was sure everyone would hear.

"Usual stuff Phil says, nothing about you back then that made you think that one-day etc. Regular guy. You, that is. Hated your father. Good student. Kept yourself to yourself, but would occasionally open a bottle and become Grouch Marx. So, that was my start in publishing. You got me fired and you got me hired. I don't know whether to love you or loathe you."

"Still the same firm?"

"Gold watch case. The young ones are disappointed I'm alive each morning. My share holding is too small to guide policy but significant enough to keep my desk."

"Business okay?"

"I built it up man, I built it. I had two Pulitzers and a National Book Prize. How about that for a failed CIA badass? I'm digging out new authors from trailer parks and finishing schools, good people, real, original talents. Then we sell part to a media company and now we do self-enhancement books and how to become a millionaire through affirmation? Short books so our reader's lips don't tire. I'm about to launch a big deal on Feng Shui for pets written by an actress who was murdered in *Colombo*."

Shota had left half a bottle of his favourite Scotch for the American guest and a Scots mist settled on Henry's brain while Max remained crystal clear over his squeezed blood oranges, an unfamiliar but useful place from where maximum information could be extracted while revealing nothing. Now Henry was in full gallop over his life. Disjointed memories lunged about in the whisky fog.

"When they opened the KGB files? Whoah, yeah – it was a real shock to discover who, Jesus! Peter! Jesus, yeah, stopped me right in my tracks, stopped me dead, even though it's you know, decades. It makes you feel... contaminated, even though you're... The world's changed, you know.

Nobody has any idea today, there are no ideas anymore. Look at Timmy,
God bless him – lovely guy, good man but... still, where was I...?"
   "Contaminated."
   "Contaminated. Yeah. How could you have been so, you know...? Peter.
Like someone I often went to for advice. Not just about the job. You know, a
war hero and a real pillar, a solid guy we thought, but..."
   "I didn't know till quite late either."
   "Really? No shit."
   Max's impression of Henry was of a man tearing through rooms where
the light was never on for him. He picked up the references to unhappy
children who never phoned; of ex-wives and lovers who had no time for
him, and remembered that even in his youth Henry had problems with
his wife. He had seemed so accomplished in every other field that this
weakness was strange and unreal. Earlier, Henry had poured out his
misgivings about the two-year relationship with a Christian fundamentalist
that he had just severed, and it saddened Max to think that a spectacular
youth he remembered so well had been boiled down by time to a bad
ending with a Jesus freak. It took him momentarily back to that age when
they all had such excitement about life.
   "You know – I mean *everything* we did, me and Mabel – had to be
filtered through Jesus and the Twelve Apostles, with His approval or...
I'd say 'Come on, let's just do this thing. Give the guy a break, give him
the afternoon off'. But no. On her knees. Then I said if Jesus ever came
back, your kind of Christian would make him blow chunks. That finished
it. I think these people are actually insane. Nevertheless, you know it's...
companionship, it wasn't all... And she was just another lost soul looking
for safe harbour but..."
   A face appeared beyond Henry, near Masha's house, a neutral
expression, half seen peering at them, ascertaining what was going on
above the candle and under the dark magnolia. Max froze. The guns were
in his case in Shota's spare room. The face was a dimness in shadows,
as if seen through a palimpsest, barely discernible, but definitely there.
It vanished as eerily as it appeared and left Max in an even worse state.
The T-shirted men had disappeared after Shorena's sexy interrogation.
But he had seen them once more, looking back from the beach. Then they

were gone again, appearing and disappearing around the bay and in some despondent inner landscape of his till he could no longer tell which was real and which was imagined. They had waited all day and now their time had come. From somewhere in the darkness he heard Shota dropping bottles and glasses into a crate.

Henry was wittering on, unconcerned, ignorant of Max's deadly drama, buoyed up on a gas of whisky wisdom. "Initially I was looking for perfection I suppose, you know, and then as I got a little older and wiser I tried to moderate. But that didn't work. Even the adequate seemed beyond me, you know, peering into goldfish bowls of dull marriages wondering how the hell they got it that good." Henry laughed at himself then finally caught Max's fraught face, flickering against the sea. "Are you okay, Max? You look a little peaky."

"Oh, just tired." Shota emerged from the shadows with his crate of empty bottles and glasses.

"I think Shota wants to pack up. Maybe we should retire. It's been quite a day."

"Hey, Shota,' said Henry. "You are the feast master of all times. This has been superb."

Shota put the crate down on the table so Henry could give him the drunk's long handshake, "Everything you have done has been beyond the call of duty."

Shota responded with a few Georgian smiles, but Max was caught by another movement by Masha's, a different texture of darkness shifting quickly, and asked Shota in Georgian if he had seen anyone and watched the fear arch Shota like a nerve gas. Gia's death gave body to the fanciful and the hysterical.

"Nothing. I saw nothing. But I wasn't looking. Maybe we should get rid of Henry."

"Henry we should get some sleep. We're going sailing tomorrow. Shota has a boat that may not sink."

"Sailing! Great!"

"There are lots of places round the coast where we can go snorkelling."

"Still swimming?"

"Oh yes, still swim.."

"Lucy's the swimmer you know. She's got it. Never used it but Peg? You won't get her near the water – won't even put a toe in now. I think it's psychological."

"Well let's see what happens tomorrow. You can find your way back?" Max gave him the candle in the jar and Henry stood, stumbled and found his balance. "Jesus, I am shit-faced. See you, Shota. See you, Max. This has been, this has been you know, really... Strange and, you know... weird and... words cannot.. Yeah! Phew, yeah! Start writing."

"I will."

And Shota and Max scuttled indoors and from a dark room watched the candle's flame and Henry's bulky silhouette make their jagged way back towards Masha's, deviating, correcting then finally disappearing behind Masha's door.

Nothing moved but the sea. They strained their eyes at absolute darkness.

"It's irrational, it's irrational, it's ridiculous. My mind is torturing me."

"Probably," said Shota but Max could see the anxiety. "I hope Henry can make it up to that gallery bed in his condition."

When Henry finally got up to his gallery bed, he wanted dreams of *Oprah* and the *NYT* Bestseller List. Max would be prone to a pretentiousness of expression, like all first-time writers; he would have to sit on him and excise the indulgence. He began to wonder about movie spin-offs. "Bill Pullman as Max Agnew. I like him. Or is it Paxton? HBO series? No Henry, slow down. A book, start with just a book." After all the watersheds of the twentieth century, they were a team again and that was a strange symmetry to ponder. But there might be money in it. "Maxie, give me something to give those twenties shit-heads at the office the finger as I say goodbye." Above him the boughs of the old bougainvillea gripped Masha's glass roof like giant talons. "Max," he said to the Big Dipper, "Keep it sexy."

Arnold paused in his reading. Beside him Peg dreamed of the Scottsdale Mall. He placed his foot against her calf and applied pressure till she shifted and stopped snoring. In the other bedroom Masha was crying. He snapped off his battery book light. Masha's sobs curled through the darkness. Hers

was a sad house in an alien world through whose history struggle ran
like an unbroken vein. He thought of his own ostentatious house in the
Biltmores, of over designed rooms filled with nothing. There had been
sadness there too. What were the lessons of sadness? He didn't know.
Perhaps there were none. He switched his book light back on and continued
reading.

Timmy woke once and wondered where he was, saw her shape, heard her
breathing. Trees rolled up a hill beyond the window. Silver trees. Stars spat
across a strip of indigo. A blinking light passing. Asleep up there. Georgian
girls with beautiful eyes. Shorena, how he would like to... He drew cartoons.
With Masha. Then she disappeared. Why? Lucy. Still sober...

Max's eyes scanned every shadow, every edge of light, his ears picked up
every sound. Is this irrational? Is it real? Is it me? In his adopted country,
death could be the price of a simple mistake. Like being honest, being a
good citizen. Mistakes. He should have thought, but he was carried away by
grief. Now his grief cursed him.

On my daughter's wedding day, I stand beneath a tree with guns. He
looked over the village. They would talk about it for years. His house glowed
in the moonlight. They were in there together. God bless them. Yes, if there
is a god, and I'm certain there's not, then bless them. Anyway.

What he did over Gia was right, even if it condemned him to behave like
a third-rate character in a gangster B movie. And what he had done today
was right. It may not have been perfect, nor executed brilliantly, but it was
right. He began to relax and be absorbed by the bay, the sounds and the
movement of the waves, the moonlight, and a certain, indistinct ease with
himself. The earth seems innocent tonight, all tucked away in the nursery.
On other nights it bristles with terror. What changes it, he wonders. Is it to
some degree a choice? Or have we no control?

On the other side of the bay, pinprick headlights switched on. His hands
tightened on the guns. The lights moved under black cliffs, picking out
trees, shacks, boulders, then, as the car took the bend they swept across
his little house, then turned. He watched the rear lights climb the hill away
from the village, the brake lights flash on and off as they avoided the cracks

and potholes. He saw the main beam pick out the summit and send an incandescence of light into the sky. Then the beam tilted and disappeared over the crest and left the rear lights hovering like ruby fireflies for a moment. They bounced violently through one last hole and were gone.

Darkness, peace, silence. Nothing but the noise in his own head. He had survived. They had come storming back: the nutty ex-wife, the energetic ex-brother-in-law, led a by an unknown daughter. Back in the family. He had a strange sense that he had never really been away. Or had been on a trip.

He looked around the bay and was aware of a new feeling; a set of different navigational coordinates, of seeing the familiar landscape in a fresh way.

Something had been offered, something new, an opportunity had come out of the frightening mess. You never knew what life had in store for you. The oddest things in the oddest places. He had been in such a state about it all. But there was another day to get through tomorrow. Don't count your chickens Max. God knows what that might bring. Those bastards might be back. Stay alert, eyes out for your stalker.

In one day Masha had become a background figure. And he felt fine about it. Absolutely fine.

Ending. That was what the strange feeling was. Not death. A sense of ending.

Next morning

The bottle's label was yellow and nothing on it made sense to her but it was alcohol, what kind and what taste was of no relevance – the effect was the same in all languages. She replaced the cleaning fluids carefully and silently, and peeped back into the bedroom to make sure Timmy was still sleeping off his wedding. The air barely moved through his lungs, he was deep in the well.

She had been woken to drink. Her body clock knew this was the heart of the night when the sleeper is at depth. Some days she woke relieved she had not gone to bed drunk; some days she woke wanting a drink; every morning she woke to the thought of a drink one way or the other. The previous night had defeated the bottle; at the last second she had tacked away through the same mystery that sometimes drove her to it, switching and steering her in opposite directions. But sometime in the night, the message had changed and woken her.

In the garden she pulled her gown about her, catching the perfumes of unknown plants and trees, and letting herself blend into the place and the early dawn. A cadence of dying summer chilled her. Light began to settle on trees and the landscape took shape. Everything was still.

The bottle label looked as if it had been designed in the days when the Czar ignored the death he was sowing for his careless family. St George proudly strutted his stuff through a foliage of Cyrillic. She slipped into the trees, away from the house. Only a couple of sips, just to bring that ease, that relief, and she could cope with the mad farce she was in. Then a swim, a vigorous one, get the breathing going hard, get it out of the system. By the time she returned to bed, any trace of booze would be washed away in the salt tang of the sea.

The bottle would be secreted in the woods so it could be returned to during the day.

Mist limply lay on treetops. She felt the damp settle on her, the silence stand back in contempt, as her fingernail pushed under the seal on the bottle-cap and teased up the end. Something caught her eye in the bottom corners of the label. The patterns around the edges moved down to a simple shape in the corner, a long, elegant movement, like an ancient un-drawn bow or a long flower leaf curling to its tip, a classic shape but one that disturbed her and at first she didn't know why. Then it dawned on her that this was the subtle shape that recurred in Gia's furniture, quietly moving through it like a motif, almost ghost like, sometimes more of a suggestion, but an unmistakeable presence. It was wound in the table in her father's living room, in the altar in the church and the chest of drawers snug in her bedroom in Santa Monica. Perhaps it was a classic Georgian motif; she had no idea, and strained to remember if she had ever been aware of it in Tbilisi.

Gia seemed everywhere and nowhere. Perhaps she was reading too much into it, but she had sensed him in the background, underscoring the warmth of the locals with grief and shock. They talked freely about him, like old people who volunteer details of their operation or medical problem unasked, and in their descriptions he embraced everything from village wide boy to sensitive artist. But they all laughed around his Casanova complex, as one charming old lady had put it.

Lucy looked round at her father's house through the wood. Gia had been in there many times, had eaten, argued with Max, no doubt, perhaps even had a sip of this kind of liquor. Or removed it to stop Max getting drunk again. Lives come and go and leave no mark but in the imagination of the survivors; the dead are handed on like puzzles. She felt his eyes on her, watching an alcoholic in a wood before anyone woke, with a bottle in her hand.

She had been plagued by a sense of loss all her life which she could hang on the peg of her father's departure, but she knew Gia was like that too; she could recognise it in others instantly, that inexhaustible capacity to feel absence, that nothing is quite enough, that you've come in the wrong door. In some loopy way he had probably died for it. His furniture was the best of him; the perfection that he lacked. He carried the gift around in him like a benign virus. All the mess was gone now; what was left was the gift.

She picked her way down the slope under the dripping tress, went back into her father's kitchen and put the unopened bottle back behind the cleaning fluids.

In daytime, the track was dusty, but in the dawn was damp and earth clung to her feet. She would wash them in the sea. As she climbed, that same signature of quiet, long curves became visible on the barn doors above her. His work stood in a Santa Monica bedroom as a memorial to their joint talent for doing the wrong thing. The memory of him had angered her, but now touched her. When she first asked Shota about the mechanics of his death it was clear he knew about her and Gia, and if he knew, the whole village knew. Moscow hoods had been his explanation. "We'll sort them. Don't worry."

"Why did they kill him?"

"Bad taste in wives."

"Come again?"

"Bad taste in other men's wives."

She left at that point since she supposed she was one of the other men's wives.

Light delicately lay on bare work surfaces. Tool racks hung empty in shadows. One end of his workshop was partitioned off with hardwood frames and chain link wire and was fastened with a heavy padlock. It was empty but for a piece of paper curled on the floor, lying as if he had left some final message. As her eyes adjusted she saw it was a page from a nudie calendar.

Behind the barn were wooden racks under a tarred, felt roof where he had weathered his wood. The grass still bore the yellow marks of long standing wood stacks. Peeping through the windows and around the racks offered a glimpse of a life beyond his own confusion, where everything was clear and simple. There still seemed a trace of him, wandering between the shadows and diffused light from the windows and skylights. Here something had his entire attention until it reached the form and grace he wanted. She could visualise him with his back to her, unaware of her watching, bent over a detail of a table or a chair.

In her current state, the empty barn conveyed a sense of peace to her, though she knew this was probably a preference of her imagination. Human comfort needs what made the dead content and not what tormented them. His workplace seemed his sanctuary away from the madness that menaced him outside, and she felt pleased he had found somewhere. This was where her chest of drawers had been conceived and made, where he had waxed his guilt into the grain and spent time and skill on a beautiful apology. Finally she felt grateful.

Below her, the village houses were becoming visible round the bay and the headland. Light green trees were still dull on its steep slopes against the grey sea, and beneath them Max, Shota, Masha, Mother, Arnold and Uncle Henry slept; her little world, imperfect, dysfunctional to the point of being an essay in human incompatibility snoozing away beneath her. Away to the right, in Max's separate house, lay someone who had dedicated his life to her twice. She did love him, she thought, she must. She really was unsure what love was. It was carried through her life as another unbroken code. And it was difficult living with a decent person; she hadn't much practice. A breeze breathed over her and through her hair. Things didn't seem so bad at that moment; they were just another fractured American family.

The door to Gia's house was the same wood as her chest of drawers now wrapped in the orange darkness of a Santa Monica night. Perhaps this was his favourite wood. It glowed in the creeping light. Tourists now slept in Gia's old home; no trace of him would be left. A person is washed from the fabric of a home with a coat of paint, or a change of curtains.

A car of some European type she did not recognise stood near the door, wet with the night's moisture. She crept quietly up to the main window. Inside everything was neat, but there was an absence of his own furniture. The subtle curve was missing from this room. Gia had never favoured himself with his own gift, and that made absolute sense to her. She could look straight through the room to huge viewing windows on the other side, and a mile away on the cliff top a plume of dark cedars mantled a peeling church dome glowing dully through the mist. For a second she experienced a brief sense of fondness.

Epilogue – Spring 2002

On the road from the airport, Max's face loomed from a litter of billboards, ten metres high, shuffled among ads for German cars, Gucci and cosmetics. His expression was studious, but the photographer had caught a something in his eyes that conveyed a subtle lightness and humour. An image of his book was cleverly worked beside him to suggest an open door, throwing light on a hidden past, inviting the reader in, and inscribed around it were endorsements from celebrities of the literary and academic world.

"Oh my God."

His driver Valya grinned at his discomfort. "Rubs against the grain for an old spy does it? You've been blown now."

"I've been blown for a long time."

"You're plastered across the ones for the conference too. All over Moscow. You and that French writer. The one who's always drunk."

Max put his head in his hands. "Its just weird seeing yourself over and over again."

"I'd kill for that kind of publicity."

In the two and a bit years since the wedding, there had been many changes. He had reacquired status but a very different strain to what he had known in his Communist heyday. It glowed from a joyously elitist world where he was a fashionable component among the champagne and lifestyle interviews that garnished it. His was a unique position as he had managed to straddle the old way and the new – "a colossus between epochs" as one gushing journalist put it – and for this he was in constant demand on TV and at all the glittering events of a society fast growing in love with itself. But the bustle of publicity that pasted his face onto billboards, buildings and TV sets from Paris to Phnom Penh kept him wary. The ghost from the past with the eyes of the devil still rose to haunt him now and again. And now he was back in the killer's hometown, soaring along a dual carriageway. He had been here before; nothing had happened. The anxiety was diluting, but he kept his radar switched on. "You're too big to kill now," was Shota's optimistic conclusion. But no one was too big for the Mafia.

"You know, my mother was a great fan of yours," said Valya, overtaking everything. "In the old days, when you were a Hero of the Soviet Union. Yeah, she thought you were very handsome. You could have had your way with her, Max. When you were younger."

"If only I'd known."

"Is there any way you could sign a book for her?"

"If we get there intact."

"Thanks. That'll take her mind off the incontinence."

"Anything to help, Valentina."

Valya was one of the many new faces of Moscow, one with rings, studs and tattooed lesbians in acts of grotesque carnality customising her body parts. Her head was shaved up to the summits where two spreads of thick, flaxen hair sat like birds wings incubating a giant egg.

"Do you set off airport security systems?"

"It's a laugh. I've got them everywhere. Oh yes, there too. Especially there. I have to strip to show them. They don't know what to make of me."

She was a stand-up comedienne with a strong line in sexual confusion, "I have this prosthetic cock that I take out and pee all over the stage. It's really

realistic, really well made and you can see they think they've got me sussed,
then that pulls them up and they're confused, calls their assumptions into
question, you know. Gets a barrel of laughs. Especially if they're out of their
trees."

Max wondered what Lenin would have made of it.

"I do the driving to subsidise the stand up," added Valya, "Irina, you
know, who's running the conference? She's my squeeze."

"Oh? I didn't know Irina was..."

She laughed. "Yeah. We don't all look like me. You never can tell, can
you?"

The car was a huge Mercedes, a courtesy car from a dealership that was
partly sponsoring the event. Fifteen different authors of fiction and non-
fiction had been gathered from all over Europe for an authors' conference
loosely bound by the theme of the alienated society and the written word.
But Max was undoubtedly the star turn. Apart from the Frenchman who
was rarely sober enough to turn up.

"Poor bastard. I picked him up this morning. He was in such a state. He
asked me if I'd go down on him. I said 'only after the opening address'." She
laughed again, happy, joyous and free.

Max's memoirs were a bestseller before they hit the bookshelves on both
sides of the old Cold War divide. Henry had stoked curiosity with carefully
placed excerpts, press releases and serialisations. The righteous and the
patriots of his old country were appalled. The furore whipped up advance
sales, an attractive infamy, and drew crowds at signings and interviews
across Europe. A Scottish company made a documentary for the BBC,
filmed at the little house by the sea, the apartment in Tbilisi, the Kremlin
and several other old Soviet locations. He even got on well with the CIA
operatives sent to check him out.

Now he was a guest on everything from quiz shows to history
documentaries. His life had a new dynamic, and there was money and he
liked it, although the scale of his celebrity sometimes frightened him. His
own safety was still a concern, but he couldn't shut himself away, he had
to operate on the assumption that the killer had just not recognised him or
decided to let sleeping dogs lie. Gia's case had advanced not one whit from
that awful morning when Max found him in the sea. There was now enough

money to take up Alexei's offer, but things had changed. Henry had made him a celebrity. The day in a Tbilisi tea bar with an unwelcome daughter had brought surprising blessings. Did he want to put those at risk by setting up a contract on the life of a cheap Moscow hood? In the moments when he was still empowered with grief, it was not easy to stick with the sensible decision. The word 'loyalty' kept repeating on him as if that last meal with Gia remained undigested. His sad eyes, his demeanour, his questioning had haunted him till the book was published; then those memories began to miraculously fade. With circumstances so radically different, and all that money now, all the risks protested. Now he had something to lose.

The timing of his success was perfect too. The rednecks were swarming out of the Washington woodwork. Now Russia was weak, all restraint was gone and there was no one to stand up to them. The America his father pined after had arrived and Max felt vindicated again. Delivered with understatement and an emphatic sympathy for those who had been lost on 9/11, whom he defined as the innocents who had paid for decades of deviant American foreign policy, he was once again part of the political debate.

Henry and he kept in regular touch and he always asked after everyone. Lucy was pregnant again after a first miscarriage and, she assured him, doing fine, but Max only pretended to believe her. He was daunted by the idea of a grandchild, but glad to have family again, and glad they were half way across the world – an ideal cushion, tucked away in the comfort of the mind and not in his face. The occasional phone call or postcard buoyed up the sensation that his world was re-populated. They were a screwed up bunch but what family is not?

He also had taken the precaution of drawing up a will. Everything would go to Lucy apart from a couple of reasonably valuable antiques that would decorate Shota's restaurant. Partly for his own safety and partly because he had finally grown tired of the little village where he spent so much time, a permanent move to Prague was being contemplated. He would be safe to invite Lucy, Timmy and his grandchild there – if there ever were a grandchild.

"You know Prague?"

"I did a lesbian comedy festival in Prague. Magic place."

Valya's postmodern approval tickled him. The book's success and
the money had replaced the despondency he felt at the end of the old
century with the prospect of an exciting future, even at his ripe old age.
He had discovered that there is little to compare with the pleasure of the
unexpected Indian summer. His pocket and his pride replenished together;
he had taken a long and strange route to respect and celebrity; hated and
feted, a hero and a villain, a rogue or an old fashioned man of principle who
had run against the current – he was a topic of debate.

Writing the book, however, had mysteriously brought everything into
question, because on each page Max was nagged by the notion that the
great risks he took as a young man were taken because there was some
other, greater risk he could not take. Something flickered in the corner
of his eye, but like the borealis, disappeared whenever he turned to look
at it. The events and characters of his youth were remembered with
complete clarity; he was scrupulously honest about everything, but when
he looked back for his younger self, there was no one there. He could recall
no sensation of how it was to be the young Max. So he had to fictionalise
himself, but in a sense that was what he had always done.

"D'you come here a lot?"

"Couple of days here and there. Usually for some bit of work."

The return to Moscow always dumped more old memories on him,
too late for the book now, but vivid and significant: memories of how
after hard nights on the vodka he was drawn to watch the suicides being
fished out of the river at dawn; of an artist in the Arbat reeking of chipped
and re-lit cigarettes, a stick man in a stained green suit from a rag stall,
without vest, socks or shoes selling him a tiny oil painting he could fit in
his hand, and which had a kind of miracle in it. It showed a birch tree on
tawny grass backed by pines under a high autumn sky and this miniature
landscape suggested something of the unfathomable mystery of Russia to
him. It reminded him too of that strange day lying under a tree in Alexei's
childhood killing fields. He would take it with him to Prague, as a reminder.

"You been to the Metropol?"

"In the old days."

"You won't recognise it now. Five star. You've got a suite there. You just
come down in the lift and you're in the conference."

"It seems to get more expensive every time I come back here."

"Maybe it needs another revolution, uh?"

He looked at her and saw the twinkle. "You really are a comedienne."

Alexei and Petra joined him for the meal in the Metropol and Max was pleased to foot the radioactive bill. It was wonderful to resurrect their relationship after the years of separation. Time had cladded Petra's extraordinary beauty with more weight and faded Alexei to a shocking frailty that saddened him. The old star who had them sitting up in the corridors of the Kremlin and the Lubyanka was a ghost. They had all lived through exciting times but they were anachronisms in the new world.

The next morning Valya and Irina took him downstairs to join the other writers for breakfast. The controversial Frenchman was already drunk. Then the great reading public of Moscow streamed in. Poles, Czechs, Latvians numbered among the locals. The new Russians took to books as if they were a designer drug. The signing was so brisk that Max's hand seized up several times.

At three o' clock, he gave his talk and for the reading selected a short chapter about a trip he and Alexei made to interview a very old Party member called Ivan. A senior official was retiring and it had been decided to collect reminiscences from all his old companions and gather them into an album as a memento of his service to the People's Soviet. Old Ivan was a survivor from the Revolution itself and was the retiring official's first departmental head in one of the many ministries that honeycombed the old bureaucracy. He had known Lenin, had waded chin deep through freezing rivers at night to ambush White Russians and had helped push tank production through the roof in the war against the Nazis. All in all, he was a man from the heart of revolutionary history, an eyewitness and participant at its key moments, but when Alexei and Max got to him he couldn't remember a thing. "Stalin? Joseph Stalin?"

Senility had wiped Ivan clean as a slate. History had gone from him. So, rather than disappoint anyone, Alexei and Max made everything up, and when the album was presented to the retiring official, he was particularly moved by old Ivan's recollections and sent him a letter of thanks that Alexei had to intercept and reply to.

The chapter brought the house down. Laughter detonated through the hotel, and in the front row by Petra, Alexei wet his cheeks with tears of laughter and pride at his moment of celebrity. His former pupil had caught that mischievous streak and preserved it for posterity. Max's readers would discover Alexei and grant him a kind of eternity. Max could see how thrilled he was and felt grateful he was able to give something back for all the years of friendship.

Then came the Q and A with the usual complement of awkward questions from the right-wingers who could never forgive what Max, Marx and their ilk had done to world freedom. But Max had the easy wit to undermine this line of self-righteousness and get the audience back on his side.

"Hey, Max, you could do stand-up. You floored those fucking hecklers like an old pro," said Valya.

"I am an old pro, Valya. What's your mother doing this evening?"

He stood beside Alexei in his chair joking with some readers who had bought copies of the book and scribbled his greeting across the frontispiece in English and Russian. That evening Max was speaking again at a dinner, to which Alexei and Petra were invited, and he suggested meeting them in the bar in twenty minutes for cocktails. "Just want to freshen up, change the suit and all that."

"My God. Two suits," said Alexei.

Showered and suited he caught a few moments in a deep, luxurious chair in his suite and watched the sun dipping behind the onion domes of the Kremlin. Stretches of austerity back in Georgia were now tempered by the brief periods of the five star life such as this, or at the behest of a Dutch television company or a publisher in Germany. He heard the drunk French author make his way past, raucously complaining to someone about something. He thought of ringing Lucy – the Conference would pay – but decided to leave it till after dinner when the time difference would be better.

Wandering along the corridor to the lift he experienced a sensation of satisfaction. If a man is favoured, he is more generous with the world.

"Mr Agnew, could I have your autograph?"

When he turned the eyes froze him. They were a dead brown under the heavy lids. No light reflected from them. He was short, broad, built for violence. Max felt a paralysis hit him like poison. He looked round. The corridor extended forever behind and in front. A thickset man was standing at the far end watching. There would be another, lurking somewhere behind him at the lifts.

"Could I have your autograph, Mr Agnew?" Max saw the opened book and the pen held out by hard knuckled hands. These were the instruments that dismembered Gia, and no doubt, countless others, and they were here to deal with him.

"Of course." He didn't bother with his glasses, he could never have got them from his case to his nose. He took the book. It trembled. The man offered a pen. Max took it, "Thank you," The bullet would come as he signed, as his eyes were turned down at the page. He could just about see what sort of a scribble he was doing and he had signed so often that day that his hands had developed a set of muscle messages. "Any name?"

"Tolya Verkovhensky."

That was the name. This was the man. No doubt. The eyes in the dark. His time had come. Only the manner remained. Please God it is quick and painless, here in the corridor. Dumbly he wrote,

'Best wishes to Tolya Verkhovensky from Maxwell Agnew.'

"Could you put the date?"

"Pardon?"

"Could you put the date, please? By your signature."

"What is it?"

"The tenth."

"Of course." He scribbled the date, handed Tolya back his pen and the book and was drawn one last time to the gimlet eyes that had haunted him for so long. He and Gia would share the same final view, because Tolya would have made sure the last thing Gia saw were those merciless eyes.

"Thank you, Mr Agnew. Have a good evening."

Max watched him walk to the lift. He moved with an animal grace, full of relaxed physical power. His fist pressed the buttons, he read as he waited and when the lift doors opened he stepped in, turned, saw Max again and smiled. The doors closed. The man at the other end of the corridor had gone. Max was alone. The dry smell of the carpet seized him; a light buzzed somewhere.

He fell against his door. His shaking hand struggled to get the electronic key in the slot. When it did he burst in and fell on the bed.

His heart felt as if it were trying to leave his chest and get back to Georgia. The fresh shirt that he had put on ten minutes before was soaked in sweat. Arteries were pounding in his ankles, the back of his head, his thighs; in places where he didn't know he had arteries.

The low sun had hit the ceiling. He could imagine the sunset over the bay, Shota switching on the bulbs in the magnolia tree, the kids leaving the beach, the raft sliding gently in the distance and he wished he were back in his little house, making coffee, peeling an orange, listening to a play on the radio, watching the light change, preparing to amble up to Shota's for a laugh and a moan.

Passing Alexei and Petra relaxing on a foyer sofa with a drink downstairs, Tolya made for home with his signed copy of Max Agnew's life under his arm.

The UnAmericans

Lightning Source UK Ltd.
Milton Keynes UK
UKOW04f1311270913

218065UK00001B/185/P